Praise
TARA

"Quinn's latest contemporary romance
offers readers an irresistible combination
of realistically complex characters and a
nail-bitingly suspenseful plot. Powerful, passionate
and poignant, *Hidden*
is deeply satisfying."
—*Booklist*

"One of the skills that has served Quinn best...has
been her ability to explore edgier subjects."
—*Publishers Weekly*

"Quinn explores relationships thoroughly....
Her vividly drawn characters are
sure to win readers' hearts."
—*Romance Communications*

Street Smart is filled with "deception, corruption,
betrayal—and love, all coming together in an
explosive novel that will make you think twice."
—*New Mystery Reader Magazine*

Where the Road Ends is "an intense,
emotionally compelling story."
—*Booklist*

"One of the most powerful [romance novels]
I have had the privilege to review..."
—*WordWeaving* on *Nothing Sacred*

"Quinn writes touching stories about real
people that transcend plot type or genre."
—*All About Romance*

Dear Reader,

I'm going to tell you up front that this is the most difficult book I've ever written. On the surface it doesn't appear frightening. On the surface it could be a safe, small-community tale of life and living. On the surface people are loved and loving, and everything's okay.

But not far below that surface, there's another world. There's another set of circumstances—in plain sight and yet unseen.

This story is fiction. And it is true. The characters and plot are figments of my imagination, but the topic is real. Facts revealed in the court cases are true.

The challenges we as a society face are real and happening in plain sight, in our own neighborhoods. As we live our lives, our actions are based on our personal perceptions and motives. But so many times, we act out of fear and call it dedication and loyalty to deep-seated beliefs.

This book is not here to judge or to educate. It's here to take you someplace you've never been. To grab you for a few hours, entertain you, maybe move you to the edge of your seat. And to leave you not quite as certain about the things you take for granted…

Rest assured, though. Because the journey will end in a safe place! And if, at the end, you want more, hang around. As I finished this book, the next one presented itself—we aren't done yet!

I love getting feedback from those who share my books. You can reach me at P.O. Box 13584, Mesa, Arizona 85216 or at www.tarataylorquinn.com.

Tara Taylor Quinn

TARA
TAYLOR
QUINN

IN
PLAIN
SIGHT

MIRA®

ISBN-13: 978-0-7783-2308-2
ISBN-10:   0-7783-2308-0

IN PLAIN SIGHT

For Sherry Stephens, who is as pure on deeper levels as she is on the surface. Thank you for your joy, your example and for a unique and treasured friendship.

Acknowledgments

Thank you to Maricopa County Superior Court Judge Sherry Stephens, her staff and Sheriff's Deputy David Parra for generously sharing their inside look at a world I'd never seen. You have remarkable strength and endurance, and the citizens of Maricopa County are blessed to have you there helping to keep them safe.

1

"Any questions?" chief prosecutor Janet McNeil asked the insolent young man slouched across from her. His cuffed hands shifted behind him at the scarred table in the private conference room.

"You said you were going to offer us a plea."

Jan shook her head at Gordon Michaels, a well-known Flagstaff defense attorney, and returned her attention to the defendant, Jacob Hall. He'd been arraigned the week before, with a trial date set for the middle of December—the maximum amount of time allowed by the law that ensured Hall the right to a speedy trial.

"No plea. I changed my mind." Staring down the defendant, she answered his attorney. *I've got you, buddy, for at least ninety days. That gives me time to find sufficient proof in the new evidence to lock you away forever.*

The green snake etched into Hall's arm flicked its black tongue in the direction of his neck. The ink elsewhere on his body was so thick that she couldn't make out specific designs.

"Come on, Jan. What's the maximum he can get on one count of identity theft?"

"By itself, four years."

"So give us a plea for three. Save the state the cost of a trial."

She didn't take her eyes off the twenty-three-year-old white supremacist. She'd been trying to convict him since he turned eighteen. How many lives had been lost in those five years? And all because, even though the cops did their job and made the arrests, she couldn't get enough on Hall to make anything stick.

"I'm adding charges for credit card and financial institution fraud, as well," she told them.

Jacob Hall didn't blink, didn't flinch—and didn't look away. The man was completely without conscience. And in possession of more physical agility, strength and intelligence than this world could withstand.

"Both federal offenses," she continued, "and with priors, they could carry up to thirty years."

Hall gave her a condescending smile. He showed no fear. Jan didn't think it was an act. The man was completely confident she'd never get a conviction.

For a second, he had her. Tendrils of fear crawled from her belly into her chest.

"You didn't make this jail call just as a courtesy to inform us of further charges, Ms. McNeil. That's not like you—you're a busy woman," Michaels said, his voice coming from her right. "And since there's no plea, I'm assuming you've got a deal to offer us."

Pulling her gaze away from the defendant, Jan focused on Michaels. She'd known him since law school and had argued against him several times. The colorless man was basically a good guy—a top-rate defense attorney, sure, but he won his cases without playing dirty.

"Yes, I do," she said, determined not to let weakness win. She turned back to Hall. "I want a list of names, places, dates. I want descriptions—in vivid detail. Give me Bobby Donahue and the people who help him run the Ivory Nation, and I'll give you consideration on a sentencing recommendation."

"You been reading too many fairy tales, *Jan*."

"I don't read fairy tales, Mr. Hall." She glanced back at Michaels. "Take it or leave it."

The two men exchanged a silent look.

"My client doesn't have any idea what you're talking about," Michaels said.

"That's your final decision?"

"It is."

Jan stood, lifted the padded strap of her maroon briefcase to her shoulder. And then the guard was there, motioning for Hall to stand. "See you in court on Monday," she said. The young man turned and sauntered out, but not before Jan noticed two things.

The black letters stamped on the back of his black-and-white clothing—Sheriff's Inmate. Unsentenced.

And the middle finger extended at her from the cuffed hands resting against his backside.

* * *

Using a clean mason jar topped with a coffee filter, the perpetrator will pour the chilled hydrogen peroxide, muriatic acid and iodine tincture into the jar...

Slumped in front of the keyboard, Simon typed, stopped, stared out the front window of his dining room office, and yawned. A nice September Friday. Blue skies. Balmy weather. The neighborhood was quiet. He liked quiet.

Iodine sales are regulated by the federal government.

The school bus had dropped off the elementary school kids twenty-six minutes before. Because once upon a time he'd been trained to observe and to protect, he'd watched them all disperse to their respective homes and waiting parents. In another two or three minutes the high-schoolers would be descending on the block.

He got in another line or two before their bus arrived. And watched them climb down, one by one, sometimes collecting in groups, as they sauntered down the street, some going into houses, others disappearing down side roads. Alan Bonaby was the only one Simon knew by name because the boy used to deliver his papers before quitting the route. Alan walked alone, pushing his glasses up his nose every couple of steps. His house was the last one before the road dead-ended into acres of pine trees.

Simon pushed his wire rims up his nose and got back to work. Law-enforcement manuals did not write themselves—which overall, was probably a good thing, since if they did, his publisher, Sam's publisher, would not pay him to write them.

Red phosphorus is regulated. To get around this, perpetrators obtain road flares in bulk and scrape off the phosphorus...

Reaching up to push against the knot of muscles at the back of his neck, Simon was briefly distracted by the hair tickling the top of his hand. It was starting to turn up at the edges. He opened the top right-hand drawer of his desk and grabbed a pair of scissors. Careful to catch the falling strands, he lopped off a quarter inch all the way around. Curls were out.

Indicators of a meth lab.

Simon hit the bullets-and-numbering key. Chose a hand-pointing bullet. **Chemical odors.** Bullet Two... A car had just turned up the street—a blue Infiniti, driven by his next-door neighbor.... **Chemical containers in the trash.** Bullet Three... She was pulling into her drive.... **Multiple visitors who don't stay long.** And on into her garage. In about forty seconds she'd be heading out to the box at the curb for her mail.... Bullet Four. **Homes with blackened windows.**

And there she was, beautiful as always, her shapely butt looking quite fine in the narrow, calf-length black-and-red skirt she was wearing; that long dark hair swinging just above her hips as she bent to peer into her box.

Simon jumped up.

"You know," he called out, seconds later, strolling across his front yard, "it'd be safer for you to drive up to this box just like the mailman does and get your mail from inside the car."

Janet McNeil smiled at him. "You see robbers waiting in the wings to take me down and confiscate my bills, Simon?"

He saw all kinds of stuff she knew nothing about. "Just passing on an observation," he said, sliding his hands beneath the loose tails of his button-down shirt and into the pockets of his jeans. They were baggy, too, exactly as he liked them. "If you're not into safety, think of it as time management," he said. "You could save a good two, three minutes if you picked up as you drove past."

"And another five without my conversation with you," she said, still grinning at him, "but then, what would I have to shake my head about over dinner?"

"I saw your name in the paper again this morning." He'd dropped the toast he'd been eating, ready to stand up and protect her, before he remembered she was none of his business. That he was no longer sworn to uphold and protect.

"Yeah, another day, another criminal," she said, sifting through the envelopes in her hand.

"Is Hall really a white supremacist like they claim?"

"Who knows?"

He rocked back and forth on his heels, watching her look at the coupons in a general delivery flyer. "You going to try to prove it?"

She looked up then, her fine features completely composed. "What do you think?"

What he thought was that she should be married and at home having babies. Sexist or not, the concept suited him far better than the idea of a nice woman like Janet McNeil spending her days with the dregs of society spitting at her.

"I hear they're not a friendly bunch," he said, keeping most of what he had to say on the subject to himself. Simon might understand how vital it was to obliterate violence and hate, but he didn't have to think about it. Or like it.

"You know, Simon," she said, tilting her head, "you should consider writing suspense instead of economics textbooks. It might suit you better."

Yeah, well, no one said she didn't have a discerning eye. He'd finished typing in the handwritten revisions on an economics textbook once. He'd done it for someone else and still maintained the fiction that this was what he wrote. It was easier that way. "Hey, you trying to say I don't look the economics type?"

"No." She held her mail to her chest. "I'm saying your curiosity and imagination are wasted on numbers and percentages."

But being considered an author of economics textbooks made a great cover. "Someday, I'll have to show you my etchings." He managed to keep a completely straight face while he delivered the tacky line.

"Are you ever serious?"

"Not often. You?"

"All day, every day."

He was glad to hear that. One moment of levity in

her line of work could lead to the missed clue that returned to stab her in the back—literally.

"Then, you should pay particular attention to your five minutes with me every afternoon," he said. "People need a bit of humor to keep them healthy and strong."

"I figured eating a good breakfast did that."

He smiled. And would have liked to hang around. "Have a good evening, Counselor," he said, backing up before he got too close.

Or did something stupid, like ask her if she wanted to go get a burger with him.

Simon didn't like to share his burger experiences. Or his life.

He didn't have enough to spare. And he intended to keep it that way.

They knew the landing gear on the jet was damaged. No one was all that concerned. Jan pulled a file from a vault in the courthouse office inexplicably housed within the airport, watching people come and go from the street. The sun was shining out there. Inside, a cast of gray infused the lighting with gloom.

Suddenly, the structure lurched. Her shoulder slammed against a wall. They were going to crash. She heard someone scream the news—a coworker. Oh, God. She was finally going to crash. She'd known her whole life this time would come.

She tried to scream, but she couldn't make a sound. Tried to tell someone they were already on the ground. And then all she heard was the screeching of metal against metal, as the plane met asphalt and she fell to the side. Things tumbled around her, breaking. She waited to die. Wondered how it would feel.

And then, just as quickly as it started, the motion stopped. Jan half lay on the floor, listening, waiting. She was breathing.

She tried to stand, slowly, straightening her limbs— waiting for them to fail, waiting for the ensuing pain. She explored her face with her fingers, assessing the damage, feeling for cuts. There were none.

She was alive—and she had to get out before there was an explosion. She searched frantically but the distressed and agitated people blocked her view. And then she saw Johnny. Her only sibling had glanced her way, but he must not have seen her. He turned toward a beam of light and dashed into it.

Scrambling over files, slipping on debris, Jan stumbled after him, desperate to get to the light before the plane burst into flames. She gulped. And her lungs filled with the coolness of fresh air. She'd made it out.

Distraught, she looked for someone she knew. She was crying. Needed to be held, comforted, and everyone was busy, unaware of her presence. Pushing through the crowd, she caught a glimpse of a familiar body up ahead.

"Mom?" she called out.

Her mother turned, saw her, and then immediately turned back to the women she'd been walking with. They were heading toward the crash. Jan wanted her mother to know that she'd been in the crash—that she'd survived.

*She said the words. And then again louder. Her mother
looked at her, nodded, patted her on the head and continued on her way, leaving Jan standing alone in the street,
sobbing. Sobbing. So hard…*

Desperate crying woke her. Sitting up in bed Jan
brushed damp tendrils of hair back from her face
and forehead with both hands, holding her head between them.

Oh, God. Would these dreams never end? Almost
thirty years she'd been having the nightmares. The situations varied, but the feelings never changed. Dev-
astation. Unanswered cries for help. Loneliness. What
did it mean? Why was she tortured like this?

With her head resting against her knees, Jan
hugged her legs. She hated the nightmares, the sub-
conscious she couldn't control, but she didn't hate
herself. She tried hard every day. She did her best.

Slowly, thoughts of the preceding day penetrated her
consciousness. The newspaper article describing Hall's
arrest. Her visit to the jail. Lunch with a law-school
classmate. A spat between the office manager at the
county attorney's office and a prosecutor who didn't
understand job jurisdiction. Simon. The quick Friday-
night phone call to Hailey, confirming their outing the
following morning. Nothing uncommon. A good day.

Jan glanced at the clock. 3:00 a.m. She considered
lying down again, trying to get some sleep. And shivered as all the horror of her nightmare resurfaced.
She couldn't chance going back there. Not tonight.

Getting up, Jan pulled her hair over one shoulder, giving the sweaty back of her cotton pajamas a chance to dry out as she walked over to the window to peer into the night. At the side of her house, more long than square, the bedroom window allowed only a partial view of the street. Not that she was missing much. Dark houses. Stillness. A couple of dim streetlights that cast more shadow than illumination. But the view straight ahead was a different matter. Light was streaming from Simon Green's bedroom window, which was opposite hers. She couldn't see through the pulled curtains—not that she wanted to.

But there was a strange kind of comfort in knowing she wasn't the only human being awake on the block. Did he suffer from nightmares, too? Somehow, she doubted it. Smiling tentatively, Jan left her bedroom and went into the kitchen to put on a pot of coffee. Simon's mind probably entertained him with stand-up routines all night. Or maybe he was working late. She'd heard that writers did that. And why not? That freed up his days to do whatever he pleased.

Jan was coming out of the shower several hours later when she heard the front bell ring. Wringing out her hair, she wrapped it in the only towel that would hold it all, an extra-large bath sheet she'd bought for just that purpose, pulled on her violet robe and went to peek out the front window.

A motorcycle was parked in the gravel beneath the low-hanging branches of the aspen tree. She didn't recognize it. Hesitated, as she stared at it. But really, anyone who meant her harm wouldn't park out front—especially in the broad light of day.

Reminding herself of the fine line between caution and paranoia, she went to the door and opened it a crack, intending to ask her visitor to wait while she got dressed, then she threw it wide instead.

"Johnny!" She reached up to give her younger brother a hug. "I didn't know you were back."

A sales rep for a major publisher of nonfiction and self-help books, Johnny was on the road a lot. And too busy to see her, most of the time, when he was in town.

He shrugged, his off-white shirt opening at the collar, revealing what looked like the edge of a tattoo just beneath his collarbone. "I just got in last night," he said.

He had a tattoo. Everyone was getting them these days—she knew that. But Johnny? Jan wanted to ask him about it, wanted him to tell her that the mark was only henna.

She invited him in instead. Offered to make some coffee.

"I can't stay." Johnny held his shiny black-and-white helmet between his hands as he stepped through the door. "I'm back on the road on Monday and I have a load of things to do before then. I just wanted to talk to you for a second." He glanced down, almost sheepishly, his longish dark hair falling over his forehead. Jan's heart melted, as it always did when her brother needed something.

"What's up?" Johnny's visits and his requests were few. She'd do anything she could for him.

"I was kind of wired when I got in last night," he said, and she wondered if he was still in the apartment by the university, where he'd lived the previous summer. Last she'd heard from their mother, he'd been planning to move to a new place out by the Woodlands. "I looked through the week's papers, catching up, and noticed the article about you and that Hall dude."

Jan warmed beneath his concerned stare and nodded.

"He sounds dangerous, sis." Sis. He hardly called her that anymore.

"Which is why he's safely in custody."

"I don't know." He bowed his head again and then glanced back at her, his dark eyes serious. "I don't like the idea of you out there digging up stuff on him. He might be locked up, but what if he does have people—and money—on the outside?"

Fear shot through her chest. Jan took a deep breath, quelled the emotion—left over from her bad night, she told herself—and smiled. "I've been at this job a long time, little brother," she reminded him. "And I'm still here."

"So why chance it? Drop the case, sis. Give it to someone else."

"I can't," she told him, torn between exasperation that the one time he came to see her it was to ask her to do something she couldn't possibly do and happiness that he still cared. "I've been following this guy for years. The history's convoluted, complicated, and

I'm the only one who knows it all. If I don't argue this, he's going to get off again, and we're not safe with him out there."

Johnny frowned, dropping his arm, his helmet resting against the side of his black jeans. "It says he's in for identity theft. That's not a matter of life and death for the citizens of Flagstaff."

No, but the longtime white supremacist was guilty of more than fraud. She was sure of it. She decided now was not the time, however, to let her worried little brother in on that fact.

"It's my job, Johnny," she said instead. "The police arrest them, and we prosecute them. Someone has to, or the entire judicial system goes down the tubes and chaos reigns."

"Just this once, sis. Can't you let go of the responsibility just this once? Lighten up. Take a vacation. I'll spring for it. Hell," he said, grinning, rubbing his knuckles against the side of her cheek, "I'll even go with you, if that'll get you out of town."

Tears welled at the back of her eyes. They'd been so close when they were younger. He'd been her best friend, in spite of the four-year difference in their ages. How many nights had he come to her room when he'd heard her cry out from a nightmare? How many nights had he sat there with her, telling her stupid jokes, making her smile, until he'd fallen asleep at the end of her bed and she'd covered him with her comforter and fallen back to sleep herself?

"Now, that's tempting, Johnny," she said softly,

even knowing that she couldn't run out on her job—not on this case. There was too much at stake. "Where would we go?"

It didn't hurt to fantasize for a moment.

"Anywhere you want," he surprised her by saying. "You name the time, the place, and I'll be there."

"What about your job?"

"I have vacation coming."

"Johnny…" She hated to disappoint him.

"Name the time and place, sis," he repeated, his voice intent as he bent to give her a kiss on the cheek. "I'll be waiting to hear."

"Johnny!" she called after him, as he spun out the door and headed down the walk without letting her tell him she couldn't go. He climbed on his motorcycle, slid the helmet down over his ears, and without looking her way, sped off.

2

Flagstaff, Arizona, was a unique place. A little too big, too spread out, to maintain the small-town feel—and too small and secluded to attract big-city folks. Simon drove along old Route 66 toward the town's one indoor shopping mall, agreeing with FBI Special Agent Scott Olsen's assertion that this city, with Northern Arizona University's rambling campus in the middle and a train station not far from the center of town, was a perfect terrorist training depot.

Entering the mall, he located the directory and the store he sought. A potential terrorist could find anything he needed here—and once outside the city limits, on any side, he'd disappear in the miles and miles of undeveloped land, woods, mountains, desert, Indian reservation. Places to get lost—forever if need be.

"Hi, Bettina, show me the best mediocre snow gear you've got on sale." Simon read her name tag and then met the salesgirl's eyes.

"What do you need it for?" She asked. "Skiing? Snowboarding? Snowmobiling? Or just building a snowman?"

Building a snowman. The last Christmas Sam had been alive, Simon had dragged him away from the half-finished economics textbook his twin had written by hand and was in the process of entering on his computer, and while consuming a six-pack of beer, the two of them had built a snow monstrosity worthy of the *Guinness Book of World Records*.

"Skiing," he said belatedly, realizing too much time had passed. He focused on the smiling young face in front of him, his vision clearing, until he was once again seeing a stranger named Bettina in the Flagstaff Mall.

She was nodding. "Too early for the good sales," she said, walking him over to a group of shelves along the side wall. "Snowbowl's season doesn't start until the holidays." She pointed up. "These are your best bet for now."

Simon grabbed a set of thermal underwear, then plopped waterproof insulated pants and a matching jacket on top.

"Where you going? Utah? Montana?" Bettina hung around watching.

Hopefully nowhere. "Where would you suggest?" he asked, adding thick socks and toe-warmers, a fleece hat with earflaps and down-lined leather gloves to the stack in his arms. He had to be prepared. Snowbowl might not have snow yet, but the resort just miles from Flagstaff was open year round and was currently drawing FBI suspicion.

Hands in her back pockets, she ran her gaze along his body. "How good are you?"

Champion quality when he'd left Philadelphia almost eight years before. "Good enough," he told the slender young woman standing before him. Good enough for anything she might have in mind.

But "in mind" was as far as it went with him.

"Hey, Ma, how you doing?" Turning on lights as she let herself into the living room of her mother's prefabricated home, Jan quickly took stock of the pulled blinds, the pillow and blanket on the couch.

"Good, sweetie, really good." Grace McNeil stood, finger-combed her scattered hair and gave Jan a hug.

"You didn't go to church this morning?"

"I forgot I was out of gas until it was too late."

Grace's clothes were wrinkled, the beige slacks and colorful blouse Jan had bought for her birthday resembling something from a secondhand shop rather than the designer outfit it was.

"How was bingo last night?"

Grace shrugged.

"You didn't go?"

"How was your week, dear?" Dropping back onto the couch on which, Jan suspected, her mother had recently been sound asleep, Grace picked at her fingernails.

"Ma, Saturday night bingo was one of our deals. Remember? I'd help out, and you'd stay busy. You promised." Her mother had been so adamant about moving to the Sedona resort.

Grace's face was lined with pain. "I ate something that didn't agree with me," she offered Jan as an explanation.

Jan wasn't sure whether to believe her or not. "What about Thursday's mah-jongg game?"

"Didn't do so good at first, but then I had Thirteen Orphans." Grace's face lit up. "That was the first time any of us saw it happen."

Jan had never played mah-jongg—she found the tiles and flowers and dragons confusing—but her mother had a passion for the game. And after her most recent suicide scare a couple of years before, Grace's passion for anything was a blessing.

"Did you play here?" she asked, glancing around the room, which was neat and spotlessly clean—except for the blanket and pillow.

"Yeah, it was my turn. Sara couldn't make it, but Belle had a friend staying with her who wanted to come. And Jean was here."

Jean lived in the modular next door—about twelve feet away from the aluminum side of her mother's two-year-old home.

"Have you seen her since then?"

"We had lunch on Friday. And she stopped by last night, on her way to bingo. We were going to ride up to the clubhouse together."

So…maybe her mother really had just had a stomachache. At sixty-two and with Crohn's disease, she was certainly entitled. Settling back into the reclining chair adjacent to the couch, Jan kicked off her clogs and pulled her feet up, cross-legged, on jean-clad thighs.

"How are you feeling now?"

"My stomach's fine," Grace said with a chuckle. "My pride would've preferred that I slept in my bed last night rather than in my clothes on the couch. Or at least to have woken with enough time to shower and change before you got here."

Jan released a long breath. Grinned. Everything was normal.

"What do you want to do for dinner?" she asked. Her mother hadn't sunk back into the darkness of depression that had almost killed her ten years ago and again more recently.

But that had been before Sedona. Before her mother had daily activities and friends to keep her mind occupied.

Since the move, the anti-depressants had been more successful.

Jan really needed to learn to quit worrying so much. To relax.

"I thought I'd make a meat loaf, since it's your favorite, and I bought fresh peaches to make cobbler…"

Jan was lucky her mother put up with her. She probably would've lost patience with such nagging years ago.

"I had one of my nightmares the other night," Jan told her mother later that day, as she finished off the last bite of peach cobbler. They'd already talked about Johnny, who'd called, but hadn't come by yet. And Hailey—Grace was anxious to meet the troubled eight-year-old Jan was trying to adopt, completely supporting Jan's need to start her own family in this untraditional way.

Grace, who'd showered, put on makeup and was now wearing a soft green pantsuit, scraped her spoon across her plate, cleaning up every remaining morsel of dessert. "Tell me about the dream," she said.

Jan did. In all the vivid detail she could remember. "I'm afraid I'm going crazy," she said softly, as she glanced at her mother.

"Of course you aren't," Grace replied, rising to stack their plates. She carried them over to the small dishwasher on the other side of the half wall that separated the living and dining area from the kitchen. "How many professionals have to reassure you before you start believing, girl?"

A million and one, Jan supposed. Since she'd already seen what seemed like a million.

"The nightmares are so real. And the feelings stay long after I'm awake. It scares me, Ma."

Drying her hands on her apron, Grace returned with a pot of coffee and filled both their cups. "I know they do, sweetie," she said, covering Jan's hand.

Jan soaked up the closeness. The security found in the touch of her mother's hands.

"The fear is what makes them nightmares," Grace continued. "But that's all they are, honey. Bad dreams. They simply mean that you have an active imagination."

She'd heard the words so many times before. And still she listened intently.

"They're nothing to worry about. You know that. If I thought differently, I would've scoured the country years ago, paid whatever it cost, to rid you of them."

"I know."

"And being upset by them is natural, too," Grace added. "Just like watching a horror movie that sticks with you for days afterward."

Yeah, only her horror movies were private—and homemade.

She glanced up at Grace, finding strength and comfort in her mother's gaze. "Thank you," she said, letting go of the fear. Once again.

"I love you, my dear," Grace said, giving her hand a squeeze.

"I love you, too, Ma."

"I'll have the barbecue chicken sandwich with coleslaw." Bobby Donahue, founder of the Ivory Nation, said, smiling at the young Mama's Café waitress on Sunday evening. "And a Diet Coke, please."

And then, the Ivory Nation brochures he'd commissioned tucked neatly in the zipped folder beside him, he made a mental note as his dinner guest ordered a burger and fries. The kid was seventeen, the nerdy type, but he had the power of his convictions. It would've been a strike against him to tell the waitress that he'd have the same thing Bobby had ordered. He needed spiritual followers, not copycats.

"Tell me about yourself," he said, holding the young man's gaze. Tony Littleton maintained eye contact. Another mental check in the "go" column.

"Not much to tell," the high school senior said. "Dad took off when I was a kid. I don't remember much about him. No brothers or sisters. Mom works a lot—has a boyfriend, nice guy, but he's into sports."

No close family ties. It all fit.

"What about friends?" Bobby expected that he knew the answer to this one. He'd figured out the basics of Tony's existence, if not the details, from his chats with him online.

"I've never been the most popular guy in school," Tony said with a shrug. "I'm no good at sports, not that great looking, I get good grades even when I don't particularly try. I'm a science whiz, and I write for the school paper. Mostly all stuff the cool kids avoid."

No close friends. Just as Bobby had suspected.

"What kind of stuff do you write?" Tony hadn't mentioned that particular talent in their previous conversations.

"Mostly editorials." Tony took a deep sip of the lemonade that had arrived while he was talking. "I see something that bugs me, and I write about it."

Bobby leaned back, his hand resting against his mouth. "What bugs you, Tony?"

"Injustice." The boy's response was strong, his expression firm.

Bobby smiled and unzipped his portfolio.

"All rise."

Pushing the heavy wooden chair back from a scarred table, Jan stood at the bailiff's direction, along with the fifteen or so other people in Judge Matthew Warren's court, just after lunchtime on Monday.

The fiftysomething judge entered through a door behind his bench. "Be seated," he said. His black robe covered the arms of his chair.

When she'd heard that the Hall case had been assigned to Warren, Jan had opened a bottle of champagne. She'd argued before him many times and had found the man to be fair almost to the detriment of his career. Matthew Warren didn't seem to care whose money was involved or how much might be at stake; he didn't respond to threats or power, and he had never played a political game in his life, as far as she could tell.

He asked if the state was ready.

"Yes, Your Honor, the state is ready."

He looked to opposing counsel for the same confirmation, and when Gordon Michaels, seated at the table across the aisle from Jan, answered in the affirmative, he called the case number. Jacob Hall stood and was released from the chain that bound him to the state's other four guests in the jury box, which also served as the courtroom's inmate seating section. He grinned as Warren's deputy led him down to the podium three or four feet below and directly in front of the judge. Michaels joined him at the microphone. Jacob didn't seem to notice.

"Gordon Michaels for the defense, Your Honor. This is my client, Jacob Hall."

The defense attorney shifted his weight a couple of times. He looked a little tense.

Jan stood again. "Jan McNeil for the state, Your Honor."

Judge Warren nodded, leaned toward the microphone set in front of him and ran through his spiel for the record, citing the case number and stating that he'd read the motions.

Jan checked her notes, rehearsing her justifications for denying Michaels's motion to suppress evidence found on Hall's personal computer.

Glancing up, she caught the defendant staring at her. And she knew he was looking forward to eating her piece by piece—in private—without clothes on. His eyes had fire in them. And a lascivious glow. It was almost as if she could hear him speaking to her—as if the room held just the two of them.

She stared back.

Warren read aloud the motion before him, asking Michaels if he had anything to say on behalf of his client. A cough came from behind her, a spectator. Someone there to watch Jacob Hall's proceedings, or a supporter of one of the other inmates waiting for his case to be called? She didn't break eye contact with the defendant to find out.

"Your Honor." Michaels's voice was clearly audible. "The warrant to seize my client's computer was based solely on a tip given to a police officer, Detective Ruple, by a supposed confidential informant. We have absolutely no proof that any such individual actually exists and, in fact, we have reason to believe otherwise. Mr. Hall lives alone. The computer in question is a desktop unit that he keeps in the spare bedroom of his apartment, and only he has access to it. Even if someone was in that room without his knowledge, that person would not have been able to access the information on Mr. Hall's hard drive, as he had it password-protected and he has given his password to no one. Further, Mr. Hall has spoken to no one about the contents of his computer. Thus, it is clear, Your Honor, that there could have been no informant who knew about that content. The constitution of this great nation protects not only my client but all of us from illegal search and seizure. What kind of society do we live in if, at any moment, anyone flashing a badge can enter a private home and take whatever he pleases? Our job is to protect the public by upholding the constitution, and Detective Ruple's search of my client's home was in direct conflict with that great document and the laws made since to support and clarify our forefathers' intent. Yes, Detective Ruple had a warrant, but one gained solely on the word of a ghost. I ask that you suppress the evidence taken from Mr. Hall's apartment, Your Honor, including any and all information found on his computer."

Jan tried to breathe calmly during the brief silence that followed, refusing to be intimidated by Hall's visual assault and hating the apparent logic of Michaels's argument. She couldn't win this case without the evidence taken from Jacob Hall's personal computer.

"Ms. McNeil?"

The judge called on her, and with a last grin, Jacob

Hall turned his attention back to the proceedings at hand. Jan stared at the defendant's back for another second or two, just to make it clear, if only to herself, that she hadn't been the first to look away. She was going to win this case.

Hands shaking, she stood.

"Your Honor, the state believes Mr. Hall is a member of the Ivory Nation." Judge Warren's nod indicated that he was familiar with the name. The Ivory Nation was one of Arizona's largest white supremacist organizations and its involvement was suspected in several unsolved murders and numerous other felonies.

"Anyone who's going to come forward with information against any member of such a group would be putting himself at almost certain risk of retaliation if his identity was disclosed—"

"Mr. Hall's private memberships have not been proven, nor are they on trial here, Your Honor," Michaels broke in.

"There was an article in the press two weeks ago and again on Friday," Jan continued, as if the opposing counsel hadn't spoken, "claiming Mr. Hall's alleged association with the Ivory Nation." The calmness of her voice belied the pounding of her heart. "The state was not responsible for that information, Your Honor, but whether the allegation is true or not, there are now many who believe it. Police officers' use of informants is common practice," she said. "Based on evidence gained from informants, we've been able to protect the citizens of this state by apprehending, prosecuting and removing from the streets many dangerous threats to society. And how can we ask these citizens, who are willing to come forward for the good of all, to do so without also granting them the protection we seek to provide every citizen? Detective Ruple has been with the Flagstaff police department for twenty years, Your Honor. His record is impeccable. He's made more arrests than anyone else on the force. But those arrests mean nothing to the people of this state if we don't support them by prosecuting offenders to the full extent of the law. The use of confidential informants is allowed under the law, Your Honor. I ask that you deny Mr. Michaels's request."

Judge Warren was reading something in the file in front of him.

Jacob Hall stood without moving, facing forward, his hands cuffed together in front. The observers behind her maintained a stillness that seemed almost automatic, in deference to the powerful man seated in front of them all.

If he doesn't grant it, you've still got ninety days, Jan reminded herself silently. *He did the crimes. You'll find another way to prove it.*

She couldn't let emotion diminish her ability to think with agility and focus.

"You both make valid points." Warren's voice cracked the uneasy silence that had fallen. "I find that I can neither grant the motion nor refuse it, with the limited information provided. Therefore, I'm setting an evidentiary hearing on this motion to be held no later than two weeks from today." He glanced at Jan, and at his frown, her heart sank.

"Ms. McNeil, bring in your cop and have him fully prepared to give specifics regarding this confidential informant."

Damn. Damn. And damn. "Yes, sir."

"Counsel, please approach."

Without so much as a peripheral glance, Jan passed Jacob Hall, and with Michaels at her side, she stood before the judge's bench. It took only a few seconds to confer over dates and the hearing was set for Monday, two weeks hence, at eight-thirty in the morning.

She had two weeks to convince a cop with twenty years on the job to do something he'd never done before. Something that could endanger his own life, and the life of someone he'd given his word to, as well.

3

The phone rang moments before the first bus was due to drop off Simon's youngest group of neighbors on Tuesday afternoon. He glanced at caller ID and then back at the screen in front of him. With a click, he maximized the manuscript he'd minimized in order to play freecell, covering the game he hadn't won yet rather than closing it. He had a ninety-one-percent win ratio and he wasn't about to see that drop because he'd quit a game.

Going rate for methamphetamine in Arizona (prices vary by state).

Simon read what he'd written half an hour before and waited for the ringing to stop. He checked the time in the lower right corner of his screen. Two minutes until the bus. Fingers on the keyboard, he deliberated over bullet choices. Made a decision. A pointing finger.

1/4 gram—$25.

One minute until the bus. The phone sounded again. Same number. The FBI agent was persistent. He picked up.

"Hello, Olsen. What can I do for you?" Simon said, eyes focused on the corner outside, waiting for the bus. After all, what else did he have to do with his day but munch on carrot sticks and watch other peoples' kids get safely home from school?

"A map found at the Snowbowl corroborates the girlfriend's story."

Simon didn't say the choice words he was thinking. "Who found it?" How legitimate was it?

"Full-time custodian. An older guy who's been there close to ten years. Keeps to himself. He was cleaning a locker and found the folded sheet caught between two pieces of metal at the bottom."

"Like it was planted there?"

"Like it dropped out of something."

The better of the two scenarios.

"Someone lost it and doesn't know where."

"That'd be my guess."

"Who used the locker last?" Not that it mattered to him. He hadn't agreed to anything.

"A student of Leonard Diamond."

The white man with the background that was apparently untraceable, or was traceable to contradicting places, who privately trained cross-country skiers and paid the Snowbowl for use of the facilities. Or so he'd said. The FBI had a tip that suggested something different.

"Was the student male or female?"

"Male."

"An old piece of paper obviously left behind. Why

did the custodian keep it? Turn it in? Why not just throw it away?" Those questions belonged to the agents and local police detective on the case, not to Simon. He didn't want them.

"It incorporated every inch of the Snowbowl property, but it wasn't like any other map of the Snowbowl he'd ever seen. The trails on the map aren't standard Snowbowl trails. The way they're engineered, only the most proficient skier could hope to master them or even make it over them alive. Turns out they aren't sanctioned, which means they shouldn't exist. The map was detailed, computer-generated, possibly one of many. Snowbowl officials contacted us."

"Someone spoke to Diamond?"

"Never saw the map before in his life." Scott Olsen's mimicking voice made clear his lack of trust in the other man's word.

"And the student?"

"Quit the class."

"Let me guess," Simon said. "The guy left no forwarding address and Diamond had no personal information on him."

"Correct."

"So how does a map of nonexistent trails tie in with a disgruntled girlfriend's tale of hearing about terrorist training?"

Simon didn't want to know. Deep in his soul, if he still had a soul, he didn't want to know.

"Marking the beginning and ending of each trail was an emblem. A circle with three crosses in the top half and a blackened dagger at the bottom."

Just as Amanda Blake—the disgrunteld ex-girl-friend of an acquaintance of Diamond's—had told it.

"I'm not the right man for this job."

"You had a master's degree in law enforcement at twenty-three and you were one of the youngest under-cover agents the FBI ever had. You have antiterrorist training."

"That was a long time ago." And ultimately all that preparation had been useless.

"I have no idea how far this thing reaches, how many people could be hurt. This gets out now, and the local police have a city in panic. I need a very discreet professional look-see. You're the only one I trust."

Simon closed his eyes, consumed with remorse. And then opened them again, seeing nothing but the clean notepad he'd pulled out of the bottom drawer. "You said Amanda Blake is a waitress at the Museum Club?"

"Yes."

"I'll go tonight."

"Glad to hear it," Scott Olsen said. "Anything you need, Simon, anything at all, you just let me know...."

Simon nodded, his throat tight. "As always, aware-ness of my role here is on a life-or-death, need-to-know basis only."

"Of course," Olsen said. "Not even the local police will know." And then he added, "Thank you."

"I'm a thankless guy, Scott. I thought you were smart enough to figure that out."

He hung up. Glanced out the window. He'd missed the bus.

* * *

"Andrew, where's the Zeidel file?" Sitting at her desk, Jan called to the attorney she'd hired straight out of law school several years before. He'd been her most trusted assistant and colleague ever since.

"I left it on the corner of your desk," the red-haired young man said, appearing at her door. As usual, they were the only two people left in the office at almost six o'clock on this Tuesday evening. "Right where I always leave everything." He came over, his brown slacks loose on his slim body, his tie perfectly knotted and dropping forward as he leaned down to sift through the pile he'd left in the box on her desk.

"I've already been through it twice," Jan told him. She'd figured out a way to get Danny Ruple to cooperate with her. And as soon as she had that piece of business taken care of, she could go home. Check her mail. And if she wasn't too late, enjoy some of her neighbor's nonsense before dinner.

"I pulled it before lunch," Andrew told her, frowning. "Right after we talked about making the deal with Ruple."

Jan was going to do something she'd never done before; charge and prosecute a defendant solely on a detective's hunch—*and* the circumstantial evidence she'd collected when she'd tried to bring the case to justice two years before. She'd probably lose and waste the state's money on a long and grueling jury trial. But if bringing in the man Ruple was sure had raped and brutally murdered U of A student Lorna Zeidel, a couple of years before would get her Hall's conviction, she figured the state would be getting its money's worth.

Andrew continued to rifle through the files.

"Maybe someone put it back," Jan suggested. Files did not disappear in the county attorney's office. And Andrew was too obsessive to admit that he might only have thought he'd put the file on her desk. He was usually too efficient to have forgotten. But he was also an exhausted first-time father—to a newborn who wasn't sleeping through the night.

"Who would've done that?" He had the entire box in one arm as he sorted through it, piece by piece.

"I don't know." She didn't. Nancy, her secretary, would never take a file from her desk. Nor would anyone else. "But could you check?"

"Maybe it fell in the trash."

From the far right corner of her desk to the near left one? Andrew's statement validated her exhaustion theory. She would've teased him, if she'd thought he had enough energy left to get the joke. Or if she wasn't bothered by his apparent carelessness.

"You check the file room and I'll go through the trash," she said instead, pulling the metal bin out from beneath her desk.

Half an hour later, Jan accompanied Andrew from their third-story office, past the potted plants on the ground-floor atrium, to their cars in the parking lot by Cherry Avenue. It was a nightly ritual, one Andrew insisted upon.

The file, containing all the notes Jan had collected on Lorna Zeidel, was still missing.

And Ruple had not been called. Jan was looking forward to the frozen dinner waiting at home for her.

Jan almost stopped at the mailbox as she drove in, rather than parking her car in the garage first. Not because she thought it would be safer or because she was turning over a new time-management leaf, but because she was thinking of Simon and he'd suggested she do so. Not that she expected anything from her friendly neighbor, ever, but tonight she was kind of depleted and could use some of his easy humor. Easy, because he expected nothing in return. No borrowed cups of flour. Or chats on the lawn. Or dates.

Of course, the cup of flour she'd be happy to give him. Jan grinned, as she waited for the automatic garage door to rise a few slow inches at a time, picturing him in the kitchen, making cookies with as much sloppiness as he showed in the way he dressed. She'd hate to have to clean up that mess.

The overhead light popped on as the door opened and Jan started to pull forward, but then stopped. What was that shiny substance on her garage floor? It hadn't been there that morning.

Putting the car in Park, she got out, not frightened but tense as she moved closer. It looked like glass. There were shards everywhere. A glance at the window showed her where it had come from—there was a hole the size of a softball through the middle of the pane. Had some neighbor kid thrown a wild pitch? It happened. And it could be fixed.

Then she saw the brick on the opposite side of the garage and her heart began to pound. No way could this be part of a ball game. Whoever had thrown the heavy object through her window had done so with enough force to embed it in the dry-wall on the far side.

"Don't touch it."

Yelping as she swung around, Jan almost dropped with relief when she realized the voice was Simon's. "I wasn't planning to," she told him. "This doesn't look like an accident, and I know better than to tamper with evidence."

"You want me to call the police?"

She shook her head. "I've got this cop friend downtown," she quoted an old play, making light of the fact that she'd just come home and found her property vandalized. It was a brick through a garage window, she told herself. Certainly not life-threatening. Or even particularly damaging.

Her nervous system was overreacting. Dialing the downtown precinct, Jan told them what had happened and was grateful when they said they'd send someone right over.

"I'm sorry I scared you," Simon said, as soon as Jan got off the phone. "When you didn't show up at the mailbox and I saw your car in the garage, I got curious."

"I'm glad you did," she admitted, a little shaky. "It's

creepy standing here alone, knowing someone was here while I was gone, vandalizing my stuff."

A window wasn't all that much. But the guy couldn't have known what else might be in the garage.

Of course, if he'd meant to do *real* damage, he'd have thrown the thing into the house, making all her possessions fair game.

"You been working on anything in particular that would piss someone off?" Simon asked, sitting beside her on the stoop in front of her house as they waited for the police. She'd called from her cell phone and was still holding it in her hand. Just in case.

A vision of the way Hall had looked at her the day before flashed through her mind. She shook her head. Twice. "Nothing out of the ordinary," she told her neighbor. No sense in giving life to fear. It only became truly dangerous when it was given the power of acknowledgment.

Besides, the Jacob Halls of the world used things that were far more dangerous than bricks. Even as warnings.

Didn't they?

"This ever happen before?"

Simon's slacks were wrinkled. She liked them that way. Unlike most of the men she dealt with on a day-to-day basis, being with him felt comfortable. Relaxed.

Safe.

Now, where had that word come from?

"Uh, no," she stammered, when she realized he was still waiting for her answer. "I've had letters at the office. Threats. But nothing that ever amounted to anything."

She glanced down the street, met Simon's gaze, and focused on the phone between her hands. "I doubt this had anything to do with my job."

"Probably not."

She looked back at him. Was he serious? With Simon it was hard to tell. "You really don't think so?"

The shake of his head was decisive. "I'd guess it's a neighborhood thing."

She took a slightly easier breath. He was probably right. It made sense. Except that she couldn't think of anyone nearby who might be mad at her, let alone angry enough to vandalize her house.

"Did you see anything?" She should've asked before. Simon was always around. Aware. How else could he know when she was at her mailbox most nights?

"Nope."

"You sound as if you think you should have," Jan said. There was something different about him tonight. Something deeper; more serious. Or maybe she was just coloring everything with the uneasiness she'd begun to feel. "You certainly aren't responsible for what goes on at my house," she told him.

"Five days out of five, my life consists of sitting at my computer staring out at an empty street. There's a school bus that comes and goes with boring regularity, and that's about it. Today, I'm not watching, and I might actually have seen something that could've been useful." He sounded disgusted with himself.

Interesting. The man was a self-supporting published author—something a lot of people aspired to but few ever managed. He was his own boss, set his own hours, dressed however he wanted, worked from home—a dream job. His work educated thousands of people. And he thought he was *useless?* Who'd have figured?

Route 66 was a lot like Flagstaff itself—an innocuous two-lane road without a high-class establishment in sight, and famous anyway. And the Museum Club, with its low-grade gravel parking lot and attention-getting giant guitar sign out front, followed suit. A comfortable laid-back hangout for locals, the bar was also on many tourist lists as a famous historical site, and according to the signs Simon read as he pulled open the door, the roadhouse hosted live country-and-western bands and dancing on Friday and Saturday nights.

He neither liked country music nor dancing.

Tuesday night was karaoke night.

Simon loathed karaoke.

Slouching on a hard wooden chair at a table as far away from the microphone as he could get, Simon glanced around the half-filled room. Not a bad Tuesday-night turnout—mostly middle-aged folks in jeans, a family in one corner, a couple dressed in matching country-and-western attire doing fancy steps on the dance floor to off-key music. And a lone woman at the bar, holding her glass as if it were her only friend. She'd had a face-lift—the line behind her jaw told him that. And she dyed her own hair; she'd missed a spot on the back of her head with the platinum solution. He'd bet his computer there was no wedding ring on her finger, but that if he looked, he'd find an oversize turquoise there.

"Can I get you something to drink?"

Amanda, according to the name tag of the young woman standing at the edge of his table. Sometimes a man just got lucky.

"What's on tap?" He gave her the slow, covertly appreciative grin that had closed more than one investigation.

With her tray balanced on a hip, Amanda listed both foreign and domestic beers. Her perfectly painted red lips moved easily, as she told him about the night's specials. "So what'll you have?" she ended, with a smile that would've locked many men's knees—including his, nine or ten years ago.

Domestic. Simon named his brand, or rather the brand he used to prefer on tap, back when he used to go out. And watched Amanda's butt in the tight, faded blue denim, as she made her way toward the friendly-looking blond woman behind the bar.

Nice ass.

Nice girl. He hoped. Ex-boyfriend with possible terrorist connections notwithstanding.

Pushing his glasses up, Simon pretended to look

around with interest, while keeping Amanda in sight at all times. Not a hard job, as things went. Though at twenty-five she was a bit young for his taste, the woman's slim figure and rounded breasts were visually pleasing. She was a good waitress, too—quick. She walked up to tables with a full tray and delivered everything without pausing to question who got what; friendly, but not really flirty.

"So, what's the most famous thing about this place?" he asked, when she brought his beer.

"Hmm." She paused as if she had all night, frowned and peered around. "I'd say the fireplace." The silver butterfly clip that secured her long amber-streaked hair, glinted as she turned back to him. "Some of those stones were dug up hundreds of years ago. And there's lava formations and petrified wood there, too."

More than he'd ever wanted to know. "No kidding." Simon gave the structure a good, long look. "You been here long?"

"Four years," she told him. "Since I was an undergrad at NAU."

"You dropped out?"

She shook her head. "I graduated. With a degree in English. I'm working on a master's now."

Bright girl. And determined enough to work while she studied.

"Got a boyfriend?"

He'd asked Jan the same question earlier that evening, when he'd insisted they look through her home while the cop was there—although he'd asked her for entirely different reasons. With Jan, even though he'd agreed with the beat cop's assessment of a neighborhood gang-related dare, he'd been hoping to find out that she had some extra protection. She didn't.

"Yeah, I got one," Amanda said. And Simon took a sip of beer, batting zero for zero.

"Been together long?"

"Three years." She grinned as she said it, letting him know that she was flattered by his interest—but not interested. Scott needed a better information source. This wasn't a disgruntled ex.

"Too bad," he told her with a warm glance. So much for getting her to spill her guts after work.

"Enjoy your beer," she said, swinging around toward the bar.

"You know anywhere a guy can get some good physical training around here?" he called after her.

Simon always had plans B, C and D, as backup.

She stopped. "What kind of training?"

"I'm getting ready for level-three alpine certification from the Professional Ski Instructors of America." He could have been. If he'd had any desire to spend his days in the cold and snow doing something he used to enjoy. Which he didn't.

He patted his belly beneath the loosely hanging wrinkled shirt, making it clear that his garment was not hiding surplus flesh. "I've got great abs," he said sheepishly, "and I can bench press twice my weight. I work out at the gym every morning." If you could call the equipment in his spare bedroom a gym. "But I need more. Something that'll put me above the rest."

An asshole at a table by the dance floor whistled, and Amanda looked over her shoulder. "I might know of someone who could help," she said, as she walked away. "Give me a couple of days."

With that, she was gone. And so was Simon. He'd gotten what he'd come for.

4

The Zeidel file did not turn up. That could be an omen. Perhaps Jan should have done what Andrew advised and cut her losses. Not only her reputation, but the state's and the county attorney's hung in the balance. It was an election year. The county attorney couldn't afford bad press or big losses. Better to let Jacob Hall go quietly on his way. After all, to her boss he was a small fish—perhaps a member of the Ivory Nation, but certainly not the leader. She'd yet to tie him directly to Bobby Donahue.

"Danny, thanks for meeting with me." She stood, shaking the off-duty detective's hand as he joined her at the table for two along one wall of Macy's Coffeehouse early the following Saturday morning.

"My favorite Ethiopian coffee and a beautiful woman. How could I pass that up?" he asked, settling his slightly overweight middle-aged body on the chair across from her. She was used to seeing him in uniform, and the jeans and flannel shirt were hard to get used to.

It didn't surprise her that when it came to coffee Danny Ruple went for the strong, rough, dry kind. She bought the coffee for him at the counter, along with one of Macy's famous muffins. And ordered a light-roast Brazilian for herself. She was picking Hailey up for breakfast as soon as she finished with the detective and she hoped that one small dose of caffeine was all she'd need until then.

"I heard about your brick encounter a few days ago," he said, taking a sip from his steaming cup.

She wasn't shocked by that. With only about sixty officers on the Flagstaff police force, the men and women resembled a big family; if one of them was called to the home of a county prosecutor, they'd all know about it.

"Officer Ramsey thinks it was gang related." Much to her relief.

Danny nodded. "There've been three or four similar incidents south of the railroad tracks since May."

"Any suspects?"

"We're pretty sure we know the kids doing it," Danny said. "But so far there's been nothing more than minimal damage, no injuries—no real proof. We've brought a couple of them in for questioning, at least to let them know we're onto them, to scare them a little. Lord knows, if we make an arrest without a full confession, fingerprints and VHS recordings, some defense attorney will start spouting rights of the accused and get him off."

"Attorneys are not all misguided, Detective," she

said with a grin. "We're just bound by laws that strangle us occasionally."

"And you call on us to cut the rope and then tie yourselves up again."

It was an ongoing debate between the two of them—in jest, but there was truth, as well. "You're a fine cop, Danny Ruple."

"Uh-oh, this isn't going to be good." He stared into his coffee, so she couldn't read the look in his eyes. Which was probably for the best. "What happened— Hall walk again?"

"Nope."

He studied her. "You're actually going to make it stick this time? 'Cause I gotta tell you, Jan, I'm pretty damn sick of risking my butt so he gets a few days bed and board on the state and then returns to the street with a vendetta against the cop who booked him. I got a wife and two teenage boys who prefer it when I come home alive."

"I know." She nodded. Took comfort from the warmth of the ceramic mug resting in her cupped hands. "And I'm going to get him. But I need your help."

"Of course, you do. Why else would you be buying me expensive coffee? What've you got?"

He thought she had a lead that needed checking. It wouldn't be the first time Danny had spent unpaid hours off duty, assisting on a case.

"An offer."

Narrowing his eyes, he sipped from his coffee, and said nothing.

"I'll charge the Lorna Zeidel case and prosecute to

the fullest extent of my ability." Even though that meant starting from scratch on a cold case, a wild goose chase that—unless she pulled off a miracle—would cost the state and ultimately hurt her reputation.

"Shit." He put down his cup with careful deliberation. The muffin she'd bought him remained untouched. "In exchange for what?"

"I need you in court a week from Monday, 8:30 sharp."

"Why?"

She didn't look down, as much as she was tempted to. "An evidentiary hearing to establish the validity of your confidential informant in the Hall case."

"They want me to testify that it's valid?"

If it was that easy, she wouldn't have needed Lorna Zeidel. Jan waited.

Ruple threw himself against the hardwood chair, almost tipping it backward. "You want me to expose my source."

She nodded.

"Knowing it's the kiss of death for a cop."

She nodded again, saying nothing as he stood.

"Do I look like a fool to you, Ms. McNeil?"

"No, Danny," she said, still seated. "You look like a cop who's really in it to get the bad guys—no matter what the cost."

She had him. At least for a second. And then, leaving his coffee unfinished, he stalked out.

Would he be in touch? Or would she have to attend

Hall's hearing still wondering if her key witness—her only witness—was going to show?

"Can we not talk about our court stuff right now?"

With an effort, Jan's smile remained intact as she fell silent. Fork in midair over her blueberry pancakes, she watched the eight-year-old across from her consume a plate of French toast without a care in the world.

"Have you changed your mind about us, Hailey?" she asked softly, holding her breath. "Because it's okay if you have. All you have to do is say so. I won't be angry with you, I promise."

Heartbroken, but not angry.

The child's short, dark curls bounced as she shook her head. "'Course not," she said, her mouth full. "Next to Mrs. Butterworth, you're the nicest person I ever met. Being your kid would be almost as good as there really being a Santa Claus."

Jan wanted to hug Hailey so tight, keep her so close that no harm could ever come to her again. "You just don't want to know about the legal proceedings?" she asked, just to be sure, respecting the little girl's reserve.

Hailey shrugged, her shoulders bony looking beneath the blue T-shirt she was wearing with a pair of faded jeans. Her sweater was wadded beside her on the bench in the booth of their favorite diner on Route 66.

"You planning to tell me what's bothering you?"

"Nothing." Hailey peeked up at her. Swallowed. And did not immediately shovel another bite of food into her mouth. "I just don't see why I should hear about the actual adoption, when they aren't going to let it happen anyway."

"Who isn't?"

Had the Ivory Nation connected her to Hailey? Threatened the child? Jan's body temperature dropped, until she realized that, once again, she was falling prey to paranoia.

"You know, the court people," Hailey said, frowning. "Judges and CPS and all that. Derek says they probably won't give me to anyone, but they especially won't give me to you."

Derek Lincoln, the twelve-year-old biological son of Hailey's foster parents.

"Why not?"

"Derek says no one wants kids like me to have regular homes, 'cause we won't fit in. They just keep moving us around from foster to foster, till we're old enough to live alone."

As quickly as Jan's blood had frozen, it burned. "Derek's wrong."

"He says he's seen it. He says it always happens that way. They talk about adoption, but every foster kid in his house just gets moved to other foster houses. He says most people don't want us kids, 'cause we're troublemakers and 'cause we're too old. He says even some foster homes aren't good, 'cause people do it for the money. He says they aren't all like his mom, who just loves any old kid."

"First off, you're not any old kid, and you're the farthest thing from a troublemaker there is, young lady,"

Jan said in a voice left over from her days in juvenile court, where she'd first met and fallen in love with Hailey Miller.

Then, sensing the debilitating fear beneath the young girl's bravado, she immediately softened. "No matter how old you get, I'm going to want you and love you," she said, leaning over so the child could hear her clearly in the busy restaurant. "I'm not adopting just anyone, you know. I'm adopting you. Specifically you."

Hailey's chin puckered.

"I've always wanted kids some day." Jan told the child something she'd never said out loud before. "But ever since college, I've worked so much I've lost touch with all my friends. And I never met a man I felt safe enough with to marry—you know one I believed would love me forever and ever."

She grinned at Hailey, and felt a little better when the child smiled back.

"I was beginning to think I'd never have my family," she continued, her voice lower as she opened her heart to this precocious and oh-so-strong child. "I don't know why, but I never even thought about adoption—maybe because I always thought marriage would come before the kids."

Hailey nodded, her gaze serious and on target, as if she could fully understand the complexity of the adult emotions Jan was laying before her.

Jan reached out a hand, covering Hailey's. "Until I met you," she continued. "Then, I could think of nothing else."

Hailey stared at her.

And then, pulling her hand away, she stiffened. "They aren't going to let you."

Because she was single? She'd already crossed that hurdle, received the legal go-ahead. "Why do you say that?"

"You put away the bad people."

Jan blinked. "Yeah. So?"

"I *am* the bad people."

"Hailey Ann Miller! You are not bad!" Jan lowered her voice. "Don't say such things."

"Why not?" the child asked, her eyes wide and clear. "It's true."

"It is not true."

"You put *me* away."

Oh, God.

After all this time, all the times I prepared for this, why did it have to happen now?

"The court took you from a place that wasn't good for you," Jan finally said. A place worse than hell for a vulnerable little girl. Jan lost her appetite, just thinking about what she'd found at the duplex rented by Hailey's mother. Dirty walls, rotten floors—a hole the size of a basketball in front of the only toilet, open to the foundation and dirt beneath. Mold everywhere. And a constant stream of horny men who paid Hailey's mother, a prostitute, a pittance for the use of a body that had once been beautiful but was now weathered and ragged.

"You took me because I stole too many times and got arrested and brought to court to be punished."

"You stole cold medicine because you were too young to buy it, and you had to help someone who'd taken care of you," Jan said decisively. "Mrs. Butterworth loved you. No matter how old or tired or sick she was, she took you into her side of the duplex whenever your mom was out too late or had…visitors."

In spite of state-ordered counseling and Jan's personal attempts to gain the girl's total confidence, no one knew if Hailey fully comprehended what her mother was— what she'd done with the various men who'd come and gone from their home. A medical exam had shown that the child had not been molested, but no one knew what she'd witnessed during the first seven years of her life.

"Till I got taken away." Hailey took a small bite and chewed slowly, no pleasure evident. When she'd finished, she put down her fork and looked up at Jan, her eyes glistening. "I am bad," she said with quiet conviction. "It wasn't just that once. I stole before, too, when Mrs. Butterworth's checks didn't come, but I wasn't that good at it and I kept getting caught. And I took candy, once, just for me. It's just that the last time they already told me no more or else, and I did anyway, and it was medicine, and now I'm taken away because I'm a troublemaker."

"You were caught, and yes, there was some punishment because stealing is against the law…" Although, in Hailey's case, Jan had recommended the punishment, probation, only as a scare tactic—and a safeguard, a way to keep close tabs on the little girl. It was highly unusual for an eight-year-old to be on probation.

Hailey was nodding, pushing a piece of French toast that was swimming in her syrup.

"But, Hailey, you weren't taken away because of that. You were put in a different home because after the court found out the kind of conditions you were living in, they had to provide a better place for you, a safer place, where there were people who would shop and cook for you and not leave you alone at night. The other times, they'd called your mother and she'd cleaned up enough to satisfy the authorities when they brought you home. But the last time, they didn't call and just went to your house. It was obvious, then, that your mother couldn't care for you as the law requires. And the judge couldn't leave you there, honey, especially after Mrs. Butterworth died."

Hailey had been pretty resigned about leaving her mother. And hadn't asked about the woman since. On the other side, Karen Miller hadn't responded to a single one of the state's attempts at reconciliation or visitation, and had, in fact, allowed severance proceedings to go forward without any objection whatsoever.

Jan got up from the table and switched sides, sliding in beside the little girl.

"You did some things you shouldn't have done, Hailey, but more important than what you do is *why* you do it. You don't do things to be mean or selfish. You don't lash out in anger or turn away when you think someone needs your help. That's what a troublemaker does. You're kind of like Mrs. Butterworth. You want to take care of things, even when you really can't. She should have moved to a nursing home where the government could have taken care of her, but she didn't want to leave you. And you took things that weren't yours because you weren't old enough to go to work to earn the money she needed. That means you have a good heart. Not a bad one."

"You really think so?" The little girl's eyes were so big and blue they seemed almost jewel-like.

"I know so."

Hailey ate a couple of hearty bites. And then, shoulders drooping, she laid her fork in the middle of her plate, the handle sinking into the syrup.

"I'm on probation," she said. "Derek says only bad kids are on probation and they don't ever get out of foster care."

Maybe the sentence had been a little harsh, but even in the beginning Jan had seen the potential in Hailey and also the determination, and she couldn't think of another way to get the point across that continued stealing was unacceptable. Telling her it was wrong hadn't worked, because in her mind her reasons had always been right and stronger. Telling her no hadn't stopped her. Threats hadn't stopped her. Eventually the habit would have ruined her life.

"Derek's pretty smart, but he's just a kid, too, and he doesn't know everything yet," Jan said, careful not to malign the boy. For now, Hailey was part of the Lincoln family, and her need for stability, a sense of belonging, were the most important factors in the child's life. The October 23rd court adoption date felt far too distant.

Jan sat back, thoughts of her own inadequacies stealing some of her confidence. She suffered so severely from nightmares—and from a consequent lack of self-trust—that she'd slowly shut herself off from all relationships that weren't work related. And now she was bringing a child into her life—a full-time resident, who would want friends to spend the night.

She could do it. She knew she could. But it wasn't going to be easy.

Would Hailey suffer while Jan worked things out?

And even after the court made Hailey her legal daughter, how could she provide this precious and needy child with stability, while she was planning to expose herself to the possible retaliation of the Ivory Nation?

Yet how could she not follow through on a five-year commitment to save the people Jacob Hall would continue to hurt, possibly kill, if he were let go? How could she turn her back on this chance to send a clear and direct message to Bobby Donahue and the rest of the Ivory Nation?

Grunting as much for show as from any real need, Simon hopped from tire to tire, up the ragged edge of the mountain. A foot into each and every one, before shimmying up the tree at the end of the rubber trail. He'd been hard at it all morning—a bit of an alternative to his usual Saturday-morning regime of lying around bored out of his skull and not caring enough to do anything about it.

"Not bad for a first run." Leonard Diamond, the

most perfect specimen of manhood Simon had ever seen, nodded from the base of the tree. "Amanda was right to send you to me. You continue to work like that and I'll have you ready to tackle any strength or skill exam they can give you—on skis or off—by the end of November, but it'll cost you. I only work with the best and I don't come cheap."

Agent Scott Olsen, and his convoluted FBI expense accounting, was paying for this—so what the hell. The sweat felt damn good.

Simon nodded. And tried not to think about the young woman who—after he'd paid three more visits to the Museum Club—had put him in touch with this acquaintance of her boyfriend's—who'd been an ex but no longer was, he'd discovered. If Leonard Diamond, the independent trainer, turned out to be providing his services to terrorists, as the FBI suspected, Amanda Blake was running with a very dangerous crowd.

With instincts that weren't quite as dead as he'd told himself they were, Simon had garnered more about twenty-five-year-old Amanda than he'd wanted to. The girl was back with her too-mysterious boyfriend, but she wasn't all that happy about the relationship. In fact, the beautiful young lady seemed more resigned than in love. And more than a little afraid, as well. Olsen, who'd received his tips from her through intricate channels, had had the same impression. Simon had practically had to give her his birth certificate before she'd agreed to get him this trial with Diamond. She said that his time was premium and he was hit on by every quack parent in the world who wanted his kid to be a star. Thankfully, compliments of Scott Olsen's connections, Simon now had a fake identity. A guy with the same name, who had been born and raised in Alaska and was a first-time visitor to Flagstaff. His alter ego even had a new apartment. If he needed a place to receive visitors.

The fact that this new game might be dangerous didn't faze him a bit.

Simon wasn't afraid to die.

An hour and a half later, after showering, securing a locker and filling out a minimal amount of paperwork, Simon turned onto his street just in time to see Jan pull into her driveway next door. When she didn't enter the garage, he wondered if she was still a bit gunshy from the brick incident earlier in the week. Then he slowed to a stop, gawking when he saw the elflike child who climbed out of the passenger seat.

Who the hell was she? In the four years he'd been living next door to Ms. Janet McNeil and in the three or so years he'd been meeting her at her mailbox, he'd never once seen or heard mention of a child in her life.

A widowed mother in Sedona, check. An unmarried salesman brother, right. No ex-husbands. No cousins or aunts or uncles or grandparents. No friends he knew of, with or without children.

The woman worked. Took care of her mother. Her home. Was friendly to her neighbors. And talked to him a few minutes every day.

She waved and Simon could feel the heat under his skin, a rare occurrence for someone who didn't care enough about anything to get embarrassed. He waved back and continued on to his driveway, but stopped just over the curb and got out.

Jan was down at the mailbox, letters in hand, just standing. Almost as if she was waiting for him.

Not good. Not good at all.

He walked over, even though he knew it was a big mistake to do so. The woman, her welfare, her guests, didn't matter to him, other than for the distant role she played in the passing of his days.

"Hey, neighbor," he greeted her, including the girl in his grin. About seven, he'd guess, based on her size. And it'd been a hard seven years. The awareness in those eyes, the chin that held back expression rather than softening in response to a friendly smile—they told a familiar story.

"Simon, I wanted Hailey to meet you." Jan's voice was higher than it usually was. She was too perceptive to be humoring this child with false cheer. Which told him she was tense about something.

"Hi, Hailey." He held out his hand. Her grip was tiny, but firm.

"Hi."

"How old are you?" Wasn't that what you said to kids you weren't rescuing from hell—or arresting?

"Eight."

A year off. Not bad for a guy who'd been off the streets for almost a decade.

"Hailey and I are in the process of becoming a family." Jan moved a bit closer to the girl.

"She's trying to adopt me, but I keep telling her they won't let it happen," the child said.

"Hailey's a little short on faith at the moment, and I thought I'd bring her to see her new home so she can start visualizing our future together."

Simon slid his hands into the pockets of the sweats he'd changed into after his locker-room shower. Jan with a child? The idea threw him. And that didn't happen often.

Why should it matter to him if she wanted to take on the responsibility, the guaranteed heartache of parenthood?

Why would picturing her as a mother affect him at all?

It didn't. He was just suffering a bit of an adrenaline letdown after the morning's workout. Mixed with a little altitude adjustment.

"Are you a cop?"

While he swallowed the need to choke, Jan chuckled. "Simon writes schoolbooks, sweetie."

Those shrewd, knowing eight-year-old eyes studied him—whether in assessment or disbelief, he didn't know. Simon smiled, slouching, completely alert.

"Nope, just a writer," he told her, his voice more relaxed than the rest of him.

"You sure you aren't a cop?" Hailey frowned. "'Cause my mom taught me to spot 'em." Her curly hair was almost in her eyes as she peered up at him.

"She says you can always tell a cop by the way his eyes see everything going on, when most people just see what they're staring at. Your eyes look all over. They don't stare."

Observation duly noted. How had he survived years undercover, if he was that obvious? he wondered wryly.

"Sounds like your mom was a smart lady," he said, cognizant of the fact that the little girl had obviously lost the woman prematurely. "And I'm sorry to disappoint you, but rather than running around the streets catching bad guys I just sit home all day and type stuff that college kids read for class."

"I'm not disappointed," Hailey said, nodding. "I don't know if I'd like living next door to a cop. I'd have to worry about him finding out that I'm not good."

Simon did choke, then. And glanced up in time to catch the pained look on Jan's face. There was a lot going on here that he didn't understand. And that was fine by him.

Except for that small, curious part of him that wanted all the answers.

"Hailey Miller, you *are* good," Jan said firmly, sounding much more like the woman he'd been meeting at the mailbox. "And I'm glad to hear that you're planning to live next door to Simon, because I'm pretty determined on this matter and once I set my mind to something I make it happen."

The white supremacist she was attempting to prosecute crossed his mind. And left him feeling tense.

"Do you have a court date?" he asked, still smiling as he glanced from one to the other.

"October 23rd," they said together. Hailey studied Jan for a long moment, one that Simon witnessed with an inexplicable pull, and then the little girl slid her hand into Jan's. "It was nice meeting you, Simon," she said.

"Nice meeting you, too, Hailey. I look forward to living next door to you."

"Thank you."

"See ya," Jan said, grinning at him as she turned with her charge's hand still firmly locked in hers.

Simon stood there watching them go.

Hailey looked over her shoulder. "Simon?"

"Yeah?"

"My mom's stupid."

He didn't know what to say to that, so it was fine that they didn't wait for him to figure it out.

So much for his ability to assess and conquer. Simon watched until they were inside Jan's house and then walked slowly into his own, to spend the rest of the day doing what he did best. Huddled in front of the computer, bored enough to write ten pages of a book that was supposed to be his nine-to-five job during the week.

5

"Hey, boss, you got a minute?"

Jan looked up from her computer. It was Monday, mid-morning. She'd had another nightmare at three in the morning and hadn't slept since. "Of course," she told her assistant. "Come in."

Andrew, dressed impeccably as always, took one of the two seats in front of her desk.

"I heard you met with Ruple over the weekend."

She'd figured word would get around. Flagstaff was a small town and Macy's was a busy place. Or maybe Danny Ruple had said something.

"I did, yes."

"Is he going to testify?"

The fact that she even had to remind herself that this was Andrew, her handpicked professional soul mate, bothered her. She had to be careful, true, but a complete lack of trust wasn't healthy.

"I don't know," she said, slipping into the navy jacket she'd thrown off earlier. She had some footwork to do over lunch—recreating as much of the Zeidel file as she could, just in case. The only key witness, a roommate, was still in town and had agreed to talk to her. "He didn't say yes, but he didn't say no."

Frowning, Andrew shook his head and said, "I'm just sick about the missing file. You know I'll do anything I can to help you rebuild the case, if he accepts your offer."

"Thanks." Jan's smile was almost genuine and her shoulders lightened. "I know your own caseload is heavy right now, and I promised you'd have time to be a father when the baby came…"

"I'm always here for you, Jan. You know that."

A life that had gone a bit out of control started to make sense again. She had to remember what she knew—not lose herself in emotions that weren't always accurate. Or trustworthy.

"I think you're about the only one who doesn't think I'm crazy for going after Hall."

"I admire the hell out of you for it." The truth of his words was reflected in his open gaze. "I hope to be just like you when I grow up."

"Hold it, buddy," she chuckled. "I'm only five years older than you. You're making me sound ancient."

"Sorry." Andrew was grinning, too. "But I mean it. You're the only one I know who consistently applies the ethics they taught us in law school to everyday life. You work for justice, not politics."

"There are a lot of us," she told him, though she wasn't as sure of that as she'd been even a couple years before. "But when people like the county attorney and the governor have the last say, and they're elected officials, politics can't help but play a part."

"And we end up with compromised justice."

Jan glanced at the news clipping she'd just pulled up on her computer—which only hinted at the gory details of Lorna Zeidel's rape and murder two years before. "It's when politics define justice that I have a problem."

Andrew leaned forward, resting an arm on the edge of her desk. "And it honestly doesn't bother you that if you push this and lose, your professional reputation will suffer?"

She shook her head. There were a lot of things bothering her. Her professional reputation wasn't one of them. "My mother's health bothers me. Hailey's adoption bothers me. The young gang members who have nothing better to do than throw bricks through windows bother me." *My awareness of my neighbor's presence bothers me.* "I'm not sure why, but my career doesn't. I think I'm on the right track."

"I don't know how you do it." Andrew expelled a long breath. "But I'm here to learn."

"You're here to teach, too, my friend," Jan told him. "You're an excellent attorney. I've bowed to your opinion on more than one occasion."

"Maybe two." He smiled and then sat back, his expression sober. "What's this about your mother's health? I thought she was doing well, keeping busy."

"She is." Jan didn't want to think about her mother right now. "I'm probably overreacting. Growing up with only one parent tends to make you a bit insecure where their existence is concerned."

"When was the last time you saw her?"

"Less than twenty-four hours ago. I went down yesterday and took her to the Blue Adobe for dinner. We had cheese enchiladas and prickly pear margaritas and talked about a mah-jongg tournament she's in."

"Sounds like she's doing great."

Yeah. And Jan had just decided to go with what she knew and not with what she feared. To quit letting random feelings control her so much. Everyone had them—those insecurities that overwhelmed common sense. She just seemed to have to work harder than other people to keep hers at bay.

By Thursday, Jan still had not heard from Danny Ruple. But she was using every spare minute she could find, in between directing the continued research into Jacob Hall's potential fraud victims and maintaining her other cases, to study police reports on Lorna Zeidel—searching for the elusive clue that might at least get her a grand jury indictment.

She'd had no word from her brother after his impromptu visit, but she'd had a quick visit with Hailey the night before. And not including Saturday, she had talked to Simon three times, twice at the mailbox and once when he was getting his paper in the morning.

By the time she got home that night, she was just plain exhausted with life. She'd seen the It's a Boy sign in the Thorntons' front yard on her way to work that morning, and felt such regret at losing touch with her friendly neighbors that she'd gone out on her lunch hour and bought them a gift. But she sure didn't feel like walking two houses down to drop it off.

She didn't want to, but as soon as she'd finished the toast and peanut butter she was having for dinner she did it anyway. And was rewarded with a greeting from Simon when she returned.

"I brought the trash out and noticed yours wasn't at the curb, so I thought I'd get it for you," he said, meeting her at the end of her drive as dusk was starting to fall. Friday and Monday trash pickup had been part of her routine for years. Today, she would have forgotten.

"My gate's locked."

"As I discovered." He walked along with her up to the house, looking so comfortable in khaki slacks and a flannel shirt with tails hanging out and sleeves rolled up past his wrists, that she wished she'd taken time to change out of the maroon skirt and jacket she'd worn to work.

The clicking of her heels against pavement sounded loud in the early-evening silence.

"You been down the street?"

"Mm-hmm." She walked up the couple of steps to her front door. Pulled it open. "Molly Thornton had her baby."

"It's not locked?"

"I was only gone for a few minutes."

"Could you see your front door every second of that time?"

"Of course not. The Thorntons are on the same side of the street."

"How do you know someone didn't see you leave and then enter your house?"

Ignoring the blade of fear that slid through her, Jan forced a chuckle. "Like I said before, you need to be writing suspense, Green. Because stuff like that only happens between the pages of a book or on the screen. I was two houses down, for goodness' sake." They were still on her stoop.

"But it only takes…"

"And during that time you were bringing out your trash."

She went inside. He stayed out.

"You mad at me now?" she asked lightly.

"No." But he was frowning.

"You just changed your mind about taking my trash out?" She'd been rolling the big can out by herself for years, didn't need his help, but she couldn't pass up the opportunity to mess with him.

It took her mind off her weariness.

"Of course not," he said. "I'll meet you at the gate."

"Simon!" She laughed out loud then. "You can come through the house."

She didn't really understand his hesitation. It wasn't as if he hadn't been inside before. He'd seen every inch of her 2,000-square-foot home when he'd trailed behind the police officer who'd searched it after the brick incident the week before.

He walked through, went out to wheel the trash to

the curb, then relocked the gate from the inside and came back into her kitchen, all without a word. He stood there, staring at her.

"What?" She'd poured herself a very weak vodka and orange juice—mostly orange juice—and leaned against the counter, taking a sip.

"It's none of my business."

"Probably not. But I'm sure you'll tell me, anyway."

He shook his head. "You know what you're doing. And you have an inside track on crime in this town."

"Yeah."

"But I'd still appreciate it if you'd be a little more careful. A woman living alone…"

"I won't live my life in fear."

"I'm not suggesting you should. Keep in mind, though, that I live right next door. And I'd like to be able to relax now and then without constantly having to listen for strangers with evil intent bothering someone who's nice."

He thought she was nice. That was all right. Because she thought he was sweet.

"Okay," she said, her mouth twitching as she held back a smile. "In an effort to contribute to your peace of mind, I will be more diligent about locking my door. Since this is the first time in years I can remember leaving it unlocked, I don't think it'll be too much of a challenge."

And she was no idiot. She was prosecuting a killer who had loyal associates. She wanted to live long enough to get him into prison.

"Thank you."

"Now how about a truce?" She held up her glass. "I have vodka to offer."

"I accept."

She was shocked. He was supposed to have made a joke and been out of there. Didn't he remember his own MO?

Turning, she took down a glass from the cupboard. A juice glass. She didn't entertain enough to justify highball crystal.

"You pour," she said, handing him the bottle and pushing the orange juice his way.

He took a splash of juice to go with his vodka, leaned back against the opposite cupboard...and suddenly she was nervous. The man seemed a lot more vital, standing in her kitchen.

"I didn't realize you knew the Thorntons all that well." He adjusted his glasses.

His eyes were brown. She'd never noticed before.

"I don't really. They drop off fruitcakes at Christmas, but I think everyone gets them."

He nodded. "Never did figure out the appeal there."

"Me, neither. But my mother likes them. I give them to her."

"Good, she can have mine next year, too. I feel like a jerk when I throw them away."

Jan chuckled with him. Took a sip of mostly orange juice and wished it was mostly vodka.

"A few years ago, my washer valve broke when I was out of town," she said. "The whole house flooded.

The Thorntons had just moved in, and they noticed the water coming out from under my doors and called the city to turn off the water. They also helped me move out all my furniture while the damage was being repaired."

"Where was I?"

"I have no idea." She smiled at him again. "That was before I'd actually met you. But I think you were gone. For about a month I didn't see any papers at the end of your drive when I left for work in the morning."

Oh. Well. It only took a second for her to realize that she'd just admitted that she paid attention. And remembered something that had happened almost four years ago. That was embarrassing.

"I took a…river rafting trip," he said, stumbling a bit over the words—as if he was finding this experience awkward, as well. "I was gone for almost a month," he continued, resting one foot in front of the other. "Must have been then."

She wanted to look away. And didn't.

"So how were the Thorntons?"

"Fine. They named him Mark."

"I hear hesitation in your voice," he said, his expression curious. "Why? Don't you like the name?"

Were all writers as observant as he was?

"Of course I like the name." She shrugged, putting her edgy reaction down to fatigue. "I'm sure it's nothing. They just seemed to go on and on about how happy they were that the baby's a boy. I got a pretty strong sense that if they'd had a girl they would actually have been disappointed."

"Maybe they wanted to please the grandparents or something."

"Maybe. I can't imagine the sex of a child mattering to me as long as he or she was healthy, but I realize it makes a difference to some people."

He switched legs, crossing one over the other. She couldn't really explain why she wasn't offering him a seat. Standing just seemed like a better idea.

"I also couldn't help wondering if my father was disappointed, when I turned out to be female." Jan's gaze shot up, stricken when she realized she'd spoken aloud. Simon didn't care about her anxieties.

And he was only supposed to see what she presented to the world. A daring, driven attorney who did things her own way, but always played by the rules.

"Did he act disappointed?" His direct gaze, the soft tone in his voice, made her knees shake.

She shook her head and took a seat at the table in the middle of her kitchen. Simon followed her, bringing the bottle and the carton of juice.

"I don't really remember much about him," she continued, telling her better judgment to shut up. She had to start working through things or she'd go nuts. And really, who was safer to think aloud with than a distant neighbor who didn't have any reason to care, beyond a generic sense of compassion.

"He died when I was four."

"He was sick?"

"He accidentally shot himself."

"*What?*" Simon's glass hit the table solidly, his eyes narrowing. "How?"

"He was drunk and got his gun out to load it, to go hunting. It was already loaded and it went off...." She closed her eyes against the assault of memories, as if doing so could erase all the blood. "There was an investigation, and the evidence corroborated events exactly as my mother had said they happened."

"Where were you at the time?"

"At home, taking a nap." She tried to swallow, but her throat was too dry. Picking up her glass, she tried again. "I don't remember the shooting at all, but I'll never forget standing in the archway leading to the living room and watching while they cut out a piece of living room carpet that was saturated with his blood."

And she'd never spoken of it, either. Jan peered over at Simon, afraid of what she'd done by telling him. Afraid of what she'd see in his eyes.

He looked confused, lost—like a man who was picturing the horrifying scene through the eyes of a four-year-old child.

"Were the two of you close?"

"I'm not sure. My mom's been emotionally fragile ever since it happened—at least I've assumed it started then. In any case, it's too hard on her to talk about my dad, so we won't."

"Seems like, at four, you'd have some memories, if you and he had much of a relationship."

Something that had occurred to her, too. "I just have flashes," she said, finishing her drink and pouring another. "I remember moments of anger, but I can't ever bring back enough to know what he was angry about or who he was angry with. I can just picture his face, red, his mouth, thin, and his eyes small and kind of black."

"That's a pretty clear picture," Simon said. "Sounds like he was angry a lot."

"Maybe. I also remember a birthday—maybe my third or fourth. I can't recall anything about the day, except that he and I laughed a lot and he threw me up in the air and caught me and said he always would."

She smiled when what she felt like doing was crying. "I like to think he's still up there, catching me. When my brother was little, he used to tell everyone he was special because his daddy was an angel who watched over him."

"How old was he when your dad was killed?"

"A few months."

"So he doesn't remember him at all."

"Nope."

"It's natural that he'd build him into some kind of hero or loving guardian, but those feelings don't necessarily have any connection to the kind of man your father really was."

"I know."

"And your mother never shared anything that gave you any indication? No story about how they met? What he did for a living?"

"Not much." Jan sighed, wanting to lay her head on a caring shoulder. For a second. "They were high school sweethearts who married fairly young. And they waited several years before having me. He worked for a trucking company, at some point. I discovered that tidbit when I moved my mother to Sedona. I was helping her get her finances together and I found documents concerning a small pension she'd been getting all these years, though it wasn't clear from the dates if he'd been working at the time of the accident. I'm fairly certain he was an alcoholic, based on something Clara Williams—she was a neighbor and my mother's closest friend—said once, when I was telling them about a friend who'd bought a fake ID and gotten drunk."

"That could explain the anger. Some guys get mean when they drink."

"Yeah." And some were nice. Please God, for her mother's sake if nothing else, let him have been a nice drunk.

"You said your mom had problems. Is she okay now?"

He was really sweet to ask. Surely he'd rather be home at his computer. Or doing whatever else he did until all hours of the night.

"She's fine." Jan gave the short version, in deference to his kindness. "She had a pretty bad bout of depression nine or ten years ago. I'd just started law school and moved into my own apartment. Johnny was seventeen and going through the rebellious teenaged crap. It was too much for her to handle alone. But she got help. And then there was a bout a couple of years ago. She wouldn't get out of bed, wouldn't eat. She finally agreed to check herself into the hospital and came out with this idea that she had to move to an adult-living community in Sedona. She did, and she's been doing well ever since."

Simon finished his drink, but didn't pour another. "You could do an investigation. To track down information about your father."

She'd thought about it a few times. "I've just never been sure enough that I wanted to know," she said. "If it turns out he was a louse, I'm descended from a louse and that's all there is to it. And if I find out he was a great guy, I lost one of the best things that ever happened to me."

Simon stood. "You're right," he said. "You may be better off not knowing. That way anything's possible."

It made a strange kind of sense. She was tired enough to accept it.

"Thanks for taking out my trash." She followed him to the front door.

"Thanks for the drink."

She started to say "anytime," but decided against it and held the door for him instead.

He began to leave, then stopped abruptly and turned, his face two inches from hers.

She could hardly breathe, struck with the completely unfamiliar desire to have wild, passionate, unrestrained and irresponsible sex. The kind you had without accountability or any thought of tomorrow.

"Lock the door behind me."

She was deciphering the words when, halfway across her yard, he turned. Jan quickly shut her door and clicked the lock as loudly as she could.

And only then realized that while she'd just told Simon her entire life story, she still knew very little about him.

6

A gentle breeze blew through the trees surrounding the old wooden cabin, mixing with the sounds of chirping birds to create a background of nature music. Bobby Donahue swelled with pride as he surveyed his acreage in the mountains several miles outside Flagstaff. He'd done well.

Reaching over, he untied the blindfold covering Tony Littleton's eyes.

"Sorry about that," he said, "but the cause is too important to risk discovery. This place is a combination storeroom, training ground and safe house. There are selfish people out there who don't want our voices to be heard because the truth of our message threatens their personal bottom lines. I have to be very careful. I can't let you know exactly where we are or how we got here. Not yet, anyway."

"No problem," Tony said, his voice eager as he glanced around, reminding Bobby of a cocker spaniel pup he'd had as a kid. That dog had been his constant companion—until his father had snapped its neck one night, when it barked during basketball playoffs.

Perhaps it was time to get another one. The experience would be good for Luke, exposing the two-year-old to deep and abiding affection, and Amanda could take care of it.

"No one comes up here—ever—without me."

"I understand. Believe me, you have nothing to worry about from me. It's like you're my personal savior. I'm so jazzed about this opportunity I lie awake at night thinking about it." The skinny young man walked a few feet in one direction and then another, as though trying to take in the whole world at once. Bobby smiled, basking in the certainty that his life's mission was the true course, the only course, and that all would be well.

This was why Bobby took in all new recruits himself—the resurgence of passion, faith and hope he gained from exposure to theirs was priceless. He'd practically had an orgasm the first time he'd felt the fire of purpose in his veins.

The air was cooler up on the mountain, feeding his lungs, stimulating him. "There's not much inside besides supplies," he said, taking a key ring from his pocket to open the bottom lock on the only visible door. And then, instructing the boy to close his eyes and not move an inch, he rounded the building, pulled a large knot out of a tree, took the lock box out of hiding, quickly worked the combination and retrieved the key to the second lock. All the while keeping an eye on Tony with the help of hidden surveillance mirrors he'd installed all over the compound.

Moving with the animal grace he'd worked so hard to acquire, he used the key on the front door and returned it to safety.

The boy passed the test. He didn't peek.

"Okay, let's go in," he said. He might have hit the mother lode with this recruit. Tony Littleton had "future leader" written all over him. Hell, years down the road he might even be presidential material.

"Wow!" Tony turned full circle in the middle of the cabin's main room. "There must be thousands of cans in here. What're they for?"

"Food storage," Bobby said proudly, grabbing one of the silver gallon-sized metal storage containers. "All essentials that will keep for up to seven years. Macaroni, dried beans, mashed potatoes, pudding, soups, spaghetti, cereal, dried milk, canned meat. We've got fifty gallon jugs of water in the shed."

"No kidding." Tony's voice reflected his awe as he read some of the labels. "Cool, you even have refried beans!"

It was as if the kid was already tasting them—seeing himself as a member of the family at the table. Bobby paused to take a couple of deep breaths, holding back tears of joy.

"It's like I've been searching for this all my life," Tony said, turning to face him. "I've always known I had a greater purpose, that I had a special job to do that would benefit the world. Something inside me recognized it the very first time I spoke with you in that chat room. Everything you said about justice and the world, about the need for men who had the courage to do God's work, about wiping out the conspirators, fighting the forces of evil and filling the world with God's true chosen people rang completely true to me. It's like you were reading inside my deepest self."

Yes. Yes! The zeal was there. The passion. The beliefs. And soon, the training would be, too. He'd start with targets today. Explosives work could come later. And by this time next year, little brother Tony Littleton would be wearing red laces in his boots.

"It's the strangest thing, Jan." Andrew came into Jan's office, closing the door as he always did when he wanted her uninterrupted attention. The other attorneys on the floor had the habit of dropping in on her to discuss cases, ask her opinion; they always seemed to assume that she was available.

"What's strange?" Friday, the twenty-ninth of September. Three days before Hall's hearing and still no word from Ruple. She could think of little else.

"I just got a report on those bank account numbers we found in Hall's computer."

"You found some commonalities? They all had business with the same bank, or bought from the same online company?"

He approached her desk. Dropped a file in front of her. "They're all dead."

That one hadn't occurred to her.

"Dead?" She stared at him, her stomach heavy. "Are you sure?"

The question was rhetorical. He wouldn't have brought the information to her unless it had been validated. She sifted through the papers, anyway. Names, socials, copies of death certificates. The victims were from all over the state.

"So this sicko targets obituaries?" It was brilliant, really. Stealing from an estate when everything was in confusion and the heirs wouldn't know what to miss— at least at first.

"It's the conclusion I'm drawing."

"That would explain why the victims haven't reported anything."

"Let's contact the families and find out how many of them he stole from. We've got him on one count of fraud. If we can add another ten to it, so much the better."

"This gives a whole new meaning to the term ambulance chaser."

"No kidding," Jan said, studying the list again. "So we know how he got the names, but that still doesn't tell us how he accessed their personal information. There's got to be some connection between these people, other than having appeared in obituaries across the state of Arizona. Once we know who he hit, let's get warrants to look at some of the victims' computers—assuming these *are* other victims. We know Hall spent a lot of time on his computer. Maybe we're dealing with a virus—something Hall or one of his brotherhood wrote that would allow them to attack other people's computers with only an e-mail address and then access their hard drives."

"That would be the most plausible way. Or maybe we're back to a common business transaction, and Hall had an informant inside a statewide company with access to billing and other personal information."

Jan nodded. "With his Ivory Nation involvement, the idea of an inside source somewhere isn't that farfetched." She stared out the small window to the left of her desk, at the weeping willow across the street. Many times she'd found answers in those long and slender branches.

They were onto something big; she was sure of it. But it would all be for naught, if she couldn't use those computer records. Unless…

"Let's make this a priority," she told her assistant. "See if we can get at least one affirmative and work backward from that victim's computer to Hall's before Monday morning."

If Ruple didn't show, if Judge Warren granted Michaels's motion to suppress, the defense attorney would then present a motion to dismiss the case based on lack of evidence. But with this new information, Jan would be able to oppose that motion and win. She'd get her time in court.

And that was when the real fight started.

"There's one more thing," Andrew said.

"What?"

"Every single one of the account owners is female."

* * *

Official FBI definition of terrorism:The unlawful use of force or violence against persons or property to intimidate or coerce a government, the civilian population, or any segment thereof, in furtherance of political or social objectives.

Simon's fingers flew across the keys. He bulleted, italicized and capitalized, without removing his eyes from the text he was typing. He'd skipped ahead to the last section of the manual.

M.O. is control by fear.

Adrenaline drove him. He was six pages behind on this week's page count, and that morning his editor had asked for the book early—they had a slot to fill. And yet, Simon had decided to add another entire section to the manual. He must be nuts.

Using the sociological preemptive appraisal for terrorist risk assessment, the United States scores ten out of ten for possible domestic terrorist activity.

He was going to have to start working nights, instead of competing in chess matches on the Internet. And he had to get more sleep, as well. Five mornings in a row at the Snowbowl had made that clear. Not that he'd found it particularly hard to get up. On the contrary, he'd been oddly invigorated that morning, when the alarm went off. It was the first Friday he could remember in eight years when he hadn't hit the sleep button at least twice.

The terrorist is a victim of mind-control tactics that can prompt good people to do evil things.

Probably from long habit, some leftover bit of internal radar, he caught a glimpse of the computer clock out of the corner of his eye. Six-fifteen. Jan should be arriving home.

Saving his work, Simon glanced out the window for the first time since he'd sat down. And watched as her car pulled up the street.

She'd survived another day. Simon stood, pushed his glasses up his nose and went out to greet his neighbor.

It was only then that he realized, he hadn't seen the school bus all week.

There was nothing unusual in Jan's mail. Not that she'd told him. He just paid attention because he'd been living with too much time on his hands for too long, apparently. And because years of training hadn't entirely deserted him.

"How was your day?" he asked when she didn't immediately turn to go up her drive. The woman looked far too good in forest-green. Or maybe he should blame the fashion industry for producing skirts that hugged hips in such an alluring way. Tailored jackets should be outlawed, as well.

"Better," she told him, apparently unaware of his inappropriate appraisal of her. "I think I actually accomplished something."

He had a feeling that was an understatement, would bet his untouched portion of Sam's trust that not one day went by without Jan accomplishing more than anyone around her.

"Not me," he said.

"You've been doing something all week." She gave him a narrow look. "Your newspaper's been gone every single morning."

"Probably stolen. Maybe it's the next gang strategy. Make us all ignorant so they can take over the world."

"And that's why I've seen your garage door open as if you were getting ready to leave? So you could go report your stolen newspaper?"

"You spying on me, Ms. McNeil?"

"My guess is you don't want me to find out you don't actually know everything and you're off doing research for that book you're writing."

Okay. He could live with that. And if you considered the chapter on perpetrator physical training methods, he supposed there was even truth in the statement.

"You seeing Hailey tomorrow?"

"I'm taking her to the zoo in Phoenix. She's never seen a live elephant before."

The barrette holding back her long hair tempted his fingers. The clasp looked interesting. He slid his hands into his pockets. They were safer there.

"I'm mowing grass."

She smirked and he tried not to notice. The woman was her own biggest threat.

"Too bad."

"My mower and I have great conversations," Simon defended with a lazy shrug. "We have a lot to catch up on since last week."

"You're an idiot." Jan chuckled. And he agreed with her completely. He shouldn't make her laugh, if he couldn't handle the sound without crazy reactions.

"I'd be happy to cut yours, too," he said, nodding toward her yard. "My mower probably won't even notice if I take longer rows. It would be a two for one."

"No way, Simon. I'm not having you do my chores. I'm not some helpless female. Or a moocher."

"Oh, I'd want something in return."

"Yeah?" She tilted her head, still smiling at him. "What would that be?"

For one split second Simon considered the word "you." Meaning, in the physical sense. And decided he needed to get some rest. Simon Green didn't want anyone. In any sense.

"I want some of those tomatoes you grow every year and never share. I love fried tomatoes, and they're best if you do them up straight from picking."

"Really?" She half frowned, as though she wasn't sure whether or not to believe him. "I wouldn't have pictured you as a fried tomato person."

"That's because you let that movie about fried tomato lovers leave you with an unrealistic stereotype."

"You mean *Fried Green Tomatoes*."

"Right."

How could he possibly be engaged in a conversation with so little merit?

"Where'd you learn to fry tomatoes?"

"From…" He'd almost told her. For the first time in eight years, he'd almost made an inadvertent slip. Almost opened up the past he'd nailed shut. "A cookbook, of course," he finished lightly. "So, we have a deal?"

She was still frowning. "Sure," she said, "but only if you answer one more question."

"Okay." He didn't say he'd answer it truthfully.

"Have you always lived alone?"

Well, by God, it was his lucky day. An easy question. "Since graduating from college?" Not many people lived alone in college.

"Yeah."

"Yep. Been on my own ever since."

She opened her mouth, as if to ask another question, but something must have changed her mind. With a nod, she wished him a good night and turned her back to head up to her house.

He waited, but she didn't look back.

The visit to the zoo was an unqualified success. Hailey's eyes grew wide, she laughed, and at one point she even jumped up and down with excitement. Jan looked forward to a time when moments like these would be common rather than rare in Hailey's life.

But the trip cost her on another front. With the evidentiary hearing looming the next morning, she had to cancel Sunday dinner with her mom. She'd used up most of the weekend and she needed to work. If she could uncover solid evidence against Lorna Zeidel's killer, she'd have a reason to call Ruple. To find out if he was going to leave her hanging. To persuade him not to. She felt cold and queasy every time she thought about facing Jacob Hall the next morning without the protection of solid evidence.

And when she thought of those bank account numbers on his computer—every single one belonging to a woman.

Many white supremacists, and members of the Ivory Nation, in particular, were known for their condescending attitude toward women. The female species existed simply to procreate.

She hoped Andrew had found a way to connect all the bank accounts.

She saw Simon briefly Sunday evening when she rolled her trash can out to the curb. He'd been coming out with his as she was going back in. She wondered if that was a coincidence, but didn't really want to know. He asked about her visit with Hailey, she thanked him for mowing her grass and they said good-night.

Nothing memorable in the encounter, at all; nothing to give her a lift. But it did.

Dressed in a conservative solid black skirted suit, with her hair clipped back, Jan waited for Andrew in the parking lot of the county attorney's office the next morning.

"Hi, what'd you find?" she asked, as he opened the door of his car. She'd been more tempted than ever to break the agreement she'd insisted on years ago and call him at home the night before.

Work was work. Home was life. They had to maintain clear boundaries at all times, or the long hours, the sometimes horrendous crimes they encountered, would begin to destroy their minds.

Her mood dived when she didn't receive an immediate answer to her question.

"Did you get something we can use?" Leather briefcase hanging from her shoulder, Jan watched as Andrew took the keys out of his ignition, pocketed his wallet, got out, then opened the back door to retrieve his briefcase. And she wanted to scream.

"I worked all weekend," he said as they headed toward the building. "I must've made a hundred calls. And I can't come up with even one person on that list who has a known family member."

"Over twenty names, and none of them left any survivors?"

Shrugging his shoulders, he shook his head. "Crazy as it sounds…"

"What about friends? Live-in lovers? *Anything?*"

"Not yet. I was just looking for heirs. I kept thinking if I stuck to the list, went from one to the next, something would turn up."

"I'd have thought the same," Jan allowed, although what she really wanted to do was lash out, ask him why he hadn't pursued the other possibilities when he knew how important this was.

Thankfully, she was able to maintain her calm. Always the peacemaker. The early-fall breeze helped cool her down a bit.

"Have you heard from Ruple?" Andrew held the door for her, their feet clattering on the tile floor.

"No." That list of women without family nagged at her. Something horrible had happened.

And damn it to hell, she didn't have time to figure out what.

"We have half an hour until the hearing," Andrew said. "We can still come up with some kind of answer."

"I'm not going to cancel the hearing, if that's what you're worried about," she told him. Going unprepared was rare for her, but it had happened before. Words had a way of coming, ideas occurring when she least expected them to.

"How's the baby?"

Andrew's face softened. "She slept four hours straight last night."

In her office five minutes later, Jan popped an antacid tablet and tried to swallow it without gagging as cold sweat dripped down her back. In fifteen minutes, she had to walk down the block to the courthouse and possibly lose Jacob Hall for a third time.

She checked her message light one more time. She hadn't missed a ring in the past thirty seconds. Ruple still hadn't called.

Simon grunted and sweated as he made his way sideways along the cliff early Monday morning, twisting and turning his skis on the makeshift ice. If he was going to qualify to train anyone else to become a first-rate skier or rescue anyone from a skiing mishap, which he'd said was his goal, he had to be able to maneuver successfully in any situation a novice might get into.

"I appreciate the time you're spending with me," he said to Diamond, who was by far the most competent personal trainer he'd ever had. Simon's only complaint was that the man didn't speak much. More than a week of hard workouts and he still had nothing of substance to report to Olsen, still had no concrete evidence that the man was training terrorists. He knew nothing about Diamond's mysterious roots. His past. His associations. His plans. He was almost as good as Simon was at diverting conversation.

"You're paying me," the man said without inflection.

"I've paid more for worse."

Diamond grunted. Unloaded another batch of instructions, pushing Simon further than he'd ever pushed himself. But pushing him fairly, always watching, closely monitoring Simon's every move, every breath.

"I noticed a couple of guys coming in when I was finishing my shower on Friday." Simon tried again on the next thirty-second break.

If he didn't know better, he would've thought Diamond didn't hear him.

"It's the first time I've seen anyone else there," he continued. "And since there was more than one of them I figured you might offer group training, as well. It's something I might be interested in."

"Can't allow it," Diamond said, looking out over the terrain. His light nylon sweatpants and T-shirt looked completely at odds with the gloves on his hands and the skis on his feet.

But, then, Simon was dressed pretty much the same.

Diamond worked him for another half hour—until he'd mastered dynamic parallel turns, with no skidding, on the worst possible terrain. And stopped at the end of the trail.

"I had some extra time this weekend and wanted to come out and test myself, but I had no idea where to go," Simon said, breathing hard. "You wouldn't happen to have a map of the trails we use, would you?"

Diamond eyed him critically. "No." He turned his back and walked off.

Simon followed him back to the main complex. He'd hit a soft spot. The day was good.

Maybe it was time to pay another visit to the Museum Club. Just to thank Amanda for such a great referral.

7

Judge Warren had a full docket of cases that morning, and at nine o'clock Hall's number still hadn't been called. His attorney was in court next door on another case.

Jan sat behind the wooden rail that separated the prosecutor's table from the spectators, avoiding the flaming glances Jacob Hall sent her way. Dressed in his stripes, he sat in the jurors' box, handcuffed and ankle-chained to the other inmates who were in court that morning. He didn't seem to notice that the prosecutor was free and he was not.

No great plan had presented itself. No argument other than the one Jan had already presented. And no Ruple.

The antacid had let her down, too.

Warren called a new case. The inmate next to Hall stood to be released from the chain so he could step in front of the judge. Along with the majority of people present, Jan watched. And Hall took the opportunity to wink at her.

If the case wasn't called soon, she was going to have

to excuse herself to go to the bathroom. He was making her sick.

She had three more cases sitting on her desk, three more court appearances that week; she couldn't afford to just sit still. Not today, not when her mind was too preoccupied with the far-reaching effects of failure and the prospect of Hall back on the streets. The cops were going to quit risking their necks to bring him in if she couldn't keep him locked up. She needed to be working out solutions, finding missing pieces, planning strategy.

She half listened as one of her associates botched a case, having failed to contact the victim as required and forcing the court to continue the sentencing that was to have taken place, postponing it for another three weeks. Another did a stellar job establishing reasons why a defendant's bond should not be reduced, as requested, and instead asking the court to increase the bond. Judge Warren agreed to do so.

Nine-twenty. The door opened, but she didn't look back to see who'd arrived, praying that it was the family member of a defendant—other than Jacob Hall. She had no way of knowing if any of the ten or so well dressed and nicely groomed men and women around her were members of the Ivory Nation, but she hoped not. As far as she was concerned, encouraging someone like Jacob Hall was tantamount to spreading germ warfare.

Gordon Michaels nodded at her. And her stomach twisted so fiercely she almost had to bend over. She now knew who'd just arrived. And her time was up. Gordon pushed through the swinging wooden gate and sat down behind the table for the defense. He opened his briefcase, but she didn't see what he pulled out. Someone stepped past her, to take a seat on her other side.

Jan stole a peek and almost wept.

The sullen-looking man in full uniform stared straight ahead, ignoring her.

"Thank you," she whispered, with her eyes on the judge.

Danny Ruple didn't even grunt a reply. Jan could have kissed him.

Hailey Miller stood at a corner of the cement playground during morning recess, watching as three of her classmates tried to play a game of four square. They were one short. Usually Tina Pratt played with them, but she was absent today. This was Hailey's chance— if she was going to be brave enough to take it.

Jan said that she wasn't a bad person; that the things she'd done were bad, but she'd done them for a good reason, and that it was the reason that said what kind of person she was. The stealing was punished and gone. That would mean that Derek was wrong about her being marked and having to be by herself all the time, unless she wanted to hang around with the bully kids and get in more trouble. 'Course, if he hadn't told all the kids about her, she wouldn't have had any marks on her, anyway.

The ten-minute bell rang and Hailey bit her lip. Now was her chance. If she didn't take it, Tina might not be absent again all year and that was a really long time to stand alone in a corner at recess. She hated doing nothing. And they made her come out here, even if she wanted to stay in and do her homework.

Pushing some curls out of her eyes, she took a step forward and stopped, holding her breath while she waited to see if anyone noticed.

No one did.

Hailey chewed on her lip some more. The other girls were wearing clogs and she only had tennis shoes for school, but maybe they wouldn't notice. If she didn't hurry, it would be too late.

And if Jan ever found out, she'd be disappointed in Hailey. Jan had enough courage to send dangerous bad guys to prison. She'd be proud of Hailey for having courage.

She took another step. And then another. And pretty soon, she was close to the girls.

"Can I play?"

Julia, the nicest one, caught the ball and held it, looking at the other two. Allie and Kaitlin didn't say anything.

"Sure." Julia stared at the ball while she talked. "I guess."

Whew! "Thanks," Hailey said, jumping into the empty fourth square. She held up her hands. "Throw me the ball."

"I'm quitting." Allie looked at Julia. "You know my mom said I can't play with *her*," she announced in a whisper so loud that Hailey heard it.

"Yeah," Kaitlin added. "I have to quit, too. I'm not allowed to play with jailbirds."

She looked over at Hailey and Hailey stared right back. She wasn't a bird. And she'd never really been in jail—not for being bad. If her mom had answered the phone that last time like she had before, Hailey could have gone right home. Instead, she'd had to stay until they could get a foster home for her.

Kaitlin was the first to move away. Hailey turned toward Julia. "We can do two square if you want," she said.

Julia shook her head, dropped the ball and ran after her friends. The ball bounced a little, rolled near Hailey's feet and stopped when it hit a rock. She watched it until she was sure no stupid tears were going to come and embarrass her.

She hated Kaitlin. And Allie. And Julia. And mostly she hated the fact that Derek was right about her. She was bad, and they were never going to give her to Jan.

Jan stood as Hall's case was called and watched while Hall was brought down from the jury box and unchained. The few feet the evil-looking young man walked to the defense table seemed to take an interminable amount of time. She held his gaze—and her breath—until he'd turned to face Judge Warren. If the man ever succeeded in winning his freedom again, she was going to have to leave the state.

Cold from the inside out, Jan presented herself and Detective Ruple, who was sitting beside her at the prosecutor's table. She listened as Judge Warren read for the record. She was going to win this case. She was going to protect the citizens of Arizona from Jacob Hall's terrorism.

She was called upon to speak first.

"Your Honor," she said, holding a pen with both hands to keep herself calm. "Due to the sensitive nature of the information to be disclosed, the state asks that the courtroom be cleared…"

Michaels objected. With spectators rustling behind her, Jan answered his objections and Warren agreed to her request and called a five-minute recess.

She was on first base.

The mind of a terrorist—he's next door, not in jail.

Simon sat back, his surroundings slipping away from his consciousness as he read.

The terrorist at large is just like you and me. He can come from and return to a normal life.

He's not the guy whose reasoning is clearly different or irrational. That guy is a loner. That guy has no one who shares his twisted way of perceiving the world. The terrorist, on the other hand, must have people beside him, working with him, in order to achieve any kind of noticeable success. The terrorist is not mentally ill.

Diamond had a group of men he trained—enough so that he'd printed maps for them. That could be considered *beside him, working with him*.

He is of above average intelligence.

Definitely.

He generally suffers from antisocial personality disorder—he has an inability to feel empathy for the pain and suffering of others.

Diamond pushed until it hurt—without compassion. And he, unlike any of Simon's previous trainers, never gave advice on treating overworked muscles.

He often comes from wealth, but just as often from a low-income family.

Check.

A terrorist does not feel that he's wrong to kill, since he is able to justify his actions as mandatory for the good of his cause. The terrorist sees his victims as the attackers of his cause.

If Diamond *was* involved with terrorist activity, Simon was not safe. Period.

Duly noted.

"Your Honor, just the hint that Jacob Hall might be associated with the Ivory Nation forces us to consider possible retaliation from among their membership. Considering that the group is suspected of involvement in the murders of multiple Arizona citizens in cold and calculating ways, we ask that the name of Detective Ruple's informant remain confidential..."

"Objection, Your Honor." Michaels jumped up. "The whole purpose of this hearing is to—"

"Your Honor, if I may finish." Jan raised her voice.

"Overruled," Warren told Michaels. He nodded toward Jan. "Please continue."

"Detective Ruple cannot possibly name his informant, Your Honor. If we are correct in our beliefs regarding Hall's memberships, we can pretty well conclude that, if identified, this informant might well be dead by sometime tonight. We would be endangering a law-abiding citizen. However, the detective has information he is prepared to give that should be enough to assure you that his informant is reliable."

The informant might still be in danger, depending on how far the Ivory Nation tentacles reached. She prayed not.

"Proceed." The judge leaned on his forearms, pencil in hand.

Detective Ruple took the witness stand and was sworn in. Jan stepped forward.

"Detective Ruple, please tell us what you can about the source you cited as cause for the warrant obtained to search Jacob Hall's home and his personal computer."

Ruple inclined his upper body to reach the microphone. "I've known my source for more than ten years. I was directly involved in his arrest and conviction. He used prison time as an opportunity to get an education and is now living with his significant other and their son, who was conceived after his release. He attributes the reason for his turnaround to something I said during the arrest. We've worked on four previous deals together, and in all four, the information given was later verified by the police."

Michaels had a turn to cross-examine the witness. Ruple was neither intimidated nor swayed. A perfect witness. And within ten minutes, Judge Warren ruled that the information taken from Hall's computer was admissible evidence.

"Any help you need building the Zeidel case, let me know," was all Ruple said on his way out.

Terrorists are often converted by social or religious brainwashing. Example: If one believes that God is peaceful, then it is man's duty to God to remove citizens who believe in or promote war from earth—which belongs to God.

Holding his glasses, Simon rubbed both eyes with the thumb and fingers of one hand. Eight years was a long time to let a skill go unused. He used to be a whiz at research.

Back then he hadn't been writing a book.

Back then he'd been…

Nope. He picked up the article, slid his glasses back on. The man he'd been no longer existed. Period.

Everyone heard the crash. But no one saw a thing. From security staff to the general public, everyone on the first floor of the county attorneys' office building or in the vicinity of the parking lot was questioned.

No one remembered seeing anyone running away from the area. No one noticed a suspicious-looking individual. No one knew how the front windshield of Janet McNeil's car had been smashed.

City police were already on the scene by the time Janet walked back from the courthouse on Monday just before lunch. She'd had a settlement conference on a domestic abuse case following the evidentiary hearing—a man had forced his wife to have sex with him at gunpoint. After a lot of discussion, some tears, and a great job of mediating by the judge, the defendant had agreed to the state's plea and Jan had pretty much floated back to the office.

To be met by this. Glass all over the leather seats of her blue Infiniti.

"There's nothing in the car that shouldn't be there," one of the officers on the scene said. "Looks like this was done with a bat of some kind."

Clever. No evidence to trace. Nothing to fingerprint.

"In broad daylight, in the middle of downtown, someone walks up, beats the hell out of my car and no one notices?" She might be tough on the outside, but Jan was trembling with fright inside where people couldn't see.

"I know it's crazy," the second officer said. "Believe me, ma'am, we aren't done here. We'll case the entire neighborhood, interview everyone in every office. But it doesn't look promising."

She was lucky. She was a government employee and the police would do the legwork. Since there was so little to go on and the amount of damage wasn't great, they'd probably have gone home if she'd been anyone else.

Andrew came running up.

"Jan, I just heard a couple of minutes ago," he said. "I told Nancy to call a repair service before I came down. Congratulations on the Hall hearing, by the way. Michaels came by an hour ago and said the computer evidence was in."

"Thanks." She gave him a grateful look, nodded at a couple of the other employees from her building who were coming out for lunch and then shivered.

"Do you know of anyone who has it in for you?" Officer Two asked—Bell, his tag read. His partner was Adams. She'd never seen either of them before, which meant they were relatively new to the force.

"She's a prosecutor," Andrew said, not bothering to hide his impatience. "She makes enemies every single day."

"I could give you a list of defendants from all my current cases," Jan said, doubting the Flagstaff police had the time or resources to follow up that thoroughly because of one broken windshield. "But I'd rather you just looked at one of them. Jacob Hall. He's in custody, but he has a lot of friends on the outside. I suspect he's a member of the Ivory Nation."

"Shit." Adams whistled. "No wonder there's no evidence. We'll see what we can do, ma'am," he finished, but his tone told Jan what she already suspected. Whoever had broken her windshield had not needed to leave a threatening note or a warning. The message had been loud and clear. Her enemies would not be found.

But she would be.

Jan had a brand-new windshield by the time she pulled into her driveway that evening. She could almost convince herself that the damage had never happened, that nothing had marred a near-perfect day. She deserved a bit of peace and celebration.

There was certainly no reason to tell Simon about the incident when she went down the driveway to check her mail. No reason to hope he didn't skip tonight. His cocky grin and nonsense might be pleasant, but so were sitcom reruns on cable television.

Ah, face it, she told herself as she made the trek to the street, the night air cool on her ankles and knees, *You're unnerved. And you need a friend.*

Not that Simon had to *know* that.

"Hi!" She smiled her first genuine smile of the afternoon, when she saw him standing there.

"Hello yourself, Ms. Prosecutor Extraordinaire. Elegant black and pearls. Today wouldn't happen to have been the dreaded hearing day, would it?"

She didn't tell him much about her work—he got more information from the newspaper. But after the brick had been thrown through her window, he'd asked about the Hall case, and she'd told him about needing Danny Ruple to squeal on his informant.

"It would," she told him, controlling her fear as she

opened her mailbox. She looked inside before reaching her hand in. And Simon, being Simon, stuck his head over the top and peered in backward.

"Wow, someone put letters in here! Imagine that!"

"Shut up!" She gave him a playful shove and reached in for her mail, thinking about how warm and solid he felt.

"I saw Molly Thornton out with baby Mark today. You didn't tell me he had so much hair."

The electric bill. Mortgage coupon. Two offers for credit cards. A letter—or bill—from the attorney representing her in Hailey's adoption. And an envelope of coupons for local businesses.

Nothing else.

"He, um…" She riffled through a second time. Still no threatening notes. "Had that little cap on—you know, the kind they always send them home from the hospital in. Something about keeping in body heat."

"You looking for anything in particular?"

The man's powers of observation were unnerving. As was the intent expression in his eyes.

"No."

He slid his hands into his pockets, rocking back and forth on his tennis shoes. "So how'd the hearing go?"

"I'm sure you'll read about it in tomorrow's paper. Unless it's stolen again, that is."

"I'd rather hear about it from you."

And if she didn't want to tell him, she could head back up to her house. These visits only had to last a couple of seconds.

"I won. The evidence is in."

The holler he let out, accompanied by a foolish jig on the gravel, made her laugh. "This calls for a celebration," he told her. "I have pretzels."

"I actually have something else I'd like to talk to you about." She needed to talk, to dispel some of the noise in her head; in the past she would've gone to Andrew. "But I'm freezing out here. You want to come up to the house for a few minutes?"

"How could any man refuse an invitation like that?"

A few minutes turned into a hastily prepared dinner of spinach salad and French bread warmed in the toaster oven.

"What do you mean there were no witnesses? Your car was parked in a government lot!"

Simon's gaze was serious, and suddenly the meal he'd been enthusiastically attacking was completely ignored.

Jan dropped her fork, as well. "It's exactly the kind of thing you'd expect out of the Ivory Nation," she said, hating how shaky she still felt inside. "They have their secret places, where they plan and store supplies, but most of the damage they do is in plain sight—and yet the perpetration is never seen. Even with the most violent crimes, there's rarely any evidence left behind. In their everyday behavior, it may be as simple as turning a back on a Hispanic customer and then claiming, if called on it, that it wasn't intentional. They teach their children to exclude black children from their games. They create propaganda in order to undermine establishments owned by blacks and Jews. And most insidious, they spread rumors through the community, via political connections, through schools and the PTA—rumors of mistrust against anyone who is not white.

"These aren't all tattooed hoodlums who'd just as soon kill you as look at you," she said, shivering again as she remembered the lurid stare Jacob Hall had sent her when Judge Warren made his ruling. "They're moms and dads who love their kids, doctors and teachers and plumbers, just like the rest of us. And if you happen to sit in a restaurant at a table next to them and allow yourself to be waited on by a black person, you could be their next victim and no one will ever know why."

"So you think the windshield was a warning because of this morning's decision?"

She was certain of it. "Who knows?"

"Yet you still want to continue with the prosecution."

"I know I can win."

"And someone else can't?"

She shook her head, and picked at the paper on the bottle of water she'd pulled from the refrigerator to go with dinner. "I've been building a case against Jacob Hall for more than five years. It's convoluted, with a lot of connections that aren't obvious. It would take months for someone else to get up to speed. We go to trial in a couple of weeks."

"And this is worth risking your life?"

Jan coughed. And tried to smile. "I don't think it's quite that grim, thank you. I'm a court employee. If they take me out, the whole state will be looking for them and they know that."

Keep it light, girl. Survive.

"Well, what do I know…" Simon said, picking up his fork. "I've just heard that white supremacists, like terrorists, justify killing for the good of the cause. They claim they do it for God."

He was right, of course. And offing a public official "for God," with all the inherent publicity, might not seem like a bad idea to Jacob Hall and his "brothers."

"That's not a God I recognize."

"No, but with terrorists their belief is so strong they stop at nothing. Think of 9/11. Those guys were willing to die."

"What I'm more worried about," she said, the fear almost choking her, "is Hailey. How can I convince the court that I can provide a safe and loving home for her if I'm in the line of fire?"

Simon chewed. Pierced another leaf of spinach. Chewed some more. "Do you think she'll be safe?"

Of course she did, or she wouldn't even consider bringing Hailey home. Jan slumped as guilt spiraled through her.

"I don't know."

Nor did she know what to do about that.

8

"I'm curious about something."

"What?" Jan slid down in her seat until her head rested against the upholstered back, peering at Simon across the table. Dirty dishes holding the remains of spinach salad lay between them. Somehow, more than an hour had passed and they were still sitting there talking.

He'd told her about the first time he'd gone skydiving and landed in a field of corn so high no one could see him. He'd stood up immediately, as instructed, to let everyone know he was fine, but no one knew where he was. Before he'd even begun to sort out the shambles of his chute, he'd been besieged by medical personnel.

When she'd stopped laughing, she'd told him again that he should write fiction.

"What are you curious about?"

"Hailey—now that you've brought her up."

"What about her?" They'd only had water to drink, but she was as warm inside as if she'd had wine.

"Why adopt? I know things have changed in this day

and age, but it still seems a little unusual to have a single-parent adoption. You're certainly young enough to get married and have as many kids as you'd like."

His question caught her off guard.

And this was why she didn't have close friends. Give them a salad and they wanted access to your soul.

She had two reasons. But one of them—the fact that she didn't trust herself or anyone else enough to risk exposing her vulnerabilities—he wasn't going to know.

"Before coming to the criminal division, I did a stint in juvenile court."

He toasted her with his empty water bottle. "I'll bet you were good at it."

"I'm not really sure how you'd measure such a thing," she told him, thinking back to those days of standing before judges to sort out the problems of children. "Unlike adult court, where the purpose is to punish, in juvenile court, the goal is to rehabilitate while there's still time. So, was I good, if I built a case that got a kid sent to detention—which is the equivalent of prison? Or better, if I found a way to justify his acts and get him probation and counseling?"

"I guess it would depend on the crime."

"What if a kid who'd been sexually abused by his father since he was a toddler and hadn't had any help to teach him any differently committed rape? Do I put this kid, who's already bent on crime, back into counseling and then out on the streets maybe to rape again, in the hope that giving him a second chance could work?"

"I have no idea."

Sometimes she hadn't, either. "I just had to judge whether or not it was too late to help, and that part of the job seemed impossible to do well."

"Is that why you left?"

"Partly." She should stop now. They were getting far too…something. Crossing lines. Changing boundaries.

And she'd given up trying to push herself to engage in a committed relationship. Hell, she'd never even been able to manage to spend the whole night with a man. The few times she'd made it as far as sex, no matter how great it had been, she'd felt more driven to get out of his bed before she fell asleep, than she'd been tempted to stay there.

"Mostly, I quit because my heart couldn't take seeing kids day in and day out, parading by me with their stories of abuse and neglect. So many of them were more confused and misled than bad. I cried myself to sleep one too many nights and I knew the job was meant for someone else. Someone better equipped to put things into perspective."

"So what does this have to do with Hailey?"

"She was one of my defendants."

"That would explain why she's eight going on fifty."

Jan frowned and nodded. "I also think Hailey was just born that way. She's a natural caregiver—it doesn't matter if her charge is a plant that was getting stepped on or an old lady who lives next door."

Jan reveled in Simon's compassionate expression— until she thought about what she was doing. And then she started to panic.

"Anyway," she continued, hoping to offset the rising anxiety. "After I left the division I kept thinking about Hailey, dreaming about her. I couldn't get her out of my mind. So I had her caseworker set up a visit, asked her if she'd be interested in getting to know me, and things progressed from there."

Which only partially explained why a single woman had considered adopting a child on her own. But the explanation appeared to satisfy Simon.

He stood up soon after that and Jan followed him to the front door, sorry he was leaving and yet glad to see him go. Balanced on a tightrope. That was her.

"I'm curious about something else," he said, turning to face her at the door.

"What?"

"Do you ever date?"

Oh, God. Was he going to ask her out? She stopped breathing. Calmed herself and sucked in air.

"Sometimes." He couldn't ask her out. She'd hate that.

"It's just that by your own admission you don't have a boyfriend, and in all the years I've lived next door to you I've never once seen a man over here."

"I go out when I date." Please leave me alone.

Simon held up both hands. "Hey, it's fine by me. You hate men and you've sworn off marriage. And you're secretly hoping that all men morph into little green gnomes by the turn of the century. I won't hold it against you, I promise."

Jan burst out laughing. He didn't care. Didn't have

any personal interest. She'd blown things out of proportion. "I've been pretty busy building a career in a field that's still predominantly male." She relented a little bit. "But I would like to get married someday, if the situation's right."

Maybe when she stopped having debilitating nightmares that made her thrash and scream. Nightmares that made her look completely unbalanced and difficult and high-strung. Maybe then she'd actually invite a man she was dating to her house for lovemaking, rather than insisting on going to his house so that she could escape when she felt the need to.

Or maybe she was always going to have the confusing urge to leave.

He nodded and turned to go without another word.

"Hey!" she called.

"What?" There was wide-open innocence all over his face.

"Turnabout is fair play, buster. You did this the other night. Get me to tell you all about *me* and then just leave without giving something back. And it's not like I've ever seen a woman visiting next door, so what is it? You hate women and you'd like us banished from the face of the earth just as soon as men figure out how to have babies?"

She wished she hadn't left her pumps in the kitchen. She felt short standing next to him.

Back of his hand to his brow, Simon sighed dramatically. "You found me out. And this is why I hate women. Their curiosity will kill you every time."

"Simon, you're not getting away with it."

"Getting away with what?"

"Prevaricating. You're very good at it, you know."

"Yeah."

"Too good, if you ask me." She gave him a shrewd glance. "Usually when someone works that hard to avoid personal conversation, he has something to hide."

"All I have to hide is an embarrassingly dull life," he said. "I like women. I've just never found one I wanted to get seriously involved with. Most recently I was seeing a cashier from the grocery store, but it ended when she went back to her husband. Okay?"

"Okay," Jan said. But it wasn't okay at all. Her mood had dipped alarmingly when he'd mentioned the cashier and she was afraid the negative sensations running through her were feelings of jealousy. As if she had some sense of ownership regarding her neighbor. Some right to his affection.

And that had to stop. She needed every emotional resource she had, to see her through the next few weeks and through a trial that could preserve the future for many good people in this city. She needed her emotions intact, in order to make the best decisions for Hailey.

She didn't need Simon.

The problem with pushing yourself, working to your full potential, was that you couldn't do it asleep. With very little instruction from Diamond, Simon moved through rugged terrain on Tuesday morning, jumping tires, making sudden turns on foot-wide trails, scaling cliff sides, balancing as he raced across fallen logs, avoiding all the knots. Tuesdays and Thursdays were all about physical training. He didn't put on skis or work on Diamond's ice. He was building stamina and strength, learning to maintain control on any terrain, in any snow condition.

Diamond was making him one of the strongest, most physically capable men in Flagstaff. If he was doing the same for terrorists...

Little bursts of steam preceded Simon as he exhaled in the early morning cold, the October mountain weather preceding the snow that would follow in the coming months. Turning, balancing, his knees moving up and down, braced for weight, Simon fell into a long-denied yet achingly familiar rhythm, his endorphins taking him back to a high he'd almost forgotten.

And his mind opened. To Diamond, his trails, his defensiveness, his closed mouth. To the padlocks Simon intended to pick that morning—his early arrival solely for the purpose of having a few minutes alone in the locker room.

He'd picked his first lock when he was nine. His brother Sam had been about to fail a strength and stamina test in gym—which would have meant the identical twins would be in different classes for the first time, and Simon had come to his aid. Sam had stayed home from school sick, pretending to be Simon, and Simon had gone to school as Sam. The plan was spectacular and, at first, it went without a hitch. They'd had no trouble fooling their mother, who, as always, had been preoccupied with the latest affair their father was having—despite the fact that the couple had been divorced since Sam and Simon were four.

Simon, the daredevil of the two, ran all the way to school, took his seat as Sam, and with the coaching he'd received the night before, had managed to keep up with his brother's math and science skills for one morning. It was when he'd skipped recess to get to the gym early and change into sweatpants before the other boys got there—just in case any of them noticed his legs weren't as scrawny as his twin's—that he had encountered a problem. The brothers had thought of everything but the fact that each boy had his own locker key. So Sam's chart and his color-coded shirt with his name on the back were not accessible with Simon's key.

Simon had panicked briefly and broken out in a cold sweat. And then he'd borrowed a paper clip from their coach's desk, straightened it, and like he'd seen on the cop shows on TV had pushed it into the back of the lock. He'd whooped out loud when the slim metal bar came loose from the body of the lock.

"That's a first."

Simon blinked, missing a beat in the rotation he was performing in response to Diamond's commands.

"What?" he wheezed.

"Never seen a guy smile while counting off lateral and fore-aft balance transitions."

Simon grunted.

And then his out-of-control memory filled his mind with a blast of light, a loud crack and a searing pain from which he knew he would never recover.

In a cantankerous mood, Simon dialed Scott Olsen during the drive back to town.

"Nothing in the lockers," he barked, when the federal agent picked up on the first ring. "No stray piece of paper, no used tissue or empty candy wrapper, not even a trial-size bottle of shampoo."

"What about clothes?"

"I would've mentioned them," Simon muttered. Not one damn thing to trace or fingerprint. Not that he could have taken possession of anything he'd found, anyway. Unlawful searches didn't go over big.

"Anything they use there is carried back and forth."

"A damned inconvenience, wouldn't you say?"

"Makes you wonder why."

"Strange that those storage compartments are never open for cleaning, and yet every single one of them was pristine. In my many years of locker-room experience, that's extremely unusual. What kind of guys are these, that there isn't even one slob among them?"

"That's what you're there to find out."

"Unless Diamond is just a private instructor, and we're playing cops-and-terrorists all by ourselves." Simon turned onto North San Francisco Street, toward home. Beaver would've been a smarter choice, less congested, but this way he could see the parking lot in the county attorneys' office. "I've been there eight times and I still have a little or nothing to go on."

"At least you're getting a good workout."

Jan's car was parked close to the building. And completely intact. "I'm a couch potato, Olsen. I have no use for trim and fit."

The young kids arrived home right on time. Simon moved a queen of spades onto a king of diamonds, further burying a two in the eight-row grid to release an ace. Words hadn't been all that forthcoming today. The cards weren't falling in a friendly way, either.

Such was life. So be it.

He won the game—eventually. And switched from cards to numbers. He'd discovered Sudoku the week before, and he found it slightly amusing. At least to while away the couple of minutes until the high-schoolers got home. And then he only had another six hours and twenty-two minutes until his Internet chess competition match. He was playing someone from Germany.

Alan Bonaby got off the bus last, as usual, pushed his glasses up his nose as he hit the ground and turned in the direction opposite home. Simon sat forward, watching as Alan walked to the Thorntons' drive and disappeared from view. The young man was probably babysitting for the couple. Good for him.

Simon fell asleep in the middle of his fourth game of Sudoku. He woke up when his head jerked forward, then went out to the kitchen for a cup of coffee, which he ground himself—a breakfast blend, but who would tell? After which, he came straight back to his desk. Jan should be home soon. He lifted the mug to his lips. After last night's visit, he wasn't going out to greet her. But a good neighbor would still make sure she got home safely.

Before he'd taken even one sip, Simon set the mug down so hard that coffee splashed over the nearly empty folder of notes beside his keyboard. A motorcycle was parked in front of Jan's home.

And a long-haired man, mid-twentyish in black leather, was walking to the side of her house.

It was broad daylight. He wasn't sneaking around. Simon left his coffee to cool.

He cut across the lawn, noticing everything from the slightly pompous tilt of the stranger's head to the expensively tooled boots on his feet. The shiny black-and-white helmet tucked between his arm and his ribs wasn't cheap, either.

"You looking for Jan?" he called out.

The man turned, no hint of friendliness in manner or expression but no particular aggression, either.

"Yeah. Is she usually this late getting home from work?"

So, he didn't know her well enough to be privy to her schedule.

"Sometimes."

The visitor frowned. "I thought for sure she'd be here." The man's voice sank with disappointment.

"Can I help you with something?"

"No." His brows were still drawn as he perused the empty street. "I need to see her."

Sounded important. Simon's senses sharpened from standby to full alert. "Who are you?"

"Oh, sorry," the man held out his hand. "I'm Johnny McNeil. Her brother. Who are you?"

Simon hunched against the cold October-evening breeze. He'd left his sweatshirt hanging on the door handle.

"Nobody," Simon said, feeling idiotic standing there protecting a woman who didn't ask for—or apparently need—his help. "A neighbor. That's all."

Johnny nodded with no real interest, already distracted. He paced a couple of steps toward the drive and back, his attention on the corner around which Jan's car should appear.

It occurred to Simon to ask the man why he didn't visit his sister more often. But he excused himself instead.

Johnny McNeil hardly seemed to notice.

"What's wrong?"

Jan started to sweat and then shivered, her heartbeat practically stopping after one look at her brother's face. He pulled her up out of her car, holding on tight for long seconds before letting her go.

"Let's go inside," he said, waiting while she shut the garage door behind them.

"Johnny." Jan fumbled her keys unlocking the door. "Tell me what's going on. Is it Mom?"

He didn't say anything.

"It's Mom, isn't it?"

She dropped her briefcase on the floor inside the door, grabbing his hand. "Tell me."

"Yeah," he said, his gaze dropping, and then returning to hers. He had tears in his eyes. "She's dead, sis. I just…" His voice broke.

"Dead!" Her heart was thudding so loudly she must have heard wrong. This was a nightmare, that was all. She knew how to handle this. She'd wake up.

"Her friend next door, Jean something, called you at home first and then called my cell. That's why I had to get here before you did. So you wouldn't come in and hear about this all alone."

"Johnny…" Jan's knees were giving out on her. Her whole body felt heavy, weak.

Her brother pulled out a chair from the table and led her to it. Took another for himself—dragging it close to hers. Taking both of her hands, he put them to his face.

"I can't believe it, either," he whispered.

Her mother was dead? The woman was the one person who knew everything about her.

"Jean found her this morning, but they think she's been dead since yesterday afternoon."

"How?"

If the Ivory Nation had done this, if she were in any way to blame, Jan didn't think she'd survive.

She wasn't sure she would, anyway.

"She… I…"

Tears slid down Johnny's face.

"How, dammit?"

She just had to hold on, go with the story until she woke up.

"I spoke with the police department an hour ago. According to the coroner, she must have swallowed every pill she had in the house." He started to name the medications found in their mother's stomach. Every single one of them had been prescribed. "When they searched the house, they found all the empty bottles lined up with a jug of water on the living room table next to the couch where she died."

She'd killed herself.

Jan's shock came not so much from the facts themselves but from the reality that descended as those facts sank in. If Johnny had told her that their mother had been murdered, it could have been a dream.

But this. This was too real. Too believable.

"Was there a note?"

"The police searched the premises to determine that her death was a suicide, not a homicide, but they didn't find a note. They said that if we come across anything when we're going through her stuff, we should call them."

She needed a note, needed to know why.

"It's my fault."

"What?" Johnny shook her lightly. "Of course it's not. Mom's been on the verge of suicide for as long as I can remember."

"I skipped Sunday's visit," Jan continued. "And she

kills herself on Monday?" She was trembling, and she couldn't stop. "It doesn't take a rocket scientist to figure out that if I'd gone I would've seen signs and been able to prevent this."

"You're wrong, sis." Johnny's voice was no less convincing for its softness. "I had breakfast with her yesterday morning. I was on my way down to Phoenix and then Tucson for a week of meetings."

Jan studied him through her tears. "And you didn't notice anything?"

He shook his head slowly. "She wanted to hear all about everything I'm doing, as always," he said with a small, sad grin. "She asked a million questions, wanted to make sure I had enough money and was getting enough to eat. Hell, she laughed out loud when she told me about something some old geezer in the park had said to her. I can't even remember what it was."

"Did you bring her anything?"

"I always do."

Johnny described the daisies and the box of dark chocolates, and Jan hung on his words, picturing their mother's pleasure. Her beautiful, tentative smile. Her love for her son.

Picturing some of her mother's last moments.

Oh, God. Mom's dead.

That was when Jan fell apart.

9

"We're all the family we've got left, sis," Johnny said a couple of hours later. They'd both cried. Talked. Held each other. And now they were sitting, numb, on the couch in Jan's living room, discussing arrangements. "We've got to stay in touch."

Jan nodded, her chin trembling as she faced the horrible emptiness looming on every side.

She'd been trying to get closer to Johnny for years. He just never returned her calls, and he rarely came to visit. Half the time, she'd only known where he was living through their mother.

"You want to stay here tonight?" Please, Johnny. Don't leave me to the darkness.

He shook his head. "I've got business to take care of and meetings to reschedule, but I'll be back first thing in the morning."

They'd already decided to drive to Sedona together, to take care of their mother's affairs and plan a service. Their father was buried in a cemetery not far from town. Her mother had a plot there, too.

"She wanted to be cremated and have her ashes spread up in the mountains," she said half aloud.

A tight mouth was Johnny's only reaction.

"Can you call your office tonight, or do you need to wait until morning?" Johnny asked several minutes later.

"I'll just call my assistant in the morning and let him know I'll be gone for a day or two."

"A day or two? Take a week or two, Jan, at least. I'm going to. We could take care of things and then head off someplace, just the two of us."

"I can't, Johnny. I've got Jacob Hall's trial starting in just under two weeks. I can't leave town."

He sat back. "You don't honestly plan to go ahead with that *now*, do you? Not so soon after...this."

His voice wobbled a little on the last word, and Jan held back tears with great effort.

"I have no choice," she told him, "but let's not talk about it now, please?" She rubbed his hand. "I can't bear to argue with you tonight."

"You're right, sis." Johnny's gaze was warm as he relented. "Now's not the time."

Listening to the roar of Johnny's motorcycle as he drove away, Jan started to sob again.

At the moment, she felt as if nothing would ever be right again. Not with Johnny; not with her.

Their mother's death just didn't make sense. She'd sounded fine when she talked to Jan on Sunday. And a visit from Johnny was usually good for weeks of better days.

Why hadn't Mom called? Trusted Jan to help her? What had Jan done wrong? Or not done? She would've been there no matter what.

Why didn't Mom know that?

It must've taken ages to swallow every pill in that house. Surely there'd been time for her to call...

It took three peals for Jan to realize the phone's ringing wasn't just in her mind.

She fumbled with the receiver.

"Hello?" Whoever was on the other end would probably think she had a bad cold.

"Jan?"

"Yeah. Who's this?"

"Simon."

Oh. She'd missed their chat at the mailbox. Had forgotten all about it. Her shocked mind was having trouble focusing on the here and now.

"I heard your brother leave. Is everything all right?"

"How did you know he's my brother?" Simon was sanity. Connection to the world of the living.

Please keep talking to me, at least for a few minutes.

"He didn't tell you? I met him outside, earlier tonight."

"No, he didn't say anything about it." Did she sound as drunk as she felt?

"I don't mean to pry," Simon was saying. "He seemed a little intent, distracted even, and I wanted to make sure everything was okay."

"No, Simon." Her reply dragged out. She wasn't

sure how to make sense when nothing made sense. "I don't think so."

"What's wrong?"

"My mother committed suicide yesterday."

The words hurt, and she cringed. Wasn't it enough for people to know Mom had died?

They wouldn't understand the rest. Hell, how could they? Jan didn't.

"Jan? Did you hear me?"

She shook her head. "I guess not."

"Meet me at the door. I'm on my way over."

If he was appalled by what she'd told him, he hadn't shown it. Hadn't asked a single, unanswerable question.

Having neighbors was nice. You owed them nothing, had virtually no responsibility to them and yet they were always right there.

Saying goodbye to the hefty fee he'd paid to enter a chess competition, Simon grabbed his keys and was out the door before he'd taken another breath.

The second Jan opened her door he knew he'd made the right choice in coming—even if regret stung tomorrow, in the cold light of day.

"Here, drink this," he said, handing her the glass of vodka he'd poured.

Without seeming to be aware of what she was doing, Jan sat stiffly on the couch, sipped and immediately choked.

Her eyes were watering, whether from the alcohol

or emotion, he wasn't sure. "Needs orange juice," she said hoarsely.

Simon added a few drops. Tonight, she needed a stiff drink. She'd have to trust him on that one.

"This is the first time you remember losing someone close to you, isn't it?" he asked, recalling the things she'd told him about herself over the past week.

Recalling, too, that after the previous night he'd vowed to stay away from her; get their relationship back to the impersonal mailbox version. But death changed plans.

"I guess so," she said in a lost-little-girl voice. "I'm not really that close to very many people. Did you know that?"

She'd finished half the glass already.

"You mentioned it the other night."

"Right. Yes." She sipped some more.

Good. The sooner she achieved oblivion, the better. And by the look of her, it wasn't going to take much.

"I shouldn't have bothered you," Jan said a short time later, her words slightly slurred. She blinked as she peered up at him, as if she was trying to focus. Her lids were drifting shut.

"You didn't bother me," he said, fighting a strong compulsion to take her in his arms. Just for the moment. "I called you."

"Oh, that was nice."

"Did you know my mother?"

She'd finished her drink and asked for another.

This time, he'd given her plain juice—which she was slurping.

"I'm sorry that I didn't." Simon sat down on the couch, a few feet away, prepared for a long night.

That first night after his brother's death was one he'd never been able to forget. Nor could he remove himself sufficiently from those emotions to allow another person to suffer the disorientation, the hell, alone.

He could only imagine the anguish that must be added because her mother had taken her own life. He'd been on the scene with survivors more than once in his previous life, had witnessed their anger at the senselessness of suicide. And their guilt.

"She was a nice lady." Jan's eyes closed, and then opened again. "You aren't asking questions."

"They aren't mine to ask."

"She took pills."

"I'm sorry." He'd learned long ago there was nothing good to say in situations such as this.

"It's my fault."

"How's that?"

"I cancelled our day together on Sunday. I worked instead. I would've known there was a problem, if I'd been there."

Guilt was insidious. He wasn't the right person to help her out with that.

"She made her own choices. You aren't responsible." He repeated what he'd been told. And never believed. Everyone lived on the same planet, breathed the same air. Everyone had responsibility for everyone else. That was how life worked—and why he chose not to engage in it any more than he had to.

Jan didn't comment.

Five minutes passed before she opened her eyes again.

"I'm fine now," she said, looking straight at him. "Thank you."

"You're welcome."

"You don't have to stay."

"I want to."

"Okay, then." Her eyes closed again.

Simon slid off Jan's pumps, wishing someone else was there—a woman—to pull off her panty hose and loosen her clothes a bit. She'd been asleep almost half an hour, needed to stay asleep and was going to feel miserable in those constricting clothes in another hour or two.

Gently setting her foot back down, he considered removing her pantyhose himself.

"Simon?" Hell, he'd woken her.

"Yeah?"

"Hold me?"

"Sure, hon."

Dilemma gone for the moment—he certainly wasn't going to embarrass or upset her by dealing with panty hose when she was awake. Simon sat in the corner of the couch, pulling her against him.

She snuggled up as if she'd been in Simon's arms countless times before.

"Stay with me?" she asked.

She'd made no discernible movement, but he felt the wetness of her tears through his flannel shirt.

"Of course."

"I'll apologize for this in the morning."

He smiled. The woman was something else. "Forget it," he told her.

But he knew she wouldn't.

If she'd had her way, Jan would have used the drive to her mother's home as a chance to talk with Johnny, to open up to him and renew the bond that had held them so close while growing up—in spite of the four-year difference in age. If she'd had her way, she'd also wipe out the burning memory of asking Simon Green to hold her. The comforting warmth, and then the awkwardness of waking in his arms.

She'd never actually gone to sleep with a man before. She'd lain down with them, had sex with them, but she'd never slept in a man's arms. Thank God there'd been no nightmares—probably thanks to the alcohol she'd consumed.

"I've got a couple of quick calls to make," she apologized, as soon as she had the Infiniti heading south on Highway 17. It was still only 7:30 in the morning, and this was the earliest she could disturb Hailey and Andrew.

"No problem, I've got work to do, too," he told her, pulling a folder out of the black leather satchel he'd been wearing over his shoulder. Did the man own anything but black denim and leather anymore? Surely he didn't go to work dressed like a biker.

She wondered if he had any aspirin.

With one hand on the steering wheel, she hit speed dial. She'd worn her favorite red-and-black cardigan because it was so soft, but now she was sweating. The car's heater was blasting. If she had a free hand, she'd turn it down.

"Hailey?" It had taken a full minute for the young girl to get to the phone after her foster mother answered and called for her.

Johnny, focused on his papers, didn't even seem to notice that she was talking.

"Yeah?"

"I have some bad news, honey." Jan tensed the muscles in her jaw. She was not going to cry. Not while Hailey was on the phone.

"You found out they won't let you have me, right?"

"No. Sweetie, please don't say that! Don't even think it. The home study's been done and approved. Mrs. Wayborn from CPS talked with Officer Standgate and she's already written her report recommending the adoption. Her superior approved it. We're just waiting our turn for the judge to make it official, okay?"

Johnny turned down the heat.

"Yeah."

Jan would have thought her heart would be completely numb that morning, but she was wrong.

"Hailey, please believe me, hon. Please? You're going to be my daughter in a matter of weeks. I promise."

Johnny seemed to give a start at that, but when a quick glance showed his concentration on the figures in his lap, she realized that her nerves were stretched to the point of unreliability. Johnny knew all about Hailey.

"Okay." Hailey drew out the word. She wasn't convinced. "So what's bad?"

Jan dreaded the rest of the conversation. What if Hailey thought she was using her mother's death as an excuse to escape seeing her?

"I'm going to have to reschedule our dinner tonight, honey," she said, rushing to get it all out before Hailey could draw incorrect conclusions. "My mother has died and I'm on my way to Sedona. I've already spoken to Mrs. Lincoln, and we're going to dinner on Friday instead. Okay? And then, if it's all right with you, I'd like you to spend the night at my house and we can have our usual Saturday together."

Johnny switched folders.

"Did you like your mom?"

Words stuck in Jan's throat. What a question from such a young child—a crime against nature that she was even capable of having that thought.

"Yes, honey," she said when she could. "I loved her very much." Tears made it hard to speak. Jan switched lanes, trying to concentrate on the mountains that towered on either side of them, the trees that made Flagstaff so different from Phoenix and Tucson.

"You didn't talk about her," Hailey said.

"I know. I was waiting until the adoption was final and then I was going to take you to meet her."

"'Cause you didn't want me to meet her early, in case they won't give me to you?"

"No!" Jan said, moving back to the slower lane. "Because I was going to surprise you with your first-ever grandma," she said. "She knew all about you, Hailey, and she was planning to see you the Sunday after our court date."

Think of the child. The road. Her brother beside her. Even her neighbor, who'd made one hellish night more bearable. Anything but the woman who hadn't hung around long enough to be a grandmother.

"I'm sorry for you."

The sweet words brought more tears. "Thank you, sweetie." And then, after another glance at the mountains, she said, "Would you like to spend the night on Friday?"

"Sure."

"Good. I'll see you then."

"Okay."

Jan took a deep breath. "I love you, Hailey." She'd never said the words aloud before.

"You do?" Hailey's voice rose, not so much with excitement as with shock.

"I do."

"Oh. Well, that's good. Bye."

The connection ended before she could reply.

Jan flipped off her phone, wondering if she was

ready for everything life seemed to be asking of her. Everything she asked of herself.

"Andrew? You the only one there?" she said moments later, when her assistant picked up his office phone.

"So far."

"Listen, I'm not going to be in today."

"What? Where are you? What's wrong?"

If she could have, Jan might have smiled at his reaction. She never missed work unexpectedly. Never. It was her unwritten code. You were paid to be there. You went. No matter what.

She hadn't realized that others noticed. Except perhaps Simon. He noticed everything.

"I'm on my way to Sedona. My mother passed away and there are some things I have to deal with," she said quickly. Each time she said the words, they made her loss real—and unbearable—all over again. "I'll be coming back tonight, but I'll probably be out of the office tomorrow, as well. I'll be in on Friday, though, for sure. I've got the Griss sentencing in the morning. And another witness to interview in the Zeidel case." Bob Griss had swindled more than fifty retirees out of their life savings. Jan was asking for the maximum sentence for each of those counts, with all his millions going toward compensation for his victims.

That's it. Think about work. About the skills she was good at. The things she could control.

"So…what happened?" Andrew's voice had softened.

"They're…not sure yet. A neighbor found her. She

was at home on her couch." She could feel Johnny's gaze on her. Did her brother know she'd just lied?

Did he understand why? Or think she was wrong?

"Listen, Andrew, I need you to do something for me. Get me on the grand jury's calendar for Friday, okay? We need to subpoena the bank records of all the dead people on Hall's list."

"Done." Andrew was there for her. She hoped. "And don't worry about anything here, Jan. I'll take care of whatever comes up. You just take care of you."

More swallowed-back tears. Maybe the missing Zeidel file had been a one-time lapse. Everyone had them. "Thank you."

"Keep me posted," he said before ending the call.

10

"Isn't Hall that supremacist guy?" Johnny asked, before she'd even clicked off her phone. "You aren't really going to proceed with all of that now, are you?"

Jan didn't want to fight. She changed lanes to pass another car.

"Why wouldn't I?"

Traffic was picking up and the sun was shining through her windshield, making her sweat even with the heat turned down. In an hour or so, she'd be identifying her mother's body.

"The trial is due to start a week from Monday," Johnny said. "At least that's what that article in the paper said."

She didn't remember the trial date being in the paper…

"That's right."

"It was going to be a tough go as it was, sis. You're stepping into the line of fire—one person against a band armed with hidden weapons."

Jan swallowed, blinking against the dizziness that

was clouding her thinking. "That's a bit dramatic," she told her younger brother, her first instinct still to protect him. "I'm not there alone. I have the people of this county behind me."

"I was worried about you doing this when you were in top form," he continued as if she hadn't spoken. "But now, after all this with Mom, you won't even be at your best."

Fear spread through her body. "Maybe the challenge is what I need," she said, wishing their turnoff would present itself and yet praying it would never come—that she wouldn't have to face what she knew was waiting in Sedona. "Maybe the need to focus on something outside my personal life will make me a better advocate."

"One screwup and that guy goes free," Johnny said. "And then what do you do?"

"He's gone free twice before, Johnny. Without screwups."

"Was it in the news before?" His papers slid off his lap as he turned slightly toward her. He left them scattered on the floor.

"No, we had a priest on trial for molestation at the same time and that got all the press coverage."

"There you go, then."

"Johnny, the general public is not a threat to me. If there really was any potential danger, it would come from the Ivory Nation brotherhood, and you can bet that if Hall's a member, they all knew I had him in before."

"But if it wasn't in the news, their name wasn't at

risk of being blackened. And Hall went free, so there was no real harm. That's not the case this time. Even if Hall goes free, the organization has taken a hit, and from the little I know about people like this, they go ballistic when their cause appears to be misunderstood. They'll feel forced to retaliate."

It was a chance she had to take. "If that's true, then they'll retaliate whether I proceed or not."

"It'll be much worse if there's a trial and details begin to emerge. Even if Hall wins, there'll still be those with doubt. Their reputation will have been damaged."

Johnny had always been passionate. About Boy Scouts—he'd been an eagle scout at the age of fourteen. College—he'd graduated in three years at the top of his class. Hobbies—his choice to wear only motorcycle gear, now that he was riding a Harley, was proof of his passion.

Jan cracked her window open an inch. "We've been through this before," she said, in as reasonable a voice as she could muster. "I'm the only one who's completely up on Hall's activities. It would take too long to brief anyone else. And I don't *want* to brief anyone else. I know I can win this case. This is my career. It's what I do. It's what I *want* to do—what I have to do. Can't you please just understand?"

"I'd like to, sis." He gazed out the windshield. "But you're the only family I've got left now. I can't lose you, too." His voice broke.

"You aren't going to lose me. At least not over this.

There's more of a chance that I'll be in a car accident than die on the job."

He didn't reply, and Jan hoped the conversation was over. And that someday soon she and Johnny would be taking that vacation he'd talked about before. The two of them and Hailey. A new family.

"But what about Friday?" Johnny's tone had become defensive again. "You don't have any idea what we'll be dealing with in Sedona, or how long everything's going to take. You might not be available on Friday."

"The grand jury is a group of sixteen civilians and most of them have full-time jobs, Johnny." She was explaining something he probably already understood. "They only serve a few times a month—and they don't meet again until after the trial starts. If I can't get to them on Friday, it'll be too late."

"All the more reason to either drop the charges or get someone else to argue it for you."

"If I get someone else, I might as well drop the charges."

"Then do it, Jan, please. I'm begging you."

The utter sincerity of his plea stopped her. Was she being too one-sided here? Too closed-minded? Was she being an idiot?

She wondered what Simon thought about it. If he thought about it.

Could she live with herself if she let Jacob Hall walk? Especially considering the new evidence? She had a list of dead people. She'd always known Hall was involved with bigger things than bank fraud. And she suspected she was on the brink of finding proof.

"I don't tell you how to do your job, Johnny," she said softly. "Please don't tell me how to do mine."

Her brother didn't speak to her the rest of the way to Sedona.

Diamond was uncharacteristically chatty on Wednesday morning—a day, more than most, when Simon would have preferred to work in silence. Jan's brother had shown up in his jeans and black leather that morning, roaring into the neighborhood before the first school bus had come. Arriving just an hour after Simon had woken Jan—still lying against him on the couch—and taken his leave.

He had an ache in his neck and his arm was stiff.

"How long you been skiing?" Diamond asked as Simon twisted and turned on a twelve-by-twelve patch of rough ice pressed on to the side of the mountain.

Since he'd been old enough to stand. The one legacy Simon had from his mostly absent father. He shifted his weight. "Long enough."

"You're not bad."

Praise? What was going on here? He pushed himself to get through the rotation—more of a challenge this morning, since he'd had a less-than-comfortable night.

Not that a little lack of sleep was going to slow him down. In his other life, he could have gone forty-eight hours without sleep and still be sharp enough to get the job done.

"A guy like you has options." Simon balanced; Diamond talked. "What makes you want to be a ski instructor?"

"Because I'm good at it," Simon said. "Too old to make it to the Olympics… Like to help someone else get there."

He'd thought up the excuse two weeks ago, and he knew that Diamond, a trainer himself, would buy it.

"Ever thought of doing more meaningful work?"

Simon didn't miss a beat. "Meaningful how?" He grunted as he voiced the words, sweat pouring down the inside of his long-sleeved cotton pullover.

"Making the world a better place."

Been there. Screwed up. All done.

"Who hasn't?"

Diamond watched as Simon finished the drill, gave him several more exercises and then dropped him off at the uphill obstacle course without saying any more.

Simon silently thanked him for that last part.

And filed away the rest of it.

They decided on a small service the following Tuesday morning. Grace McNeil's closest friend, their old neighbor, Clara Williams, would handle the plans, as it would be held at her church in Flagstaff. Jan and Johnny had been to the mortuary, identified the body and made the necessary arrangements there. They'd talked to the police and to Jean, next door, and were back at their mother's home, looking for papers that needed immediate attention. There was no will. No direction from their mother about what should happen next.

No plans had ever been discussed concerning their mother's eventual death.

"I think we should sell most of this stuff," Jan said, walking around aimlessly, touching things, vacillating between moments of productive calm and helpless tears. "And anything that doesn't sell, we can donate."

"Fine with me." Johnny was going through a drawer in the kitchen, collecting bills that were due. He was going to pay them out of his own account and then they'd sort out the finances later.

Jan had offered to pay them. He'd insisted it was his place.

"Unless there's anything you'd like to have?"

"Not particularly." He didn't look up. "But take whatever you want."

She wanted it all. Because it had been her mother's. Because she'd lived among some of these things. Seen them every day. Touched them.

And at the same time she wanted none of it—no reminder that the woman she'd loved above all others had not loved her enough to hang on to life. Had not trusted her enough to ask for help. She wanted no reminders that she'd let her mother down.

"I should've been here last Sunday," she said, half to herself, sitting down at the kitchen table. "I'm so obsessed with this case that I forgot what was most important."

She was never going to forgive herself for this.

Johnny glanced up at her, his dark eyes—at least what she could see of them beneath his long hair—warm and loving. "You *have* become slightly obsessed, sis."

His words were like a knife. Her work, it seemed, was the only place she had succeeded. Her personal life certainly wasn't a success. She had no significant other, her closest friends were her work associates, frequently she was estranged from her brother, she'd failed her mother and she'd even screwed up a perfectly good friendship with her neighbor by asking him to hold her.

At least there was Hailey. She was definitely not a screwup.

"I'm telling you again, Jan, I think you should drop the case."

She probably should. But she couldn't.

"My obsession with it might have cost Mom her life, Johnny. But I have to win this case. It's one way I can make Mom's death matter."

Johnny's reply was a disgusted shake of the head.

"I want this."

Jan, sitting in the middle of the floor surrounded by photographs, glanced up when Johnny came in from their mother's bedroom.

She saw the pistol in her brother's hand and started to shake. "Where'd you get that?"

"Mom's closet, in a shoebox."

Jan could hardly breathe and was sweating so much that chills shook her body. "Why did Mom have a gun in her closet?"

"It was Dad's gun. Don't you remember?" Johnny asked, his voice filled with emotion.

She couldn't speak, so she shook her head.

"It was his favorite hunting pistol. Mom showed it to me when I turned seventeen. She told me one day it would be mine."

At least it wasn't the gun that had gone off in their father's hands, killing him. Her mother would never have kept that.

"I wish you'd just get rid of it, Johnny. The sight of that in your hand gives me the creeps."

"It's just a gun," Johnny told her, coming closer. He held the weapon out. "Look at the workmanship on this handle. And the barrel…"

"Johnny!" She hadn't meant to sound so sharp. "I don't want to see it."

"It's Dad's!" Johnny said, lowering the pistol. "There's no way I can get rid of it. He loved this gun. And we have so little that was his."

Johnny didn't even have memories of the man he'd made into a heroic idol.

"Then take it," she said.

She didn't want anything to do with it.

Simon debated about making the phone call. He'd seen her headlights come up the road and turn into her drive a little after eight. Had heard her brother's motorcycle roar away almost immediately afterward.

He had no reason to call. Nothing to offer her. He wanted it that way.

The terrorist's mind is closed. He is good and right; his victims are wrong and bad.

Simon dropped the article he was reading and picked up the phone.

"It's Simon," he said as soon as she answered, wandering into his bedroom as he spoke. Her light was out. "Were you asleep?"

"No." He'd never heard her so tired—lifeless, really. Not even the night before. "I brought some pictures home with me. Clara thought it would be nice if we had a collage at the service."

"Clara, that old friend of your mom's? The one who told you your father was an alcoholic?"

"I can't believe you remember that."

Once upon a time he'd remembered everything. Obviously, the habit was still with him. Or, at least, some of it was.

"So how'd things go today?" It was polite to ask, given the circumstances.

"Fine. Good."

Her erratic breathing came over the line. "Really?" he asked.

"No." He hated hearing her cry. "It was awful. But it's done and I don't have to go back tomorrow, so that's good. I arranged to have someone auction off her things. Whatever is left will go to a Flagstaff women's shelter."

Great idea. A clean sweep.

"You didn't want anything?"

"I brought everything I wanted back with me."

He wondered which of her mother's things had meant the most to her, what memories she had attached to them. And backed away from his bedroom window. It didn't matter. Couldn't matter.

She couldn't matter.

He didn't have what it took to allow that.

Simon saw the light come on in her bedroom. He'd been in bed for an hour—running through every trick he had for finding oblivion. Thinking of chapters one through three in the book he was writing; counting imaginary chess pieces; planning his day, any day. Exhausted, he punched his pillow. Rolled over. And he lay there long into the night, smelling her scent on his skin from the night before—in spite of the two showers he'd taken that day.

Bobby was tired. Stumbling into his bedroom late Wednesday night he considered the phone call he'd just made, convinced he'd made the best decision for the good of the greatest number.

Being a leader was hard work. But the rewards were worth it. God was plentiful in his blessings and Bobby was looking forward to enjoying one of them right now.

Her body was a shadow in the dim light of their room, huddled under the covers as if they could protect her from the ills of the world. Amanda was a sensitive soul, one of God's chosen. And now she was Bobby's.

Dropping his clothes by the bed, he lifted the hand-made quilt and slid in behind her, lifting her gown. Good girl. She wasn't wearing any panties. It was a requirement he wouldn't compromise on. A man needed sex available to him if he was to be capable of clear thinking.

Her crotch was already the slightest bit wet to his touch.

Bobby fingered her softly, reverently. God had sent him a beautiful woman and he would show her his respect, love and devotion every day for the rest of his life.

She groaned and he smiled. Soon she would be awake, moaning as she moved beneath him, on top of him, beside him, whichever pleasure she chose. He brushed his finger over her flat stomach and below, getting her ready.

Getting himself ready. With one hand he spread her legs, rolling her onto her back and slid up her body, taking her gown with him until her breasts were fully exposed to the night air. To him. Her nipples grew taut and Bobby latched on to one, suckling her as she'd been made to be suckled.

"Bobby?" Her husky voice fueled him. "It's late, baby."

"I know."

Her hand touched him, squeezed, just the way he liked. "You need it, huh?" She spoke so lovingly, he almost came then.

But he needed more than an orgasm. He had to fill her, to be her king, to know her in ways no other man had.

He turned her over.

And from the monitor on her nightstand, Luke's whimpering, the child's buildup to a full-blown wail, filled the room.

Giving him a long wet kiss, Amanda moved away from him.

"Don't go."

"He needs me," she said, yanking her gown over her nakedness.

Bobby grabbed her arm, drew her back down and pushed his hands up the sides of her body, removing her gown completely.

"You coddle him too much," he said, taking both of her breasts in his palms. "He's got to learn there are times when Daddy has first dibs on his mama. He needs to know he can expect the same attention from his wife."

Amanda didn't fight him, didn't deny him access to the body God had given him, but she turned her head, denying him her heart. That hurt.

"I'm not your wife."

"In all the ways that matter you are," he said. She understood he had a higher purpose. Although he encouraged members of the Nation to get married, he felt he couldn't be legally bound. He couldn't be tied to one family, because of his responsibility to the entire nation. They'd been through all of that. She'd thought she could leave him, had tried as a means of forcing him to marry her, but God had shown her that she couldn't. After a week on her own without Luke, she'd come back to Bobby. "If I marry, I become encumbered, and you know I can't afford to do that. If you take my name, you and Luke could be in danger of retribution from the system simply because of my name. I can't make the decisions I have to make, do the things I might have to do, if I think that you'll pay for them." He kissed her.

And again.

"You have all of me, Amanda. More than most wives." He moved back to her nipple, running his tongue over it until it hardened again. "Your body is the only one I touch. The only one I want. I provide a good home for you and Luke—buy you whatever you need and want. You work because you want to, but you will never have to do so."

"Mama!" Luke's cries were getting louder. Bobby's fault. He should have remembered to mute the monitor. She pushed his mouth away from her breast.

"Bobby, he's scared! Let me go to him."

"My son will not be a coward," Bobby told her, spreading her legs with one knee and driving into her cold. If she wasn't going to give him love tonight, he'd settle for sex.

"He's not your son."

Where he'd meant to be gentle, to coax her body's response, her words pushed him deeper, harder. "Don't you ever say that again," he demanded through gritted teeth. She made him crazy. Her body. Her mouth.

"He's not!" Her voice got louder as the toddler's cries subsided. She bucked against Bobby and he lowered his mouth to her breast. "You're sterile, Bobby. Did you forget?"

He sucked. Moved to the other breast.

"You gave me to your friend," she continued to talk. He continued to pump into her. "Luke is Jacob's, Bobby. Not yours."

He almost laughed at that last bit. It wasn't like that at all, and she knew it. She was a good woman. God's woman. It was her job to procreate, to bring to earth white boy babies who would further the cause. As long as the seed was pure, it didn't matter whose body released it. The only important thing was the man who raised the child.

Jacob Hall was not, and never would be, father material. He didn't even like kids. But his seed was pure, and for that Bobby loved him.

"I want another child," he told her, getting close to the edge.

Amanda didn't answer. She came instead. And Bobby followed her, giving her all of himself. His love. His loyalty. His cause.

And when it was over, he gently dried her tears.

11

The rain was coming down so hard she could barely see out her window. She thought the street was there—and her mailbox. If she could just get the mail, she'd be fine. She stared so hard her eyes hurt, and sometimes she could see the box—but each time it would fade away. And somehow she was out there, only the rain had turned to snow and dusk to darkness. Sliding on the ice, she fell, cracked her head, wondered about the pool of blood, but knew she had to continue. Her head could hurt but she couldn't stop. She had to get to the mailbox or she'd be locked out of her house forever.

She slid again as she reached the end of the drive and grabbed for the wooden post. Splinters pierced her arms and still she held on. Pulled on the latch. The door wouldn't open. She yanked at the mailbox latch with both hands, crying as the metal stuck to her skin. It didn't matter. Nothing mattered but getting in.

The door wouldn't open, but somehow her hand reached inside the box, anyway. Something was there. Something she recognized. Something she needed. It was *as cold and hard as the latch that wouldn't open. But heavier. She dragged it out and immediately dropped it.*

The gravel was clear, warm and well lit where the revolver lay.

Thursday morning, dressed in her most colorful blouse and her green suit, Jan went to work.

"What are you doing here?" Nancy, her secretary, asked as Jan walked by. "Andrew said you were out until tomorrow. And I'm so sorry about your mother, Ms. McNeil. So sorry."

I'm here because I've been up since four o'clock this morning, walking around my house, and I realized that if I didn't work I would have nothing else to do. "I finished in Sedona sooner than I thought," Jan said, eager to get to the safety and privacy of her own office. "And thank you. I'm sorry, too." She almost started to cry.

The middle-aged woman who'd been with her since she first began work at the county attorneys' office, nodded, her lower lip trembling. "What happened?"

"A mix-up with her medication," Jan said. She wouldn't lie again, but there was no reason to besmirch her mother's memory. "She died quietly at home." With no note to her survivors. No message for Jan or Johnny, except the obvious one delivered by the death itself—you aren't worth living for.

"When is the service?"

"Tuesday morning," Jan said, naming the church.

"I'll put a memo out, if you like," Nancy offered. "Everyone's been asking."

Why that surprised her, Jan didn't know, but it did. She hadn't realized her personal life was of any interest to her coworkers.

"People care about you, Ms. McNeil," Nancy said, apparently reading Jan's reaction in her expression. "You're the best prosecutor this town's had in years. You're dedicated, you're fair and you're always willing to help out."

With tears in her eyes—perhaps an indication that she hadn't been ready to come to work—Jan nodded. "Send a memo, then, if you think it's appropriate," she said. She was touched by Nancy's compassion.

"Will you please find out what time slot we have on the grand jury's calendar tomorrow?" she asked, focusing on the one thing she hoped would hold her grief at bay.

"Sure," Nancy said, making a note on the pad to her left. "Also, we heard from Judge Morris's JA on the Griss sentencing. They didn't get your recommendation on the pre-sentence report."

"I wrote it a month ago."

Nancy nodded. "Andrew found it immediately and hand-carried it to his chambers."

Andrew had come through for her. Thank God.

Dripping wet and wrapped in a towel, Simon trudged from the shower to his locker on Thursday morning. He'd stayed beneath the spray for an extra ten minutes, ostensibly to let the heat work on a sore shoulder muscle. With another ten to dress, he should be good for five minutes of conversation with Diamond's next clients and still get home in time to write a few pages before the first school bus arrived.

"Good work this morning." Diamond surprised him as he came around the corner.

Simon didn't like being caught unaware.

"Thanks," he said, wondering if he had a death wish he didn't know about. What in the hell was he doing, letting his guard down? Even for a shower?

"You're welcome to join that group session you asked about last week."

He dropped his towel. Slid into his briefs and nylon running pants. "Thanks."

"It'll cost you another couple of hundred a week."

Olsen would be glad to hear about that. "No problem."

Watching him for a long moment, Diamond nodded. "Hours vary, depending on the day's routine. We start every morning at nine."

Simon slid a long-sleeved cotton shirt over his wet head. There was no longer any reason to wait around. Diamond had just given him his other clients on a plate. "Fine."

"We're planning an overnighter tomorrow."

"For what?" It would've been a fair question, even if he hadn't been suspicious of everything the man said or did.

"Preparation." Diamond's tone clearly said Simon should've known that. "Avalanches happen. People get stranded. You aren't worth the salt on your skin, if you can't make it through the terrain at night."

Simon had been through high school sports training, police academy training, FBI specialized training—and he'd never had to do an all-night session. "Sounds good."

"I'll put you through your paces tomorrow. You might not be ready for it, but we'll see."

Shaking his head as a token attempt to dry his hair, Simon slid into the nylon jacket that matched a pair of pants in his dirty-laundry pile at home. "I'll be ready."

After one last perusal, Diamond was gone.

Simon called Olsen on his way home and hit him up for more money.

"Ms. McNeil?"

Jan glanced up from her computer screen as Nancy opened the office door.

"I can't find you on the grand jury's calendar. Are you sure you scheduled it?"

"I'm sure," she said, preoccupied with the information she was finding. So far, running searches on the names from Hall's list, she'd found potential matches for every single one. Every woman was an Arizona business owner. But it might not matter. These might not even be the right matches. There could be other women with the same or similar names. Neither was she ready to dismiss any of this as coincidence, however. "Andrew did it." She followed up on the conversation she was having with her secretary.

Nancy shook her head. "If he did, he must've confused the day. They have a full schedule for tomorrow and you aren't on it."

"It's for the Hall case."

"None of your cases is on for tomorrow."

Frowning, Jan asked her secretary to send Andrew in. There had to be some explanation. She had to be on that calendar. Period.

And she couldn't afford to doubt Andrew right now.

"I'm sorry, Jan." Andrew burst into her office a couple of minutes later, his red hair sticking straight up. He'd already been in, half an hour before, offering his condolences and asking if there was anything he could do. "Jenny called yesterday just as I was getting to the grand jury schedule. She said the baby was breathing funny. I rushed home to take them to the hospital and completely forgot that I hadn't finished what I was working on."

Shit. What was she going to do now?

"Is the baby okay?" she asked, genuinely concerned.

"Yeah, she has a little bit of apnea, but nothing to be too worried about. They put her on a breathing monitor."

"They kept her?"

He shook his head. "It's a mobile unit."

"Poor Jenny. That must've scared her."

"It was rough going for a few hours," Andrew said. "But that doesn't excuse my lapse here." His expression underscored his guilt and frustration. "I've let you down and I'm sorry."

"Don't worry about it." Jan gave him a smile that felt strained. "You did the best you could." And for several years his best had been near-perfect.

"Nancy says the calendar's full. I wish there was something I could do."

"I know." Sympathizing with his distress, she thanked him for the Griss catch and for the three or four other things he'd taken care of in her absence.

And now she had to track down James Kistle, the attorney who was overseeing the grand jury clerk, call in the favor he owed her—which she hated to do—and get Hall's case on that calendar. She hoped the process didn't have to include dinner. Divorced, for the third time, the year before, Kistle had been dropping hints all over the place suggesting he'd like to get to know her better.

But Jan was not the least bit interested in the handsome, independently wealthy womanizer.

Her headlights appeared, turning into her drive, at 7:45 p.m. Simon, who'd been watching since 6:15, was glad to see she'd made it home safely and he went back to his game of spider solitaire. There were blacks and there were reds, and never the two should meet.

If he wanted to win.

"I'm not calling her."

Simon stood shirtless, cell phone in hand, at his bedroom window, watching her bedroom window. Her light had been on and off three times in the past hour. He'd been on his bed in workout shorts most of that time, playing chess on his wireless laptop until he'd signed off five minutes ago.

"No, you'll stand here and talk to yourself." He didn't even bother changing positions, as he sometimes did when having a particularly heated conversation with himself.

"You started that."

"I did not."

"Sure you did. Two years ago. You'd just slept with what's her name and were tempted to do it again."

Ah, yes, he remembered. Staying away from Anita had called for drastic measures. Conducting the conversation in his head just hadn't done the trick—the words hadn't been loud enough to be effective.

He almost dropped his phone when it started to vibrate. Who the hell would be calling him? He'd already spoken to Olsen. Who else did he talk to?

On the third ring, Simon glanced at the caller ID on the tiny LED screen.

"Hi, neighbor," he said. He'd spent the dinner hour—and the one after that, too—working out in his spare bedroom. His mistake had been not putting in a third hour, after which his muscles would've been too shaky to hold the phone.

"How'd you know it was me?"

"I recognized your number."

"You've called me once."

"I put you on speed dial. When you call, my ID shows *Jan*."

"Oh."

Her bedroom light was still on. What was she doing

over there—getting ready for bed? Or had she already undressed?

Or was she crying.

"I wanted to thank you for bringing up my trash can."

He'd done that after coming back from the Snow-bowl. He'd forgotten.

"Just as easy to do two as one."

"Except that they go to different places. Anyway, thank you."

"You're welcome." He spoke to the light in her room. Time to hang up now.

"Did you have a good day?" Fine and dandy. If you didn't consider the fact that he'd been itching to tell her about Diamond's offer. The urge was a death knell for him. Even in his old life he'd been a complete loner when it came to his work.

"Alan Bonaby is definitely babysitting for Mark Thornton."

"Who?"

"Alan Bonaby."

"Who's he?"

"The kid who lives in the house at the end of the street. Used to deliver my papers. I've seen him go to the Thorntons' after school, and today he had the kid all bundled up and in a stroller."

Jan chuckled, reminding him that he hadn't heard the sound for a few days. "You have far too much time on your hands, Green," she said. "I'm telling you, you need to write a suspense novel. Or take up juggling or something."

"I already know how to juggle."

"You do?"

The light was still on. And she wasn't crying. Was she sitting on the bed? In a nightgown?

Or did she sleep in the nude?

"Mm hmm." He didn't give a damn about how she slept.

"Is there anything you don't know?"

"Probably, but how would I know?"

Her chuckle sent seductive chills up his legs. But only because he was standing at a cold window in his shorts.

"I had to have dinner tonight with the biggest jerk."

She'd been out. With another man. That was good, very good.

Yep. That was good, all right.

"Since when were dates mandatory?"

"He wasn't a date."

He should change into pants. He had a pair hanging on the bathroom door. Or maybe draped over the shower rod. He couldn't remember which.

"Who was he?"

"Another attorney at the office."

She told him about her grand jury predicament, and it occurred to Simon that Jan was the first woman he'd ever conversed with who didn't eventually, at some point or other, bore him to tears.

"So what'd you have to promise this jerky attorney to get onto the schedule?"

"I promised to think about asking him to work with

me on a case sometime. And I did. I thought I'd do it when hell freezes over."

Simon's bark of laughter surprised him. It was the second time that day he'd been caught off guard.

He'd better watch his ass, or it'd be shot off before he missed it.

Shifting his weight, Simon told himself to get away from the window. Sit down. Find a computer to distract him. His legs were going to be sore from all the work.

"Did you hear from your brother today?" Simon didn't like the way the guy ditched his sister for long periods. Couldn't Johnny see how much she cared about him?

"I did."

"Good. What'd he have to say?"

"He knows Hailey's spending the night tomorrow and he called to ask us out to dinner. He thinks it'll help still her fears about the adoption not going through. Give her a feeling of family and solidarity."

"I'm impressed." Simon spoke from the heart, without thinking.

"Yeah. Me, too." Her voice grew gentle.

Might be kind of nice to have that tone directed at him.

"Johnny was always such a sensitive guy," she continued. "Until he graduated from high school. I don't know what happened after that. Testosterone interference, I guess. He seemed to get angrier and angrier, and I could never figure out why."

"Have you talked with him about it?"

"I tried a few times. Never got anywhere."

"What'd your mom say?"

"Mostly, she said I was imagining things."

Maybe she was. Simon doubted it. "So the reason you keep nagging me to write a novel is because that's *your* secret desire and you're trying to satisfy it vicariously through me. Right?"

"Good night, Simon."

"Night."

He stood at the window until her light went out.

And wondered where a man went for strength when he had no faith.

Unable to rest her mind, Jan was up most of Thursday night, sitting at the computer in her guest room, tracking names on the Internet. By the time Andrew arrived at work Friday morning, she knew she was onto something big.

Knew, too, that she couldn't trust it to anyone but him. She wasn't a hundred percent sure she could trust even him, but she needed his help. If what she suspected was true, this case was going to be bigger than she'd ever guessed.

"You wanted to see me?" Andrew closed the door behind him and took a seat.

"Look at this." She handed him the pages she'd printed and compiled. She had two copies. One set for herself. One for him. She wasn't taking any chances on someone tampering with proof before she could put it all together.

"Have you matched social security numbers, to be sure these business owners are the same women on the list?"

"No," she said. "But once I get the bank records, I may not have to."

He glanced up. "How're you going to get them?"

"I called Kistle and got on today's calendar."

Andrew's attention returned immediately to the sheets.

"It's okay, Andrew." She looked him straight in the eye. "You're human. And no harm was done."

He nodded. But glanced away.

"So what do you think?" She gestured at the papers.

"They're all Caucasian women who own small businesses that cater to the general public."

He didn't disappoint her.

"And how much do you want to bet that they either service or employ minorities?"

He regarded her thoughtfully. "So what are you getting at?"

"I'm not sure yet, but we already know that subjugating women is part of the Ivory Nation philosophy. They've clearly got all the old-fashioned ideals that women should be subordinate to men. I read a pamphlet once that spoke about God and Jesus as men, appointing men to further their cause. And like Rachel and Sarah in the Bible, women were God's precious mothers to God's sons.

"Bobby Donahue wouldn't like to see women out running businesses, when they should be staying home raising their sons. And it would further incense him to see some of society's business dollars in the sole control of women. If we can prove that these businesses all had some significant Jewish, black or Hispanic association, we can completely tie white supremacist motives into the fraud. With the connections we have to Jacob Hall, that would all but give us the Ivory Nation." She tightened her lips. "I'd like you to get the coroners' reports on every single one of those women."

Andrew paled. "You think Hall killed them?"

The thought had crossed her mind. "I'm not saying that. I just want to know how they died."

"You want to know how Hall knew they were dead."

"Yes."

"To find out if, for instance, he has some connection who's got access to death records and reports to him when a single business woman passes on," Andrew suggested. "Assuming, of course, that we're correct in our assumption that Hall was targeting women."

"That's what I'm suspecting."

Nodding, eyes so focused she could almost see his mind working, Andrew continued. "He then takes their money for the cause."

"I'm guessing."

"It would certainly serve the Ivory Nation's notion of justice."

"Completely."

"This puts us in a far different place." Andrew sat

forward, hanging his head. He stood up and paced to her window. "Do you have any idea what kind of danger we'll be in if word gets out that we're this close to exposing them? They've been talked about for years, but no one's ever been able to prove anything." He shrugged helplessly. "Who knows how far-reaching the Ivory Nation is? What neighborhoods they've infiltrated, appearing like every other mom and dad?"

"That's why there are only two copies of this report. One for you and one for me. This goes nowhere, Andrew. Not yet."

"And when it does? What then? I have a wife and daughter to think about."

She understood that. "If this turns out to be half as big as I think it will, I'll take you off the case. I'll argue this one alone."

He spun around. "I can't let you do that."

"I'm chief counsel. You'll have no choice."

Andrew leaned down on her desk, meeting her gaze, quiet for too long. And said, "Then pull me now."

Jan stared at him. "Do you mean that?"

Pushing away from her desk, Andrew swore softly. "Hell, I don't know what I mean." He yanked at his neatly knotted tie.

She'd never seen him so conflicted, so unsure. And she couldn't blame him. When you went to law school, decided to fight for justice, you didn't expect that doing your job could force you to choose between your family and the greater good. He was a brand-new father. He suddenly had a lot to lose.

"I'm happy to do it, if you decide that's what you want," she told him.

"Can I let you know Monday?"

"Of course. Take the weekend. Talk to Jenny."

She sympathized, because she continued to fight the same battle herself.

But for her, there appeared to be no choice.

It had become life or death. She had to proceed.

12

"How come they're letting me spend the night with you when you don't have me yet?"

Hailey, wearing jeans and a T-shirt, light-blue sweatshirt and tennis shoes, stared out her side window as the Lincolns' home grew smaller in the distance.

"You've been allowed to spend the night since they did the home study on me." Jan paid particular attention to her speed, her turn signals, every road sign, as she always did when she had Hailey with her. "I just thought it would be better to wait until CPS had approved the adoption before bringing you home. So from the very first time you were there, you could feel like it was really yours."

She hadn't wanted to set the child up for more disillusionment.

"But the judge can still say no."

"He isn't going to."

Hailey peered at her from beneath her curls. "Do you know him?"

She nodded. "He was in juvenile court before he

moved over to family court, and I appeared before him several times. He's a very kind man."

The little girl's features relaxed the further they got from the Woodlands, the housing development where the Lincolns lived.

"Derek says that boys are better than girls because they have more muscles, and no matter how hard we work at it we'll never be as strong as them. It's because God already decided we couldn't be, so He made us with not as much muscles."

Jan had a thing or fifty to say about that.

"You want to know what I think?" Hailey asked, without giving Jan a chance to comment.

"I do, very much."

"Boys are so busy thinking their muscles are so great that they don't use their brains, so they'll never know what to do with their so-great muscles. Girls pay attention in school while boys are horsing around, and we'll have to run the world."

"I think you're right, sweetie," Jan said, holding back the laugh that had almost burst forth. "Some boys are definitely like that."

"Derek is."

Figuring that Hailey knew what she was talking about, Jan held her tongue. And counted the days until she could have her new daughter away from Derek's influence for good.

Johnny was waiting for them, sitting on his motorcycle on the street in front of the house.

"Who's that?" Hailey's tone was guarded, almost defensive.

"That's my brother, Johnny. I told you about him. He's coming to dinner with us."

She'd called Hailey that morning before school regarding their plans, to give her a chance to voice any objections.

"Oh, yeah."

"Let's go check if there's any mail."

Leaving the garage door open behind them, Jan took the little girl's hand. Hailey was watching Johnny.

"He doesn't look much like a brother."

Johnny, who had his helmet under his arm, waited at the street.

"What do brothers look like?" Jan asked, intrigued by the way the child's mind worked.

"I don't know," Hailey said. "Nice."

"When I was growing up and I had bad dreams, Johnny always came to my room and woke me up and stayed with me until I felt better. He'd even sleep at the end of my bed all night."

They were almost at the end of the drive. Johnny was waiting, dressed all in black, as usual. He'd pulled his hair back into a ponytail.

"Do you still have bad dreams?"

Another one of the things she and Hailey would have to talk about—before bedtime tonight. She didn't want to scare the child if she cried out.

"Sometimes."

"Me, too."

* * *

"Hey, peanut, nice to meet you." Johnny bowed to Hailey as they were introduced, the child gave him a tentative grin and Jan breathed more easily again.

"You want to sit on my motorcycle?"

Jan opened her mouth to object. Motorcycles weren't safe. She didn't want Hailey introduced to them—ever.

"Okay."

"You'll have to put this on," he said, handing the little girl his shiny helmet.

"Just to sit?"

"Yep."

Jan reached for the handle of the mailbox as she watched the expensive-looking helmet swallow up her little girl's head. She loved Johnny for the care he was taking with the child.

"What do I call you?" she heard Hailey ask, as she reached in for the mail.

"Uncle Johnny, I think…"

Heart pounding, Jan peeked at the envelope with no stamp, no return address, no postal stamp—and her own return address label pasted in the middle of it.

At first she thought she'd left it there by mistake. That she'd forgotten to address something she'd sent. But the mailbox had been empty the night before, and she hadn't visited it that morning. Besides, she always dropped her outgoing mail in a collection box. Which meant someone else had done this. Today.

She couldn't believe it, couldn't stand the thought

of it. How had anyone gotten hold of her personal labels? The one on the envelope was identical to the ones she kept in her desk at work—and at home.

Were they telling her they'd been in her house?

Had they stolen some mail she'd sent? Had they been right there at her box? Or did they work someplace where she'd sent mail?

She couldn't tell if the label was fresh, but it wasn't taped on.

Fingers shaking, she stared, her face hot, her body cold.

Aware of Hailey's voice, asking questions about the bike, and Johnny's muted replies, Jan slid open the envelope. She briefly considered the need to preserve fingerprints, but figured that whoever had done this was smart enough to wear gloves.

Turning her back, not wanting anyone else to know what was happening, she peered inside. And saw nothing. Absolutely nothing.

The label was the warning.

Because of the grand jury decision earlier that day? But who would've known?

Jan tried to think about where she'd sent mail recently and couldn't remember a single place. She paid her bills on-line.

Where was Simon? He usually checked the mail with her.

"Can I have a ride?" Hailey's question sank through the heavy fog suffocating Jan.

No. But the words didn't come out.

"Nope, too risky." Johnny took care of it for her.

Could he take care of this, too? Figure out who'd done this to her? What she had to fear?

Slipping the envelope between two others, Jan pasted a smile on her face and turned to watch as Hailey climbed down and took off the helmet.

She couldn't tell Johnny about this. At least not until she had a chance to think about it for herself. She couldn't handle any more pressure from him right now.

She glanced over at Simon's house. No sign of life there.

She'd have dinner, calm down and put Hailey to bed.

And then she'd call Ruple.

Johnny took them to a popular Italian restaurant not far from downtown—one where they'd eaten many times as kids. Known for its good food as well as its reasonable prices, the place drew families. She shared a smile with Johnny as they were seated, Hailey on her side of the booth and Johnny across from them.

Being a family again felt right—even if her world was frighteningly wrong.

"Are you going to have to change schools?" Johnny asked Hailey while they waited for their dinners to be served.

"I dunno." Hailey, who was chewing on a piece of bread, turned to Jan. "Am I?"

"That's up to you," Jan said, taking comfort from the ordinary people around them, the buzz of conversations, the plans for a future together with Hailey. "Your current school is in a different district, but I'm willing to drive you there if you want to stay. At least for the rest of this year."

She'd be willing to drive to Phoenix and back, if it meant the girl would feel happy, secure, loved.

"I'll move," Hailey said.

"What about the friends you've made?" Jan asked, not that Hailey talked about any of them.

She shrugged, ripping off a piece of her bread and sticking it into her mouth. "Don't have any."

The matter-of-fact way the words were delivered broke Jan's heart.

"So, how'd the grand jury thing go today?" Johnny seemed to be enjoying his lasagna.

Hailey was wolfing down her macaroni and cheese, putting her napkin in her lap without having to be reminded this time.

Jan's spinach manicotti was mostly untouched. Her stomach knotted as she stared at her brother. "How'd you know about that?"

"The phone call in the car the other morning, remember?"

Oh, right. Of course. She could not afford to be paranoid.

But then, she'd told herself she was worrying too much about her mother, too, and as it turned out she'd been absolutely correct in her first assumption—that she had reason to worry.

"It went fine," she said now, not wanting to think about work, Jacob Hall or the envelope in her purse. She also didn't want to say too much in front of Hailey. The child had seen a lot in her young life, and to Jan, that seemed all the more reason to protect whatever innocence she had left. "They granted the subpoena I was after."

Johnny stabbed a piece of meat and some pasta. "I don't like it, sis." The low tone didn't disguise his harshness.

"Johnny..."

"I mean it," he said, his gaze intent. "How can you sit here with her—" he pointed at Hailey who, while she might appear to be fully engrossed in her food, was almost assuredly taking in the conversation "—and still pursue this case?"

Chest as tight as the fingers she clenched in her lap, Jan said, "I don't see how they're connected."

"It's one thing to put yourself in danger, but what about her?"

Damn him. Jan couldn't believe he was doing this, trying to force her hand in this way.

And she understood. He was scared. For her and for himself.

He knew how much she loved Hailey. And none of his other tactics had worked.

"It's a job, Johnny." Jan had no idea how she managed the lightness in her tone. "I've never heard of a single instance in Arizona where a prosecutor or his family was harmed because of a case."

"There's always a first time. Look what happened in Chicago. And then Georgia."

She recalled the Chicago incident immediately—a judge's family had been attacked. And in Georgia a judge had been killed. She'd had a horrible nightmare right afterward—and had seen Johnny the next morning.

"Pulling out all the stops, are you, brother?" she said with what she hoped was an easy grin. *Not in front of Hailey,* her eyes pleaded with him.

"I'm fighting for your life here." His eyes glistened with moisture—and conviction.

"I know you *think* you are."

"Why won't you listen to me, trust my judgment instead of your own for once in your life?"

A couple at the next table glanced over.

Hailey put down her fork. Slid a little closer to Jan.

"I trust you, Johnny. You know that. But I know more about my job than you do. I've been working at the county attorneys' office for more than a decade."

"I'm not talking about being a lawyer," Johnny said, lowering his voice. "I'm talking about the things you can't see because you're so caught up in doing your job."

He had her there. How did you argue about what you couldn't see? Or were told you couldn't see… How did you know if there was anything to see, if you couldn't see it? How did you know if you couldn't see because there was nothing there, or because you really were blind to what others were trying to tell you?

In all the years she'd worked with Andrew, she'd

never seen him hesitate on a case before. And he was thinking about taking himself off this one.

The letter in her purse loomed in her mind.

Maybe she wasn't listening, seeing.

Maybe she should drop the charges, or find someone else to take the case.

But if that was the right answer, then why did she feel this burning compulsion to go forward? Why was it so crucial to risk her own life to save others?

Why couldn't everyone understand that this was the only code by which society could live, people willing to risk themselves for the greater good. Policemen did it every single day. So did firemen—they all had families.

Where would civilization be without their protection?

Even white supremacists and terrorists did it, for their own perception of the greater good.

Or was there something she was missing?

After just a few hours with the two other men in Diamond's group, Simon knew he was going to be earning his keep. These young men might not be terrorists. They might not be doing anything illegal at all. But they were far too serious about every step they made, too focused on every aspect of the experience, to be ordinary citizens bettering themselves merely for personal gain. They were obviously preparing for something bigger than ski-trainer certification. Or even a shot at the Olympics. The simmering intensity with which they moved set Simon's nerves on edge.

All three of them had run up the side of the mountain, including the obstacle course, in the pitch black, with Diamond silently following them—ready to pick up the pieces, if there were any, Simon surmised.

The small pistol in a holder on his hip, was on the forefront of his mind that night. His elastic waistband allowed for immediate access.

But what about his reflexes? Simon might still wear a gun out of habit every day, but he hadn't pulled one in years.

"I sent the other two to find flat ground with shelter," Diamond said, coming up as Simon slid down the tree he'd shimmied up at the top of the course.

"What about food?"

"What about it?"

"Do I need to find some?" Simon asked.

"You hungry?"

"Not yet."

"You know where there's any food?"

Simon considered the terrain they'd covered. "Purslane weeds two bends ago. Lots of beta-carotene, potassium, iron, magnesium and omega-3 fatty acids." The stems, leaves and seeds were all edible, but he'd prefer his with salad dressing.

The whites of Diamond's eyes glowed in the moonlight. "You're a good student, Green," he said.

Simon continued to move around the plateau, keeping his blood flowing so his sweat wouldn't freeze. "Getting up here was easier with no snow," he said, "but keeping warm tonight's going to be harder. No insulation."

Diamond nodded in the direction the other two had disappeared. "They'll find a wind shelter. And enough brush to keep us alive."

Simon didn't doubt that. Nor did he think that any searching he did after they went to sleep would turn up any useful information. He'd search anyway. And wait. And listen.

"I hear about jobs sometimes." Diamond motioned for Simon to follow where the others had gone. "People looking for fearless men to save lives."

"What people?"

"Can't say. The work's too vital—and sometimes sensitive—to be jeopardized. But when I see someone like yourself, someone who could make a real difference, I put him together with a job. If he has any interest."

Simon tread carefully, and not because he was climbing a mountain at night.

"Where's the work?"

"Nothing more to be said, other than you're interested or you're not."

"I'm interested."

Unable to relax and fall into a deep sleep for fear of having a nightmare, Jan was up early the following morning, cleaning the oven, disinfecting kitchen counters, wiping out the refrigerator and waiting for Hailey to wake up. And she was thinking about the envelope still in her purse. Last night, enjoying her time with her soon-to-be daughter, getting used to having someone share her private space and time, talking about how they'd decorate Hailey's room, she'd tried to ignore it. Today she would turn it over to the police. No point in bothering Ruple.

Move on to the idea of sharing her home. She'd fully considered the logistics of having a full-time family member, of course. Had seriously considered the ramifications and consciously chosen to go ahead with the adoption.

The reality of having the child in her home was unlike anything she'd imagined—both wonderful and a little discomfiting. She'd been alone a long time. Had grown used to having a place where she could hide undetected.

Cry if she needed to.

Live unseen.

She'd grown used to being lonely.

Having someone else in her home, even for one night, had brought more life to the place than she'd dared hope for. Already the thought of possibly losing Hailey was unbearable.

Six-thirty, and her kitchen was sanitized. The living room was next. Grabbing disposable dust cloths, Jan slid open the drapes to watch the sunrise as she worked and saw headlights instead. Simon's car slowed as he turned into his drive. His hair was standing up all over and his chin was dark with whiskers.

It looked like he'd been out all night.

With a woman?

She'd planned to stop by her local precinct on the way home after dropping off Hailey that afternoon. But thinking of the junior officers she'd dealt with when her windshield had been shattered, she'd gone straight home instead, returning to her original plan. She'd give the envelope to Danny Ruple on Monday. It wasn't immediately life-threatening, if it was life-threatening at all. It was a warning. A scare tactic.

Nothing more.

And she wasn't going to be scared off.

Simon sauntered out, as Jan drove up to her garage. Although she was tempted to push the button on her visor and shut the garage door before she got out of the car, Jan turned off the engine and headed down the drive. A little idiocy was too tempting to pass up, at the moment.

"How'd it go with Hailey?" he called as she approached her mailbox.

"Great. Better than I'd hoped. She wants her room done in butterflies. My trunk's filled with the results of today's shopping. I hope by now she's at least a little bit convinced that the adoption's really going to happen."

She was jabbering, dammit.

Simon nodded, a hand resting on the top of the mailbox. She should be yanking on the lever. Reaching inside.

And she couldn't.

"I saw you come home this morning." Jan bit her lip. Stellar, McNeil. Can you think of anything equally brilliant to add?

"You were up early."

"As much as I want Hailey, it's kind of weird to have someone in my house after all this time living alone. I didn't sleep all that well. Sounds crazy, huh?" What did it matter if he thought so? He *was* crazy.

"No."

"You've lived alone for years, too. How would you feel about sharing your space?"

"Can I spit in the living room if there's anyone else around?"

Chuckling, Jan shook her head. Simon didn't look like a spitter.

"Then alone's the way for me."

"What about family?" She studied the latch on her box again. "Don't you want one someday?"

"My computer games figure they're all the family I need."

The man was impossible. And easy to be around. Much easier than the mailbox at the moment.

"Where'd you grow up, Simon?"

"Philadelphia."

"So that's where your family is?"

"My folks are dead, Jan. No siblings, either. So I get to spit all I want, thank goodness."

He really was alone. Why that knowledge made her sad, she didn't know. Didn't want to know.

"You could always get married."

He took a step back, threw up his arms with such force he knocked off his glasses and then caught them in midair. His horrified expression was so over the top, she laughed out loud. "Don't let my grass even hear those words," he whispered. "I've promised it there'd be no little feet stomping it to death and in return, it grows quite obligingly." He looked over his shoulder a couple of times as he said the words. "I mean, look at my grass compared to the rest of the neighborhood. Its color, its depth, are far superior to the rest."

His yard was turning brown for winter, just like all the other yards.

"Grass aside," Jan continued, pushed as much by her fear of the mailbox as by some need to engage him in personal conversation, "you might find someone who'd let you spit."

What did it matter to her? Was she so insecure that she needed him to want what she wanted—a family— just to validate her choice?

"No way. I'm not looking."

"Why not?"

"It's too big a step and I've got little feet." She glanced down at his size eleven shoes and shook her head.

13

"You ever going to open that mailbox?" Simon's tone was playful; his intent scrutiny was not. "It's part of the routine," he continued. "We meet, you open. If you don't, we can't leave and we'll freeze to death here waiting—if we don't starve to death first. The neighbors will drive by, staring, convinced we've gone mad…"

Jan yanked on the latch. Reached inside. Trying to keep her shaking hands from his perceptive gaze, she fumbled through the envelopes.

All bills. And a solicitation.

Jan almost wept with relief.

"You are now free to get warm and eat," she said to her neighbor.

"Uh-uh."

Mouth open, she peered up at him. "What?"

"Not until you tell me why you were scared to death to open that." He pointed at the box between them.

"We got that routine thing going, Green," she said. "Just imagine the warp we'd be caught in if we…"

"You've had a hard week and you look like you need a friend."

The sudden compassion in his eyes, his voice, almost caused her knees to buckle.

"I don't need any more complications in my life." She was thinking out loud.

Simon held out empty palms. "No complications, I swear," he told her. "Remember? I like to spit."

And he'd spent the night out—presumably with another woman. If she hadn't already been so depressed, or worried, or whatever she was, the awareness of his involvement would have put her emotions at rest as easily as it did her mind.

"Do you have time to come in for a minute?"

"I'm sure my grass and computer games won't mind."

Disoriented by emotions that seemed to be all over the place and by a lack of confidence even in herself, Jan led him up to her house. And tried not to feel too good about having him there.

"It came right after your grand jury win?"

Blood surged through Simon's veins, stimulating every reflex he had. The sensation was instantly recognized, instinctive—a long-lost friend.

Jan nodded, reaching into her purse.

Focused completely on the envelope she pulled out, he sensed that danger was imminent.

"Who knew you were meeting with them?"

"Any number of court staff, my assistant, my secretary, the detective who's working the case with me, Danny Ruple, and anyone he might have told."

"Is that all?"

"Except for my brother." She held the frightening piece of mail out to him and just that quickly he remembered who he was—the guy who'd finished an economics textbook because the author was no longer alive to do so. The guy who lived alone writing law-enforcement manuals because those who can, do, and those who can't, teach.

The adrenaline racing through him slid through unseen cracks, a friend no longer. A bitter enemy instead.

"I'd better not touch it," he said. "You always hear about them needing fingerprints."

Anyone doing a job like this was far too professional to leave such a clear calling card.

"I doubt there are any."

She was no novice here, and she didn't need him.

"You should still call the police, report this. If nothing else, they'll know to watch out around here. Maybe they'll even put an extra car in the area."

"I intend to give it to Ruple on Monday."

She dropped the envelope back into her bag, leaving him no reason to stay beside her. At least not a valid one.

"That's another day and a half."

"Yeah."

"Their message to you is that they know where you live, right?"

She was so close he could see her throat move when she swallowed. "Seems pretty clear."

Simon couldn't remember ever needing to pull a woman against him, the way he did at that moment. Not for sex—though he was still human and she was beautiful and he wouldn't mind that, if circumstances were different—but because it seemed somehow necessary for both of them.

"So why not get immediate protection?"

Her eyes clouded. He was scaring her, dammit. Yet what else could he do?

"They might put it down to a prank."

"Not with one of your personal labels on it. Someone either had to go to a lot of trouble to produce an exact replica of that or they stole one of yours."

"I'll call Ruple. You want to wait?"

There was no reason for him to be there. He shouldn't want to be.

"If you don't mind, since I'm around all day, I'd like to hear what he has to say. There might be something in particular I could be watching for."

He noticed that Jan didn't make her usual comment about his overactive imagination or suggest he should consider writing suspense.

Danny Ruple was home watching college football, but when he heard what Jan had to say, he came right over. The detective was there for less than ten minutes, taking the envelope with him in a plastic bag, but it was long enough to frighten the hell out of her. Both Danny and Simon were acting as if she was completely helpless, a sitting duck in the middle of a rifle range.

She almost wished she'd kept the whole thing to herself.

"You should do what he suggests and find someplace else to stay for a little while," Simon said, standing inside her front door when Danny Ruple had left.

"This is my home."

He took her by the shoulders and it felt so good in a day that seemed so utterly black.

"You told Ruple you still have another week until you go to trial."

"That's right." Her gaze was resolute as she looked up at him. She was not going to give in to the fear. All her life she'd been fighting its insidious power, and all the counselors she'd seen had told her the same thing her mother had said her entire life—the only thing she had to fear was fear itself. Survival meant not letting it beat her.

"And the trial's scheduled to last a week?"

"Based on the number of witnesses, the defense attorneys and I are predictiong it will take that long." And if her suspicions proved correct, there'd be more charges—another trial.

"So you're only looking at a couple of weeks. What would be so bad about staying in a bed-and-breakfast, just to be on the safe side?"

Letting fear win, that was what. "They know where I work, Simon. If they want to find me, they will. If I stay somewhere else, what's to stop them from following me wherever I go after work?"

"Then come home and I'll take you out to eat every night and drop you off at a different hotel."

She smiled, genuinely warmed by his ridiculous suggestion. "So the villain gets to eat out at a different place every night, before he follows us to where I'm staying? What are you going to do—stay there with me, too?"

She'd been going with the flow, finishing his painting for him, and she wanted to bite her tongue when she heard the words slip out of her mouth.

"It's not a half bad idea." His expression was completely serious.

"No!" She could feel the heat spreading up to her face, and knew she was turning red. "I mean, no, thank you." She lowered her voice. "In the first place, you have work to do at home. And so do I, Simon. I'm in the middle of a very important investigation, building a case, and my law books are here. I'll take the precautions Danny suggested, have an alarm system installed, not go out alone after dark, keep my car doors locked, even in the garage. I'll do it all. And the police are adding an extra patrol, but beyond that, short of dropping the case, there's not much I can do. And I'm not dropping the case."

"I'm not saying you should," he said, although judging by the lines of doubt on his forehead, she suspected he might like her to do just that. "I'd just feel better if you weren't alone."

"With you right next door guarding the neighborhood?" She wasn't going to tell him how damn good that felt right now—didn't want him to know how close she was to giving in and running away to hide. Flagstaff had some wonderful bed-and-breakfast inns.

But why risk putting anyone else in danger?

"You don't have to do everything alone, Jan. You've just lost your mother, and now this happens. At least let me go into the house with you when you get home."

Another suggestion from Danny—that she not enter her home alone. One she felt she had to refuse simply because she wanted so much to agree. What if she spent her days looking forward to going home just because she knew she'd be seeing Simon?

This was getting complicated, and she'd said only an hour ago that she had no energy or emotional stamina for any more complications in her life.

He was a man destined to remain alone.

He liked to spit—or at least talk about spitting. And she had nightmares.

She was adopting a child. He'd promised his grass he wouldn't have kids.

"Only if you'll let me bring you dinner sometimes."

"Chinese?"

"I have it once a week."

"It's a deal."

It is? Oh, good. Oh…hell.

Profile of a terrorist.

Simon didn't usually work on Sundays—not for any spiritual reason, but because he used the "day of rest" as an excuse to escape into old war movies on the couch, in between lifting weights and sleeping late. He also cooked on Sundays, just for the hell of it. In his old life, although he wasn't much of a chef, he'd insisted on hosting Sunday dinner for Sam and Shannon any time he wasn't on shift.

Some habits didn't seem to die, no matter how hard he tried to kill them.

Simon glanced out his window for the hundredth time that morning. No one had come or gone from Jan's house.

More often male than female.

Diamond didn't train a single woman that Simon knew of.

Most common age: twenties.

The two men he'd spent Friday night with had been no more than twenty-five.

Fulfilling a need to belong.

Surviving together in the mountains was a bonding experience.

Self-actualization is reached by serving a cause.

The job that meant more.

Hearing the now-familiar roar of Johnny McNeil's motorcycle, Simon watched the black-suited young man pull up in front of his sister's house, dismount and saunter up to her front door.

He wished he was relieved about the fact that he could now relax and not worry about his self-appointed responsibilities next door. Wished he didn't envy the man who was having Sunday dinner with her. Wished it didn't matter that he was no longer needed.

Disgusted with himself, Simon went to work out again, using physical aggression to wipe all feelings of envy from his body.

And when Diamond called Sunday evening offering to arrange a meeting Monday morning regarding a potential job, Simon accepted with relief.

By the time Jan went to work Monday morning, she had convinced herself she didn't care whether Andrew decided to take himself off the Hall case. She'd be perfectly fine either way.

Johnny was back in her life. She had her neighbor's kind support. Soon she'd have a daughter. Hall was going to be convicted. And time and hard work would one day dissipate the dark cloud that hung over her heart as a result of her mother's death.

"I can't let you down, Jan." The words poured out of Andrew as he walked into her office just before eight. "As long as you're going ahead with the Hall case, I'll be right by your side."

Jan took a second to breathe a sigh of relief, concentrated on the one piece of lint she could find on her navy suit, assuring herself that she had no reason to doubt Andrew. He'd put in too many good years to have his job compromised by a couple of mistakes. Especially since he was a new dad and his preoccupation was understandable. And when she was certain her emotions were in check, she glanced over at her assistant. "Did you talk to Jenny about it?"

Taking his usual seat in front of her desk, he shook

his head. "Once I figured out that I couldn't turn my back on what we've started, I didn't want to worry her with possibilities."

She understood that. "I got a pseudo threat over the weekend." Jan described the envelope she'd found in her mailbox. She couldn't let him continue without knowing it all.

"What did Detective Ruple say?"

"That we'll never trace the envelope. And it's too much of a coincidence that the thing showed up on the same day as the grand jury ruling."

"That's it?"

She gave him the entire rundown of ideas the detective had had for her safety.

"So are you going to hide out someplace?"

"No."

"But you are going to be careful," Andrew said, showing open concern as he leaned forward. "Don't blow this off, Jan."

"I'm not," she assured him. "I've got someone meeting me at the house every night, so I don't enter the place alone. I won't be going anywhere by myself after dark. And the alarm system is being installed this afternoon."

Her answer seemed to satisfy him.

"So, you're still sure you're in with me?"

Chin resolute, he met her searching gaze head-on. "Absolutely."

"I can't guarantee that it won't get ugly." Or dangerous.

"I wasn't born yesterday, boss."

Regarding him for another long moment, Jan finally nodded and scooted her chair up to her desk, organizing the papers spread there.

"We have one week until trial starts. Any suggestions?"

As a concession to Monday morning's interview, Simon made sure that his loose pants and wrinkled shirt matched each other. And at the last minute, he ran a comb, rather than just his fingers, through his hair. Whether or not he got the job only mattered in relation to whatever information he might gain. About Diamond. Terrorists. Anything that might give validation to—or disprove—the finger Amanda had pointed.

He arrived at the upscale chain breakfast place just before the appointed hour of 9:00 a.m., asked for the recently vacated end booth and slid in facing out, his back to the wall.

His breakfast companion would be in his thirties, tall, dark-haired and wearing a beige pullover sweater with brown Dockers.

Not quite the underworld look Simon had expected.

Tom Davenport arrived right on time. Had a strong, steady handshake. And apparently liked breakfast as much as Simon did.

"I manage a private protection-services company," the short-haired man said as he dug into his scrambled eggs, potatoes, biscuits and gravy.

Anticipating the omelet he was still waiting for—

he could scramble eggs on his own—Simon started in on his side order of pancakes first and listened.

"Our clients range from politicians to picketers, with an occasional fearful old lady thrown in, although we try to stay away from babysitting. The goal of my company, Pure World Protection, is to keep the way safe as others step forward to make this country a better place—and to cover our overhead."

"Lofty goal," Simon said. "I respect that."

Tom's scrutiny turned to an approving glint.

"What about you?" The man wiped his mouth and carefully placed his napkin back on his lap. "You must have goals."

"To be the best damn ski instructor I can be—and to leave a positive impact somewhere before I die."

Simon almost lost his appetite as he got carried away. That last had hit too close to a truth he'd once believed. A truth that had cost him everything, except the one thing that didn't matter. His own life.

His goal was to live in such a way that he would never again be responsible for the pain of another living being—which was why his only living companion was grass.

Tom Davenport forked up a piece of sausage, chewed and swallowed. And sat back with a friendly smile and a nod when the waitress came over to refill his coffee. Simon nursed his orange juice.

"You have any particular beliefs that would get in the way of your performance on a job?"

"I believe in staying out of jail."

"Would you consider yourself a conservative?"

Davenport's fork was suspended in air. The man didn't move, waiting for Simon's answer.

It would be good if he gave the right one.

Terrorists always had a cause to which they were deeply committed.

"If you mean do I have faith that the ultimate goal for this universe will prevail and evil will one day be wiped out, then yes, I guess I'm a conservative. I don't have a lot of patience with a chaotic, free-for-all way of life."

He was so full of shit. If his brother Sam could hear him, he'd be beating his head in despair. Simon's live-and-let-live (within the boundaries of the law) philosophy had been the one difference between the identical twins. Sam had worried about things like global warming and had stressed himself out with his fears about scarcity.

Simon had been hell-bent on protecting the constitution—and on drinking.

"How are you with a gun?"

"I own one." Even if he didn't have special clearance—which he did—civilians could legally carry concealed weapons in Arizona as long as they were registered.

"You interested in some target practice?"

Scooping omelet onto his fork with a piece of toast, Simon shrugged. "Sure."

By ten that morning, after having vetoed many of Andrew's suggestions for opening arguments and accepting his multiple apologies for coming to work with another sleepless night behind him, Jan agreed to let him brainstorm some strategies on his own and get back to her. While the majority of their daily work entailed focusing on facts, her opening and closing arguments were, to a large extent, artistic creations and they took a different kind of concentration.

"I'm going to be a mother soon, myself," she told Andrew with a smile. "And I fully expect you to cover for me when Hailey gets sick and I forget to come to work."

"Like that would ever happen."

"Parenthood is more important than anything else in my book, Andrew. No need to apologize to me for being a dad." *Please, God, let that be all it is.*

He nodded, still tight-lipped, and Jan wished there was more she could do to reduce the sting he was apparently feeling at the realization he wasn't superhuman.

"I'm moving all my files on this case to the office." Jan decided to change the subject. "I've cleared out the bottom drawer in my desk, just for Hall material, and I intend to keep it locked at all times. I'd like you to do the same with yours. I don't want anything concerning this case in either of our homes. I've asked Nancy for her keys to both desks, so you and I will be the only two with access." As a final protective measure, she was backing up everything on a flash drive and keeping it with her at all times. She wasn't going to risk any more disappearing files.

He nodded, but he was still frowning.

"It's okay, Andrew. Truly."

"I hate the position I find myself in," Andrew said, meeting her eye to eye. "I'd never do anything to hurt you, you know that...."

"Of course, I do."

His gaze dropped to watch his hands slowly rubbing together. "Yet over and over lately I seem to be letting you down."

"You have a life, Andrew!"

"I know." He glanced back up, his face resolute. "And I have to be there for them, no matter what."

"Of course you do."

"So you aren't tempted to replace me?"

"Of course not!"

He sat back, not looking happy, but a little more relaxed. "I'll make it up to you."

"You can start by finding me some answers," she told him, feeling, for the most part, satisfied with the conversation. Andrew had been acting out of character—at a particularly unfortunate time. Her uneasiness was to be expected.

14

"Have you heard from Ruple regarding the bank statements?" Andrew asked his fifth question in as many minutes, as if trying to prove to Jan, despite her assurances that his job was not at risk, that he was worth his paycheck.

"He's coming by to meet with us late this morning," she said, glancing over the items they'd just discussed, looking for other pieces that might be missing. She was reassigning a couple of his cases, freeing up his time for fatherhood and the Hall case.

"Do you intend to tell him about the list you showed me on Friday?"

Jan didn't even hesitate. "Not yet. Until we're more certain of what we're suggesting, I don't want to take a chance on any leaks. Can you imagine what would happen to this state if someone started spreading word that female business owners and anyone else who did business with minorities were in danger?"

"You don't trust Ruple?"

"Of course, I do. But he has his superiors, to whom

he has to report, and there are also clerks who handle paperwork. If even one of them has a conversation about this with someone he trusts and a janitor overhears, or someone in an elevator or at the next table at a restaurant does, all hell could break lose."

Andrew sat forward, his gaze potent despite the weariness that was also evident. "You really think it's going to be that big?"

"It could be."

He nodded, looking more resigned than surprised.

"For now our only goal with any evidence we find is to try to establish the Ivory Nation connection and motive. We should be able to do that on our own, so I'd like you to start researching these businesses."

With a yellow pencil in hand, Andrew jotted on the legal pad he had propped on his lap.

"I'll take the top half of the list, if you want to take the bottom," he suggested. "We make our individual notes but keep copies together in our desks whenever we aren't actually working on them."

"Agreed."

Andrew glanced at his watch, and then looked back at the pad. "So what have you decided to do if, as we suspect, Ruple brings us evidence of fraudulent activity on the thirty other bank numbers? If we charge Hall with more counts connected to the same scheme, the defense is going to move to have them tried concurrently."

Because if Hall was convicted on the first three counts and had a second trial for the rest of them, the first conviction would be treated as a prior, and the jury would be privy to that information and more likely to return a guilty verdict. And, of course, the sentence would be stiffer.

"And if he wins that motion, which presumably he will, the start of the trial will be continued for six to eight weeks."

Six to eight weeks in which anything could happen. Now that they were this close—and she could see the dangerous pieces falling into place—Jan didn't want to give the defense any extra time.

"It might be better to use the information at sentencing," Andrew said, seeming more like his normal self. "Instead of charging him with fraud, we could use proof of the other accounts as aggravators, and go for a maximum sentence."

Jan agreed completely.

The pistol grip was unfamiliar to him, but Simon had never met a gun he couldn't shoot. Aiming with one eye closed, he emptied the first round into the center target his potential employer had nailed to a tree fifteen miles outside the Flagstaff city limits. When he was done, he pushed his glasses up his nose and turned around. Davenport stood, hands in his pockets, shoulders huddled against the cold, rocking back and forth in his buffed leather shoes, not smiling but with a respectful expression on his face.

Simon emptied another round—perfectly—before returning the gun. If he wasn't mistaken, and he very rarely was about these things, he'd just earned himself a job.

"You have any problem with traveling?" Davenport asked, as they traversed the stiff, brown grass back to their vehicles.

"Later, no. I'd rather not right now. I intend to finish my training and take Level III certification, no matter what."

"I can appreciate that." Tom's breath was gray vapor in front of him. "I like a man who finishes what he starts."

Simon had figured as much.

"But you're interested in taking local jobs in the meantime?"

"Yeah." Simon wished he'd brought a jacket. The flannel shirt might be okay for going from his house to the mailbox, but it wasn't too effective against the open-range wind. "I'd need to know what the pay is."

Davenport named an amount that was far higher than Simon had ever earned risking his life and shooting guns in the past.

"You said you're a manager," Simon said, after agreeing to the wage. They were standing between their SUVs. "Who owns the company?"

"We have a silent investor, someone who wants to remain anonymous for his own reasons." Davenport gave the first answer Simon really didn't like.

"No problem," he said, reaching out to shake his new boss's hand. "I'll look forward to hearing from you."

* * *

Jan and Andrew spent the rest of the morning considering arguments, discussing case calendars, going over witness testimony, working together as the solid team they'd been for the past few years. Jan called a halt for a fresh cup of coffee when Ruple phoned to say he was expecting to be able to give them paperwork on all thirty accounts, but not until the next day.

"I'll be out of the office in the morning," Jan told him. "But my assistant will be here." She raised her eyebrows in question to Andrew and when he nodded, she continued. "Andrew Tuttle. You know him. It's really important that you hand the file directly to him. And no one else."

With the detective's calm assurance that he'd do as she asked, she hung up.

The lines on Andrew's face, around his eyes, were still pronounced, but he actually smiled at her when he sat back to sip from the mug she'd just brought him.

"You're a hard person to live up to. Are you aware of that?" he asked, his tone taking any criticism out of the words.

"Me? You've got to be kidding."

"Look at you, not even a week after your mother passes away and you just cleared up two days' work in a morning."

"So did you."

He acknowledged the comment by raising his mug.

"So how are you doing? The memorial's tomorrow, right?"

She focused on the willow tree outside her window. "I'm okay." Some of the time. "I still can't believe she's gone."

"I remember how it was after my father died," Andrew said. "Life went on, but there was this sense of unreality, an awareness that nothing was going to be the same again."

"That pretty much describes it." Except for the propensity to cry at the least provocation, and the guilt eating away at her.

She'd chosen to work a week ago Sunday instead of going to see her mother—telling herself she was being foolish for thinking her mom couldn't survive without her. She hadn't missed a visit since moving her mother out of the city, because she'd known how crucial it was. But last week she'd let her mother down.

"Has your brother been in touch at all?"

"Yeah," she said, the grip on her heart loosening just a little. "He had dinner with Hailey and me on Friday, and then he dropped in yesterday and ended up staying until evening. He knew I'd been spending every Sunday with Mom since she moved to Sedona and he didn't want me to be alone."

"And he didn't give you a hard time about anything?"

Andrew knew a little about her difficult relationship with Johnny.

"He was the sweet boy I grew up with. Talked about his life on the road—about books he's read that he wondered if I might like. He asked if there were any repairs he could do around my house. Asked about

Hailey, offering to be a surrogate father figure to her."
No matter how many times she thought of it, she
could hardly believe the day had happened. Even if
Johnny didn't follow through on his promises, having
him there—not brimming with pent-up anger, intending to be around more—was enough. She'd given
him her new alarm-system security code, just in case
he did come by.

"So something good might come of your loss."

"I hope so." Jan forced herself to focus on that
thought. It was one she could share.

The self-loathing that had come with her mother's
suicide, she bore privately—and in her dreams.

After his big breakfast, Simon never got around to
lunch, and he was hungry again by five o'clock. He
could throw in a frozen pizza. Run out for burgers.
Have a peanut-butter-and-banana sandwich.

Instead, he ground some Sumatran coffee and sat
down to a game of freecell while he waited for Jan, instead. He wasn't counting on dinner with her or
anything—he just wanted to be available when she
got home. She'd probably go in alone if he wasn't
there to escort her inside.

He'd never before met a woman so bent on not asking for help. If it wasn't damned infuriating, he'd probably admire her for it.

Five-thirty came and went. So did freecell. He was
on to Sudoku. By six, he'd pulled up the latest copy of
his manuscript.

He chose a bullet—the pointing finger again.

Terrorists and Politics:

A new breed of terrorist has hit the United States. Instead of the vigilante, we're finding politicians...

Those were Jan's headlights coming down the street.

Simon closed the document and headed outside.

Simon went in first. The second he stepped through the door and punched in the alarm code, he knew no one was there, but he checked each room, anyway. With his instincts in high gear, the job took him about ten seconds per room. Except for the one where she slept.

When he found himself checking behind doors that were fully open and against walls, and staring at her bed, he made himself get the hell out.

She had a fully cooked roasted chicken from the grocery store cut and on a platter in the middle of the kitchen table. A tub of mashed potatoes and another with vegetables sat on either side of the platter. Two plates, with silverware and napkins, told the rest of the story—dinner for two.

And because the meal was obviously too much for her to eat alone, and because he couldn't let her hard-earned money go to waste, Simon helped her get drinks and took the seat she offered him.

"How'd it go at the office today, dear?" he quipped.

"Just fine. And how were the children?"

"School buses were right on time," Simon told her, enjoying his first bites of the meal.

She seemed tired. In need of a stronger libation than the water she'd opted for. In another life, Simon would have urged her to eat all she could, done the dishes himself and pulled her into his arms to keep her safe for a few hours.

In this life, however, he finished eating dinner and then excused himself.

Before he forgot that he'd already lived the first life, failed miserably at it and could never, ever have this woman—for comfort or sex.

Two hours later, Simon's body was still buzzing. Jan's bedroom light had gone on and then right off again. He didn't think she'd gone to bed.

Davenport called just before nine, asking him to accompany a far-right candidate for the Arizona gubernatorial race, which was due to be decided in another few weeks, to an appearance. The man's most recent attempt at a public speech had ended violently with a group of gays and lesbians challenging his homophobic beliefs. Since that time, he'd also made enemies of pro-choice voters. Simon was to escort the man to a campaign rally in Phoenix the next morning.

He accepted. Studying the still-darkened window across from his bedroom, he changed his clothes and drove down to the Museum Club. It couldn't hurt to pay Amanda Blake another visit.

The young woman barely glanced at Simon when he came in. She asked another waitress to take his order. And when he stopped to have a word with her as he left half an hour later, she didn't smile—or even appear to be acquainted with him.

What in the hell was going on?

Simon wasn't sure, but one thing he did know. As far as women went, he was 0 for 2 tonight.

"Dearly beloved..."

Did funerals and weddings start the same way? Jan sat in the front pew of the almost empty church, shoulder to shoulder with Johnny, focusing on simply getting through the next half hour. She analyzed, summarized and compartmentalized, until she was pretty sure she'd removed herself from everything but the physical proceedings.

Until...

"Please stand with me and sing Grace's favorite hymn."

And as the twenty or so people gathered there—including a row of her coworkers toward the back—began to sing, "When I, in awesome wonder," Jan started to cry and couldn't stop.

Mom, why didn't you turn to Him, if you couldn't turn to me? Why didn't you call me?

Johnny's hand slid into hers. It was big, warm, steady.

Mom, can you hear me?

A tissue appeared beneath her nose.

Are you there, Mom?

Johnny's voice slowly faded away, as the others sang on. He squeezed her hand.

*I'm sorry, Mom. So sorry. For not being there for you.
And for being so angry with you for doing this.*

The song ended and the small congregation sat down.
Jan found no forgiveness.

A lunch had been arranged in the church hall.
After saying good-bye to her coworkers who weren't
staying, Jan stood with Johnny, both of them in black,
smiling as a few of their mother's friends came and
hugged them, said how sorry they were, how much
they'd loved Grace.

Jan wondered how many of them knew that she had
taken her own life.

Clara Williams, her mother's longtime best friend,
was last.

"If you ever need to talk, or need a mom or even a
dinner date, don't hesitate to call me," she said in
Jan's ear as she gave her a hug. "I promised your mom
years ago that I'd take care of you."

Jan held on to the older woman, sobbing. And was
moved by Clara's own shudders of grief.

As Clara moved on, Johnny took Jan's hand and led
her to the lunch table. He waited while she put mea-
ger portions of salad and turkey on her paper plate,
took a glass of punch, a cookie and a rolled-up napkin filled with plastic utensils.

They sat alone at the end of one of two long tables.
Her mother's friends sat in small clusters at the other.
The pastor who'd performed the service stopped to talk
and offered to help the two of them in any way he could.

"I expected to see Hailey with you," Johnny said as he cleaned his plate.

Jan pushed salad around on hers. "She didn't know Mom."

Johnny regarded her seriously. "And you were afraid someone would mention the suicide?"

No, I wasn't. "She's only eight, Johnny."

"You don't have to be ashamed of it, sis," Johnny said, as though reading her mind. "Mom was ill, just like someone who had cancer."

"I love you, Johnny," she said, tears brimming in her eyes again.

"I know. I love you, too."

She hadn't heard those words from him in years.

The drive to Phoenix with the long-winded, intelligent and frighteningly bigoted client he'd been hired to protect taxed Simon's nonexistent urge to be social. The man was articulate, soft-spoken, loved America and claimed that a return to "family values" would save "this great country." He firmly believed that in order to achieve that, women should once again take their traditional place in the family. He partially blamed women in the workforce, women who weren't at home, supervising and raising their children, for higher crime rates. Judging by the hundreds of people who'd come out to hear him, shouting agreement and clapping, others shared his beliefs. He used convincing and persuasive words, which made his views of women sound reverent rather than demeaning. He was also unequivocal about his antigay and antiabortion beliefs. He played on people's fear of change in a fast-changing world, manipulating with emotion and pleas for a better society.

He did not, however, invite or incite violence. Neither did he hint at stepping outside the boundaries of the constitution or the laws of Arizona.

Those who showed up to voice their opposition were louder than he was, less polished, more vulgar, but also nonviolent.

The entire morning left a bad taste in Simon's mouth.

The first thing Jan did when she arrived at the office Tuesday afternoon was send an e-mail, thanking her coworkers for their support. The second thing she did was call for Andrew.

"Are you sure you want to be here?" Nancy asked, as Jan stood in the doorway waiting for her assistant to appear.

Hugging her arms around herself, Jan nodded. "My brother was heading out of town and it's better that I'm here, being productive, and not home alone with too much time to think."

"If there's anything I can do, just say so…"

Jan smiled her thanks, and then disappeared into her office with Andrew right behind her.

"How was the service?"

Her door was shut before she noticed he was empty-handed.

"Where's the file from Ruple?" The trial was due to

start in four days and she needed a clear idea of how far-reaching this case was before she decided on the tone to set for the jury.

"He didn't bring it. We've got Lord knows how many dates and transactions to make sense of, and I've spent the whole damn day sitting here waiting."

"*What?*" It was two in the afternoon. Detective Ruple had said they'd have the full report by ten. He might be surly, he might not like her much, but he'd always been dependable. "Did he call?"

"Not that I'm aware of and I've been here all day." Andrew sat down. "I didn't even take a lunch."

"Did you phone him?"

"Of course." Andrew sat forward, his elbows on the arms of the chair, facing her as she dropped down to her seat. "Several times. His office and cell. He doesn't answer."

"He must've been sidetracked..." The man was a cop. Emergencies happened.

Andrew nodded, clearly not happy. He asked her again about the funeral and then left her in peace.

Ten minutes later, Jan had Ruple on the phone.

"It was there by nine," the detective's gravelly voice assured her. "I brought it myself."

Rubbing her forehead with her fingers, Jan took a deep breath. "Where'd you leave it?" she asked, glad to know that the file was in her office even if Ruple hadn't given it to Andrew as she'd asked. A day's work had been lost and she was going to have some late nights, but she wasn't expecting to sleep well anyway.

"You asked me to hand deliver it to Tuttle," the cop reminded her. "So I did."

Not prone to headaches, Jan wasn't handling her current one well. "You're saying you gave the file directly to Andrew Tuttle this morning?"

"I'm not just saying it. That's what happened."

Why would Andrew lie to her? Or was Ruple the one who'd lied? Perhaps covering up carelessness or negligence...

"Do you have another copy handy?"

"Yeah."

"Mind if I stop by for it on my way home?"

"Be my guest."

"Thanks, Detective." Jan was sure there was more she should have said, suspicions they should have discussed, but she wasn't in the right frame of mind to communicate clearly.

"Andrew?"

Jan stood in the doorway of his office.

"Yeah, boss?" He glanced up from his computer, frowning. He had his half of their confidential list in front of him. She'd started on hers at home the night before, had slept with it by her bed and had stopped by the office early this morning to lock it up safely. So far, she'd searched the Internet for any information on the first businesses on the list and had made notes but drawn no conclusions.

"Ruple says he gave the list directly to you at nine o'clock this morning."

Without hesitation Andrew shook his head. "Wasn't me." He dropped his pencil onto the legal pad to the right of him. "We've only met a couple of times. He must've confused me with someone else."

There was no one else by the name of Andrew in the building. Nor was there another redheaded male on staff at the county attorneys' office.

"He's sure he gave it to you." She had to push. Too much was at stake.

"We've lost an entire day's work on a case that has my butt squarely on the line," Andrew said, looking her straight in the eye. "Believe me, if I'd seen Ruple, I would've been thrilled."

She believed him. And wished she felt better about that.

Walking past her secretary's desk on the way back to her office, Jan turned around.

"Can I get you anything?" Nancy asked.

Jan shook her head, but continued to stand there.

"Nancy, did you see Detective Ruple here today?"

"No, ma'am."

"What about Andrew? Was he here all day?"

Nancy nodded. "He even had one of the girls bring him lunch."

So Danny Ruple *was* lying to her? On a case she was prosecuting for him?

Why on earth would he do that? she wondered again.

But then, why would Andrew lie? The same questions went round and round in her mind. Did he want to make her look bad? But then, he looked bad, too, and what would he gain by that?

None of it made sense. Unless he'd been bought... Oh, God! Surely not...

One thing was certain. Jan was going to be watching all of them. Taking nothing for granted until Jacob Hall was convicted and sentenced.

15

Simon wasn't in the best of moods that evening, but he perked up when he saw Jan's car coming up the road toward home. Something about that woman brought out the happy-go-lucky guy he used to be.

He met her car at the garage door when it opened, entering before she did and standing aside as he waved her in.

"How was the service?" Not exactly an innocuous question, but today's circumstances were an exception.

"Nice," she replied, reaching inside the car for her leather satchel and purse before closing her door.

"The minister talked about the grieving process more than he did about death. It was almost like a counseling session, and I appreciated it." She was still talking as they walked down to the mailbox. "He skated around the whole suicide issue pretty well."

Her voice caught on the word. *Suicide.*

"Suicide isn't a curse," he said without forethought. "It's a last resort for a mind that can't rationalize. A soul in so much pain and distress that there's no other reality."

They'd reached her box by then and Jan didn't respond. She opened it, waited for him to look inside, and at his nod pulled out the day's delivery of junk, propaganda and bills.

"How do you know so much about suicide?" she asked as they headed back up the drive side by side.

"Just what I've learned in passing," he told her. Thinking of grieving family and friends he'd encountered as he processed scenes and oversaw the removal of bodies during a number of professional episodes. "I'm no expert."

"So that bit about not being able to rationalize... You don't know that for a fact?"

Okay. He could give her this much, since she seemed to need it so badly. "I've done some reading."

"And it's possible that she didn't call me because she couldn't rationalize her way to the phone? Couldn't think things through enough to know there was help on the other side of the darkness? 'Cause I gotta tell you, Simon, I'm finding it hard not to be angry with her for it. After all we'd been through together, all the times I came running, she just turned her back and walked out."

"Anger's a healthy part of grief, in general," Simon said slowly. "And even more natural when suicide's involved. But to answer your question, from what I've read, you're right. They can't see help on the other side of the darkness, because at those moments nothing but the darkness exists."

"Even though she told me a million times that the darkness is only an illusion?"

"You ever been in that darkness?"

They'd stopped in the garage, at the door leading into the house.

"Maybe."

"And while you were there, did it feel like an illusion?"

"Of course not."

"Were you able to step outside it long enough to remind yourself that it *was* an illusion?"

"No."

Taking the keys she handed him, Simon unlocked the door to her house, went in and punched in the alarm code before he could ask what had sent her to dark places.

On Monday night Jan had been busy bringing in groceries while Simon searched the house. Tonight, with nothing else to do, she followed him around. It didn't take him long to give what appeared to be a cursory glance over each room, though she waited outside as he checked her bedroom.

His bedroom window was visible from there, and she'd spent too many hours lying in bed watching his light to face him in that room.

He was coming out, when her satchel—with the recently retrieved file from Ruple tucked inside—fell off the chair in her spare bedroom. She had no idea how Simon got from one doorway to the next so quickly. She hadn't even seen him move.

Nor had she seen him pull the gun he was now

holding. One second he was in the doorway of her bedroom, and the next he was standing across the hall—with a gun.

"It's just my bag," she said slowly, gaping at the small, lethal-looking pistol he was pointing toward her computer.

He seemed to take in the entire room—even parts that weren't visible. And then, relaxing, he dropped his hand.

Jan stood there, unable to move.

Nothing made sense anymore. Her mother had committed suicide. Ruple lied to her. And Simon had a gun.

"Is that loaded?"

She couldn't stop staring.

"Yeah. Wouldn't do much good to point an empty gun."

It had sure scared her.

"Where'd it come from?"

She had no idea what Simon was feeling. She wasn't looking at him. But she knew his arm was still hanging at his side, with the gun held loosely in his grip.

"The back of my pants."

Not something she'd pictured when she'd imagined that part of his anatomy.

"You have to have a permit to carry a concealed weapon in Arizona."

"I have one."

"Why?"

"Because you have to have one to carry a concealed weapon."

She didn't have the patience to deal with his pre-varication. "Why do you have a gun?"

"I'm taking the threats against you seriously."

She glanced up then. He didn't hide from her. "You *just* got it? Because of me?"

"No."

"Then when?"

"After 9/11. But don't worry, I've read everything I can find on weapon safety, including when not to pull one. I've also spent quite a number of hours at target practice."

"You don't seem like a man who'd spend his time worrying about defending himself against terrorists."

"You're the one who keeps saying I should write a suspense novel."

He was right about that.

And so was she.

"You want to call out for pizza?"

"Sure." He was still standing at the end of the hall.

"Would you mind putting that away?"

"Not at all." Simon lifted his oversized wrinkled shirt, reached behind him, and the gun was gone.

At least from sight.

Jan wasn't sure what they talked about while they waited for the pizza. Books they'd read. Computer games they played to unwind. Movies they'd seen. Simon poured them each a glass of wine. And when dinner arrived, they ate.

She wasn't hungry—hadn't had much appetite all

week—but she needed her strength. She had a job to do, and she planned to do it well.

Just as soon as she got through this day.

"Thanks for staying," she said as she put away the leftovers and Simon threw out the pizza box.

"Thanks for asking me."

He was leaving, and she was going to be alone.

"I know you're busy, I…"

"Jan." He was directly in front of her. Only inches away. "It's okay. Today was a little rough. I get that."

She was afraid she was going to cry again. Trusted herself to nod.

Simon held her shoulders, giving her a gentle squeeze. "What are friends for?"

"Oh…" She was about to make a fool of herself. She felt the train wreck coming on. And couldn't find the strength to stop it.

"Hey!" He lifted her chin. "You wanna come watch my grass grow?"

She almost accepted.

"Or have a spitting contest?"

She tried to smile. "Would you mind staying?" she managed instead. "Only for a little while?"

"You got the stuff to make chocolate chip cookies?"

"Yeah."

"You know how?"

Jan chuckled then. "Yes."

"Can I watch?"

"If you want cookies, you can help, buster," she

told him. But she figured they both knew she'd kiss his feet, if it meant he'd stay.

A batch of cookies and a tear or two later, Jan put away the towel she'd used to dry the last of the baking sheets.

"You've got flour in your hair," Simon said, brushing his fingers lightly across the top of her head.

It took everything Jan had not to lean into him. He was so close. And warm.

Vital and real.

The easiest, happiest person she knew.

She waited for him to move away. Braced herself for his departure, for the long, dark hours ahead. She was going to try to work—to look up businesses and hope to glean a stray article here, a Web site with pictures there, that might lead to some connection.

"Why am I so tempted to take you in my arms and have my way with you?" he murmured.

She wasn't sure she'd heard him correctly at first. And when she'd replayed his words a second time, she was fairly certain he'd been teasing her.

Until she saw the honesty gleaming in his eyes.

"I don't know," she said, shocked and yet not really caring that she was. "I wouldn't say no, if you did."

If she'd been more composed, she would've died right then and there—before she could proceed with the biggest mistake of her life. As it was, when he stepped closer, she fell into him, wrapping her arms so tightly around his neck that he had no choice but to lower his lips to hers.

She wasn't sure if her first gasp was a sob of shock or pure pleasure, and she didn't think much after that. Giving herself over to the tiny bit of heaven being offered on this faithless day, she allowed herself to be slowly undressed.

Simon had had plans. A computer game open on his computer, just waiting for him to conquer. He had obligations to himself—a promise not to allow anyone to care deeply for him ever again. No exceptions.

But Simon wasn't listening to his head that night. His body, some emotional part of himself that he'd assumed was long dead, simply took over. He couldn't look at Jan's lost gaze and walk away.

Tonight, she was in the same kind of private hell he'd lived in for the past eight years. Tonight, she just needed—and he needed—to allow a connection with another human being.

If she got the wrong idea, if he had to extricate himself, tomorrow would be soon enough.

Their clothes made a trail behind them as they found their way to her room. Jan surprised him by turning on a dim light as she passed the dresser. He would've thought she was strictly a love-in-the-dark kind of woman.

He'd always enjoyed the light.

Pulling back the comforter, she lay on the bed, reclining against the pillows by the headboard, and Simon got his first real look at her.

His body's reaction embarrassed him.

The woman was absolutely beautiful. The golden glow of her skin drew him close to the bed, where he stood for a moment, pacing himself, so that the experience would be good for her, too.

She was watching him, her eyes half closed but not at all sleepy.

"I don't know what you like," he said, settling beside her, running a hand along the curve of her waist, over her thigh and back up. Her breasts were firm, full, bigger than he'd expected, her nipples puckered—inviting.

"To be touched," she said, her voice husky, as if she'd just woken up. "Everywhere. Touch me everywhere."

The invitation practically sent Simon over the edge before he'd even begun. *Slowly*. His brain managed to communicate with him briefly.

With unsteady fingers, he explored her cheeks, tracing her lips, her brows, wiping away tears that were no longer there. Those he'd seen her shed and more that he hadn't seen.

And he sucked in air as her fingers slid softly down his spine and over his buttocks. Her hair was far softer than his, falling over his fingers; her neck was slim, appealing and so vulnerable.

Simon was almost in agony, and in ecstasy at the same time. He stroked her throat, her neck.

"That feels so good," she moaned.

"*You* feel so good," he told her, watching his hands

as they moved over her. "Your skin is silky and soft—smooth, where mine is rough." He brushed his fingers down her shoulders.

Jan moaned and her eyes closed as she lay there, letting him touch her, explore her, where and however he chose. The closer he got to her breasts, to her thighs, the harder he got. And when he'd touched her everywhere else, her stomach, her calves and feet, when there was nowhere else but the parts of her that were strictly feminine, his groin was pulsing to the point of explosion.

Simon leaned over her, studying every inch of the body he'd been fantasizing about for months. For once, reality was far better than anything he'd imagined. This was going to be a problem later. He knew that. To be here, like this, and then gone would be hell.

But a hell worth enduring for this chance—a time out of time.

He bent to kiss her, taking her lips gently. He hoped to sustain the experience, to prolong it. But as soon as her lips opened beneath his, his restraint broke and his lips and tongue fastened to hers with a passion he'd only imagined before.

He'd supposed, until that moment, that the fire in a kiss was all acting, but not now, not tonight. Touching his tongue to Jan's, exploring the inside of her mouth, feeling her teeth nipping at his lips was driving him out of his mind, making his body hurt with pleasure.

"Now it's my turn."

He blinked and fell back as she pushed against him. *What?*

"You've loved me and now I want to do the same to you," she said, her sultry voice causing his hips to buck involuntarily.

"I'm ashamed to say I might not be able to last that long," he admitted with a shaky grin.

"I don't expect you to."

Her response was as unexpected as she was and Simon gave himself over to her.

Jan didn't restrict her exploration to her hands as he'd done. Where he'd used fingertips, she used lips—touching him everywhere but his groin. But he'd been so far gone he hadn't needed direct stimulation. As his erection started to pulse with an orgasm that pulled a scream from his lungs, she grabbed hold of him, caressed him, rode the waves with him.

When he was done, Simon lay there, bemused, embarrassed and feeling slightly robbed. He'd come and gone, and he hadn't even been inside her yet.

Before he could follow that thought or even look at her, Simon felt her fingers against his penis, stroking him with light touches, and he laughed out loud.

"Oh, woman, this is going to be a night to remember," he told her, rolling on top of her.

"That's what I'm hoping." He saw the desire burning in her eyes, the smile on her lips, and then he experienced nirvana as he buried his face in her chest.

Usually Hailey hated her meetings with Officer Standgate, because mostly they made her feel she was bad since she had to have them. But she was kinda glad to be going down to the school offices on Wednesday morning because she got to miss recess.

"'Course now everyone's gonna know where I was and remember I'm too bad to play with," she mumbled to herself, looking around before she reached for the door handle.

"What was that?"

Hailey jumped as she heard the woman's voice behind her. *Officer Standgate*.

"Nothing," she said, waiting while her probation officer opened the door for the two of them. She took a quick peek down both sides of the hallway. Empty. Phew.

"So how've you been?" the pretty black woman asked, as soon as they were sitting in the little room with just chairs and a kid's desk. Officer Standgate's uniform was the only scary thing about her—not like those cops who'd taken her in their car to the kid jail place.

But she wasn't a cop. She didn't even have a gun.

"I haven't broken any laws," Hailey said. "I do everything Mrs. Lincoln says I have to, and I don't argue, and I go to bed and close my eyes when she says I have to sleep."

All week she'd been thinking about the butterflies she and Jan had bought. The quilt and the lamp and the sheets and even a trash can. Maybe she'd be allowed to live there. At least for a while.

Officer Standgate nodded, but she didn't smile. Did that mean she could tell Hailey was hiding something?

She might've cried right then, if she was still a little kid.

Still, she'd figured out a long time ago that it was better to confess than to wait for them to tell you they already knew what you'd done wrong.

"I can't help it, I really can't," she said. "I do close my eyes, I really try to sleep, but I just can't!" she said. "Mrs. Lincoln comes and checks on me and she isn't happy when I'm still awake, but my head just thinks of stuff and…and…won't let me go."

"What kind of stuff?"

She couldn't tell her that.

But would she be breaking the law again if she didn't?

"What keeps you awake at night, Hailey?" Her probation officer leaned way down to look at Hailey's bent head, her eyes.

"Do I have to say?"

"Yes, I think you do."

Hailey sighed. Wished she could tug at her jeans where they were creeping up her butt, and hugged her sweater instead.

"Just mom stuff."

"Tell me about it."

She swung her legs, wondering when she was going to be big enough to touch the floor without scrunching forward. Wondering if she'd ever have clogs like everyone else was wearing now, instead of just tennis shoes.

"I'll bet your mom made chocolate chip cookies," she told the woman.

"Nope. My mom had seven kids and had to work two jobs to support us," Officer Standgate said. She'd folded her hands between her knees and Hailey could hardly picture those hands being tough on a bad kid. "My older brothers and sisters watched out for us young ones." She kept talking. "I hardly ever saw my mom."

"What about your dad?"

"I never knew him. He left when my mom got pregnant with me."

Another kid who didn't get the real kind of mom. But still, she'd been taken care of by brothers and sisters.

"Do these questions have anything to do with the reason you can't sleep?"

"Maybe. I dunno."

"Talk to me, Hailey. It's why I'm here."

Hailey thought about that. Derek said Officer Standgate came to make sure Hailey wasn't being bad. And maybe it'd be better to go to jail than to talk, anyway.

"Do you think I'm ever going to get a different mom?"

"Different than who?"

"My real one."

"Yes, of course I do." Officer Standgate seemed so surprised, Hailey almost got excited for a minute. Like it might really happen.

"Do you think it might be Jan?"

"Absolutely. It's been approved. And your court date is only a couple of weeks away."

Yeah, everyone kept saying that.

"Then would it be against the law if I just wait and talk to her about, you know, stuff?"

The officer bent over and got her face real close to Hailey's. "Do you promise me you'll do that?"

Hailey nodded, too scared to speak.

"The very next time you see her?"

Hailey nodded again.

And almost peed her pants when Officer Standgate stood up and told her she could go.

16

The copies of the death certificates she'd asked for showed up by courier late Wednesday morning. She called Andrew immediately.

And spent the two minutes until he got there not opening the envelope but thinking of Simon.

Of his body inside hers.

And the hours she'd lain awake thinking about him after he'd finally left the night before.

Andrew's arrival saved her from herself.

"How're you progressing with your investigation of the businesses?" she asked, as soon as he'd closed her door. She'd concentrate on her job. Jan could always do her job.

In addition to thinking about Simon, wondering how on earth she was going to face him that evening, she'd spent the morning collating information from the file she'd picked up from Ruple the night before.

Andrew opened the folder he carried and pulled out a legal pad. "I'm about half done."

"Any conclusions?"

"I think this involves more than doing business with minorities, Jan." His face serious, Andrew leaned forward to place a handwritten spreadsheet in front of her. "I pulled up public records from the Department of Economic Security, to see the list of employees each of these business owners purchased unemployment insurance for."

Jan had done the same.

"Once I had names, I did Internet searches to see if any of them had home pages or other public information. I also searched marriage, divorce and property records."

"I haven't gotten to property records yet."

"Not much showed up there."

"Did you search public records from the Small Business Association?" The federal program gave loans to small businesses who employed minorities.

"I did," Andrew said, passing her his spreadsheet. The man she knew and trusted was back. Thank God.

He'd marked a column "employed minorities." And for every single business he'd investigated, the column was checked. The employees' names were in another column.

Jan passed over her own chart—not as neat and clean as Andrew's, but with identical information.

"Our women didn't just serve minorities, they employed them. Paid them," Jan said, adding, "we've got to get through the rest of this list. I want every single one of these businesses verified as a minority employer before we do anything. Since this part is all circumstantial, if there's even one of them that doesn't fit the pattern it weakens our case."

He nodded.

Jan welcomed the adrenaline that was pumping through her veins, even as fear crept up her spine. Her biggest professional hope was coming true. She was finally coming up with something substantial to hang on Hall—something that would ultimately expose his supremacist activities and ties.

And to do that, she'd have to engage in open combat with the Ivory Nation.

"I've been going over Ruple's file," she continued. "I'm not through all of it yet, but so far I've been able to trace money from several of our business owners' private accounts to the account we know Jacob Hall used in his other fraudulent activities. All transactions took place the same day as the victims' deaths. Once I see the death certificates, we'll be able to ascertain whether the fraud occurred before or after the time of death. I'm guessing they'll all be after, which will be another hard coincidence for a jury to ignore."

Andrew nodded again, his face pinched.

"Right now I'd like us to split up this pile." She tore open the envelope, pulled out thirty pieces of paper and gave half of them to Andrew. "Let's see if we find any correlation in causes of death."

"Are any of them being investigated?"

"Not as far as I know."

It didn't take her long to see why. The only common denominator in the cause of death was that none of them was obviously murder—not that she'd really been expecting murder to play a part in this particular scheme. It was more likely that Hall had illegal access to records, had a list of all female small business owners who employed minorities in the state and was informed when any of them died.

Still, she hadn't ruled out the possibility of murder.

"Accidental overdose of prescription medication," she read aloud. "Falling off a ladder. Diabetic coma."

"Here's a woman who slipped in the shower," Andrew added.

Another was killed in a hit-and-run accident. There was a case of anaphylactic shock. One died in her sleep, apparently of natural causes. Someone had a heart attack.

Mind speeding ahead, Jan started to see pieces fall into place. And rejected them even as they fell.

"There's even a rattlesnake bite," Andrew said.

Jan frowned, trying to ignore the nervous energy crawling under her skin. "I have an elderly woman with a black widow sting." Black widow bites weren't all that common to begin with, as the spider wasn't aggressive, but they could be lethal for small children, the elderly and those with respiratory problems. "Am I crazy to think that these deaths were carefully calculated, premeditated, planned with each individual in mind?" She glanced over at her assistant.

"I have to admit a rattlesnake bite and a lethal black widow sting on a list of thirty seems questionable."

"By themselves, each death seems plausible, but

when you consider them all together..." Her heart pounded.

"We're looking at a possible murder conspiracy here." Andrew's eyes widened as he stared at Jan.

Simon had assumed he'd reached the depths of self-hatred eight years before. He discovered on Wednesday that he could dig a little deeper. Eight years before, he'd had no idea of the damage he'd do. Last night he'd jumped in, fully knowing that he might create pain.

For himself—so what? But for the woman he'd slept with... He should be shot.

Pounding his computer keys until he thought they might break, he eventually realized he was typing garbage and went to make himself a peanut butter sandwich. He hadn't eaten since his morning workout at the Snowbowl. Maybe the food would improve his mood. Or choke him.

And while he ate, he stood at the window of his dining room office, watched the trees freeze and remembered Jan coming in his arms. She'd laughed and clung to him. It had gone on and on.

He'd tried all morning to dredge up a different memory, but he had to acknowledge that those seconds with Jan had been the high point of his life.

But his memory of last night didn't have the roar of a motorcycle for accompaniment. Simon frowned at the interruption and watched as Jan's brother pulled up in front of her house.

In the middle of a workday.

Didn't the guy know his sister was never home on a workday?

Dressed in his usual black, Johnny jumped off his bike, jogged up to Jan's front door and let himself in.

Her brother had a key.

He didn't know why, but that came as a complete surprise to Simon. Until recently he'd never even met her brother—and it certainly hadn't occurred to him that Johnny and Jan were close enough to have keys to each other's homes.

He couldn't imagine what reason her brother would have for being there now, unless she'd asked him to fix something. Simon wasn't aware of anything that needed fixing.

Of course, she'd only had sex with him once. She wasn't obliged to tell him about her household repairs.

Except that he was there every day, making sure she was safe… You'd think she would've mentioned it if something needed fixing.

Simon put down his half-eaten sandwich, and considered walking over to find out what was going on. He dropped the idea when the scenario he played out got to the part where he told her brother he had a right to be there because he was Jan's lover.

He'd made love to her. He was not her lover. One was an act. The other a life.

He watched, fought with himself, and in the end the decision was taken away from him. Seven minutes after he'd arrived, Johnny left.

There hadn't been time for him to fix anything.

Unless he needed a spare part and would be back. He hadn't brought any tools.

She could have a supply of them, for all Simon knew.

He could call her and ask if her brother was supposed to have been over.

If he and Jan hadn't made love, he probably wouldn't even be thinking like this. He was getting possessive, and it had to stop.

What had he been afraid her brother was going to do over there anyway? Rob her?

Simon paced. Swore. And eventually sat down at his computer. He had no business getting involved in Jan's affairs. No reason to call her, bother her, nose his way in.

He pulled up his favorite search engine. Typed in John McNeil. Just to be sure.

And because no one would ever know of his weakness.

Once a detective, always a detective.

Jan told herself it was her choice that Simon was in and out of her house within two minutes for each of the next couple of nights. She purposely didn't bring dinner home.

She brought work.

On Wednesday night, when they went in and saw the book Johnny had left on her counter—a book about dealing with grief—with a note saying he'd only been in town for an hour but wanted her to know she wasn't alone, she'd told Simon she'd recently given him a key to her place.

He couldn't have seemed less interested.

In the book. Or her.

He'd left just as quickly on Thursday night.

She was glad they'd agreed that their night together had been just that—one night—without getting into some major discussion about whether they'd ever have sex again. Or not.

At least, most of the time she was glad. When she got into bed at night and thought about his leaving without even a goodbye kiss after checking her house, when she saw his bedroom light come on and knew what he looked like when he took his clothes off, she cared.

She had nightmares both nights.

And she got a lot of work done. By Friday, when she was meeting with Andrew to finalize opening arguments, possible defense strategies and their potential answers, she had two freshly completed lists of all the current information regarding Hall's other frauds.

She'd arranged for Hailey to spend the night again on Friday. With the trial starting the following Monday, she didn't know how much free time she'd have before the adoption was finalized.

Perusing the lists again, Jan ignored the feeling that someone was out to get her. These people instilled fear and then manipulated their victims with it. Instead of becoming one of these victims, she forced herself to focus on what she knew.

Names. Times of death. All of which preceded the fraudulent bank transactions, although there hadn't been enough time for anyone to have officially known of the deaths. Employee lists for each business which all included minorities. Victims' banks were listed—and they weren't all the same.

With Andrew present, she destroyed the original lists she'd prepared for the two of them and asked that, until they decided exactly how they were going to proceed with the information they had, he continue to keep his list locked in his desk when he wasn't using it. She was still a bit hesitant with him.

She had no idea why Ruple would lie to her about dropping off his lists and assumed that if he had, the reason was personal rather than anything to do with her. But she still wasn't ready to reveal her findings to him.

"There's one more thing here," Andrew said, standing behind her at her desk as they were going over the sheets. "I noticed a number of independent bookstores on my half of the list."

With a quick perusal, she saw that he was right.

"I'm not sure what it means," he added, "but it's curious, isn't it? Especially since, with the influx of major chains, so many of the privately owned ones are going out of business."

"What it proves is that Hall wasn't just doing this for money," Jan said. "If he'd chosen his victims randomly, he wouldn't have known that some of those accounts were small. But there are too many similarities here for this to be a coincidence. Which means he handpicked his victims. Books, and by association, bookstores, influence a lot of people. Which gives them power. The white supremacist mission is to destroy anyone with power who is not loyal to the cause."

If what she now suspected was true—that all thirty of these women had been murdered before they were robbed—some of them had died for less than five thousand dollars.

Johnny McNeil had no criminal record. He wasn't in any fingerprint file. As far as Simon could tell, from the myriad sources he still had access to, the man didn't even have an outstanding parking ticket.

The only interesting thing he turned up at all, was that, as of a week ago, the man was no longer employed by the publishing company he'd worked for since graduating from college. He'd already applied for unemployment.

Simon wasn't able to confirm, so far, if the split had been amicable or not.

His phone rang just before the first school bus was due on Friday afternoon.

"Davenport here." His new employer. He'd already seen the caller ID.

"Yeah."

"Got a group on campus handing out flyers at three. My guy canceled. Can you make it over there?"

Simon glanced at his watch. Two-forty-five.

"For how long?"

He had a mandatory prior engagement at six.

"An hour."

"I'll be there."

He didn't want to know what was on the pamphlets.

For the first time in her career, Jan took off early Friday afternoon. Although she knew that lack of sleep was probably the cause, she'd spent the entire day looking over her shoulder, waiting for something bad to happen, and she had to change her environment. Get some fresh air.

Furthermore, she wanted to go to the grocery store and spruce up the house before she picked up Hailey. There were still cookies left from the other night, but if Hailey wanted to they could bake more. Or go to the mall. Or watch movies.

They could work on the butterfly room.

Entering her drive with a carload of groceries at four, she paused long enough for Simon to see her and then pulled in. He wasn't there when she got out of the car. Not surprising—he hadn't been expecting her.

He couldn't spend every minute of his day at the computer, staring out his window.

Feeling a little guilty for going into her own house unescorted, she closed the garage, unlocked her door and punched in her code for the newly installed alarm.

"Hello?" She added some extra volume to her voice the second time she called out—and then counted to thirty, giving anyone who was there a chance to escape out whatever window he might have come through.

Which was ridiculous, considering that the alarm hadn't been deactivated.

After a couple of deep breaths and a firm admonition to herself, Jan held her shaking hands together in front of her and walked through every room of the house, turning on lights—and a television—as she went. She was doing it again. Allowing fear to control her.

Her mother would tell her to relax.

Her mother had killed herself.

Fifteen minutes later, Jan had put away the groceries and was throwing Hailey's new butterfly sheets in the washer. She wanted the bed made up and ready for Hailey when she brought her home. She'd just dumped in the soap when her front bell rang.

Telling herself to remain calm, she closed the washer lid, set the dial and pushed the button to start the load. And breathing deeply, she walked to the front of the house.

Was Simon home? Had he seen whoever had come up her walk?

Would someone who meant her harm march right up to her front door in broad daylight?

Wasn't the fact that white supremacists worked in plain sight of those around them part of what made them so frightening? There were no signs, no obvious indications of danger. You didn't know you couldn't trust them until it was too late.

She glanced at the alarm button blinking on the wall opposite her front door. Thought of Simon close by. And peered through the peephole.

A woman was standing there, looking lost. A beautiful woman. About her age. Flyaway blond hair. Petite. Expensively and stylishly dressed in a black linen suit, hose and pumps.

Her purse and jewelry were the only colorful things about her. They were both red.

She rang the bell again and Jan, shaking herself, opened the door.

"I'm sorry to bother you." The woman started right in. "I was just wondering if you had any idea if your next-door neighbor's in town."

Even her New England accent was elegant.

"Simon?"

"Uh-huh. I wanted to surprise him and it's only now occurred to me how stupid it was to come all the way across the country without first making sure that he'd be around."

Simon was always around.

"He is." Jan couldn't help staring at the woman. How on earth could he ever want her if he could have *that*?

"I'm sorry," the woman said, reaching out a hand. "I'm Shannon Green. Simon's wife."

17

Simon had a sick feeling in his gut the second he saw the rental car in his driveway. Eight years, and he'd never had a visitor. No one he knew would disrespect him enough to go against his wishes.

"Simon," Jan called from her front door. "In here."

He jogged over, trying to imagine who might be there with her. Praying that she was okay. Wondering why she was home early and sounding so sharp. And hating that he hadn't been there to check the house for her.

He'd have preferred his own death to the scene that awaited him.

As soon as he recognized the tentative smile on the face of the sweet woman standing up from Jan's couch to face him, his world crashed at his feet.

"Shannon?"

"Please don't be angry with me..." She walked slowly toward him and all Simon could see was the pain he'd caused her. The lives he'd ruined.

"Never," he whispered, hauling her against him,

holding her there as if he could make it all go away by just holding her tightly enough. "I could never be angry with you, sweetie. You know that."

A noise from behind reminded him that they weren't alone. He had no idea what Jan knew, what Shannon had told her.

Shannon drew back, wiping tears from her face. "Your neighbor was nice enough to let me wait here rather than in my car."

"But I can see you two have a lot of talking to do and I've got to go get my daughter, so if you'll excuse me…"

Jan wouldn't even look at him. She gripped the edge of her front door.

"Thank you so much for taking pity on me," Shannon said, as she preceded Simon through the door.

He needed to say *something*. And couldn't come up with a single word that would do any good at all.

"Don't you think it would've been a good idea to let me know you were married *before* you had sex with me?" Jan whispered, as he passed.

"Yes," Simon said, wishing there was some way he could take the stricken look from her eyes.

But there wasn't.

"I've met someone, Simon."

Sitting with Shannon at the kitchen table, sipping wine, holding her hand, Simon drank in his wife's happiness.

"Who is he?" Relief was almost as palpable as guilt. Almost, but not quite.

She gave his hand a squeeze, but didn't let go. "A cop, of all things."

His shock must have shown on his face.

"No one you know," she added quickly. "He's a detective from Maryland. I met him at a fund-raiser for police widows…."

Simon nodded, sipped. Let the silence fall between them again. He didn't know she'd been involved with police widows. She wasn't one. But it made sense.

They hadn't seen each other or spoken for more than six years. In some ways, lifetimes had passed. In others, mere minutes.

"Your neighbor seems nice."

Too nice to be anywhere in his vicinity. "She is."

"She mentioned a daughter. Is she married?"

"No."

"Divorced?" Shannon always had to know the details. The habit used to irritate him as much as it had charmed Sam.

"No. She's adopting an eight-year-old girl she prosecuted during a stint in juvenile court."

"She's an attorney?"

"Yes." God, it felt good to see her smile. To feel her hand steady inside his.

"I'm impressed."

Jan was an impressive woman. And he'd hurt her.

"You interested in her?"

"No."

"You ever going to let yourself live again, Simon?"

"I live."

"Jan says you're home all day long. She describes you as an easygoing, slightly lunatic guy who makes her laugh."

Exactly as he'd have wanted her to see him. "That's me."

"Only on the surface." Shannon brushed back the hair on his forehead. "You're a passionate, caring man, who needs to save the world."

"I was a kid, Shannon," he said now, emptying his glass. "I grew up."

She opened her mouth, ostensibly to say more, and Simon knew he had to stop her. "I want to meet him."

She didn't ask who he meant.

"I told him you would. He's waiting at the hotel—probably in the bar, if I have my guess."

Simon frowned, finding it difficult to stay in his seat. "He's a drinker?"

"No more than you are," she said with a soft chuckle. "But consider this from his position," she said. "He's worried about me. And figures he doesn't have a chance in hell of living up to you."

"He killed his brother, too?"

"That's enough of that." Shannon let go of his hand, coming to stand behind Simon, rubbing his shoulders like he'd seen her do for Sam countless times. "Sam's death was due to a freak set of circumstances, that was all."

"I was working undercover with terrorists." Simon couldn't sugarcoat the facts. "I knew that guy was after me. I had plenty of warning. I ignored the threats."

"Threats were a way of life for you. You couldn't possibly have known that one was different."

"I was an FBI agent, Shannon," he said, unable to conceal the self-loathing he felt. "It was my job to pay attention to every threat I got."

That wasn't the point, anyway. He'd been a hotshot. Believing he could conquer the world where others had failed. He'd never considered the price his identical twin might have to pay for his ego.

"I can't believe you fell for a cop," he said now, dragging his thoughts back to Shannon and things that could change.

"He's not Sam," she said, emotion filling her voice, and her hands still on his shoulders. "Nobody's ever going to be Sam, you know?"

He nodded, bending over to rest his elbows on his knees, rubbing his eyes. He'd never be able to wipe away the memories.

"I'll always love him."

Her words were blades to his chest. He'd suffered every day for eight years with the awareness of how he'd hurt this woman. Of the life he'd stolen from her.

"But I'm still alive," she said. He could tell she was crying. And he felt tears prick his eyes, too.

"Please forgive me, Simon."

What the hell? He glanced over at her face as she once again sat beside him. "Forgive you? For what?"

"Falling in love with someone besides Sam."

"Oh, sweetheart." He pulled her onto his lap, cradling her, wiping away her tears. Letting her do the same for him. "Don't you waste one second of your life feeling guilty about that, Shannon. Not one second," he said as fiercely as he could, considering the grief and regret and remorse choking him. "Why should you and your cop be denied happiness because Sam died? Where's the sense in giving up three lives because one was lost?"

She sniffed, smiling at him with tremulous lips. "I'll always love him. You trust that, don't you?"

"With all my being."

"I just never thought it'd be possible to love two men in one lifetime."

"So what's his name?"

"Bradley Hunter. Would you like to meet him now?"

"If he plans to marry you, he has no choice."

She grinned and looked up through her wet lashes. Then she stood, and glared at him, her chin resolute. "Don't be too much of a tough guy with him, Simon," she said, her voice half begging. "He'd heard of you before I even met him. You're a legend back home, even if you don't want to believe that. He's probably drinking himself into a stupor over this whole thing."

"If he's worthy of you, he'll be stone-cold sober," Simon told her.

And when, half an hour later, he met his almost ex-wife's future husband, he wasn't disappointed. He signed the divorce papers they'd brought for him to sign and agreed to fly out for their civil service as soon as the divorce was final.

* * *

Hailey became Jan's entire world Friday night. Any time her mind wandered—to work, thirty dead women, Ruple's lie, empty envelopes with her return address label, Simon's wife—she'd focus on the child who was more important than any of them, and more talkative than Jan had ever known her to be.

Over dinner at a popular burger joint, she'd told Jan all about the tests she'd aced that week. And about Tina, a girl at school that Hailey didn't appear to like much, who'd failed the math test.

In the car on the way to the mall, she'd given Jan a rundown of Derek's latest negative predictions regarding Hailey's educational and social success—based solely on the fact that the little girl had a probation officer.

Over ice cream, she'd talked about Mrs. Lincoln making noodles from scratch.

And when Jan brought Hailey in to help make the bed with her newly dried sheets and comforter, the little girl promptly stopped talking.

"What's wrong?" she asked, as Hailey just stood there staring at the bed. "Don't you like them anymore?"

Kids changed their minds a lot. She was okay with that.

"Oh, yeah. I do." Hailey's eyes were wide as she stared up at Jan. "They're the coolest."

"So what's bothering you all of a sudden?"

"Nothing." Hailey sat on the edge of the bed, staring at her tennis shoes.

Moving purely on instinct, Jan settled beside her and waited.

"I want clogs someday."

That was it? New shoes?

"Tomorrow soon enough?"

Hailey's head popped up and she studied Jan. "I don't have the money for them," she said so pragmatically that Jan almost started to cry.

"Kids don't worry about things like that, sweetie. Moms do."

Still watching her, Hailey nodded slowly. "From the state, you mean?"

"No, from their jobs."

"But I'm a ward of the state. They have to support me."

"Technically, but only until the adoption is final."

The child's brow furrowed. "And then you won't get any money for me?"

"Of course not!"

"Mrs. Lincoln does."

"She's not your mother. I will be."

"Oh." Hailey seemed to be considering that. "So they won't give you money for all the butterflies?"

"No."

"Did that make you mad?"

"On the contrary, it made me very happy."

Hailey frowned, her gaze intent as she studied Jan, and then she sat back. "Okay."

"So that's all that was bothering you? Your shoes?"

Silence was her only answer.

"Hailey?" She waited until the girl looked at her. "If this is going to work, you and me, I mean, then you're going to have to talk to me. I'm brand-new at parenting and I'm not going to be very good at it without your help."

"I'm a good helper."

"So let's start now with you telling me what's on your mind."

"I had to talk to Officer Standgate today."

The woman, who usually dealt with surly fifteen- and sixteen-year-olds, adored Hailey.

"And?"

"She says I have to talk to you."

Jan's heart dropped. Had Hailey stolen again? She'd promised she wouldn't. She had no reason to now. Jan had firmly believed the little girl just needed a change of environment.

"So talk." Perhaps the Lincolns hadn't been enough of a change. Regardless, she and Hailey would get through it, whatever it was. There were lots of programs available and—

"It's about that I have troubles sleeping at night."

Her mind slowing to focus solely on the moment, Jan took Hailey's hand.

"So tell me about it." Sleeping problems she could handle. She was a pro at them.

"My head thinks a lot, and what's in it scares me and then I can't sleep."

Jan completely understood.

"Then we should talk about what's in it."

"But if I tell you, I won't be the same kid you think I am and I won't get to have you for a mom."

Jan's eyes blurred as she helped the little girl onto her lap. "Of course you're the same kid, Hailey," she said. "You aren't what you did, or even what happened to you. There's so much more to you than that. You have a heart, and reasons and feelings. Remember?"

The pressure of Hailey's head nodding against her chest was an unexpected comfort to Jan. The child's short wayward curls tickled her neck.

"I know stuff other kids aren't supposed to know yet." When Hailey finally spoke, the words were mumbled and Jan could hardly make them out.

"What kind of stuff?"

"About…about sex and stuff."

Jan sucked in a breath, bracing her heart. *Please God, no*, she thought silently. Then she said, "Why don't you just tell me what you know and then we'll both know and be done with it."

Jan had no idea where she found the courage, the strength, to be so calm. But she was thankful it was there.

"No mom's ever gonna have to tell me about the birds and bees 'cause there aren't any birds and bees," Hailey said, sounding more sad than appalled. "There's just a man's dick that gets big, and he sticks it in a woman's hole, and they grunt and move around and get sweaty and then they're done."

Oh, sweet God in heaven.

Jan knew all about the atrocities that happened to

children every day in every city across the nation. She was a prosecutor. Probably a quarter of her cases were sex-related. There was little or nothing she hadn't heard or seen pictures of over the years.

She'd worked in juvenile court.

But when it was your own…

"See, I'm not the kind of kid a good mom wants, huh?"

"Oh yes, sweetie," Jan said, holding the child tightly against her. "You're exactly the kind of kid this mom wants. You're honest and sweet, and no matter what life brings you, your heart keeps trying to do good."

"That doesn't sound like the me I see," the child said skeptically.

"It's the you I see, and the you Officer Standgate sees, and the you Mrs. Lincoln and Ms. Wayborn see."

"But they don't know what's in my head. Except you."

"What's in your head is a criminal act, Hailey, but you're not the one who committed the crime," Jan answered with conviction. "Now I need you to tell me how that stuff got in your head."

What level of counseling did the child need? How could she best help her?

The evidence they had against the child's mother had been enough to remove Hailey from her home, but not enough to convict her on criminal charges. The standards were much higher for that. In a system that had its flaws.

"They made me watch." The childish voice was soft, sweet. Hesitant.

Jan held her breath. "They never touched you?" Medical reports attested to the fact that she hadn't been penetrated, but there were other ways to sexually abuse a child.

"Nah. One time a guy wanted to, but Mom wouldn't let him. Which is good, 'cause I don't have boobs yet and he liked Mom's a lot, so he wouldn't have liked me anyway."

As much as the child knew, she still had no idea. Thank you, God.

"That's good, because no one is allowed to touch you until you say so," Jan said. "And not until you're all grown up, because right now it would be against the law. And when it does happen, when you're a legal adult and it isn't against the law, it will be with a man you love very much and who loves you and..."

Hailey tapped at Jan's shoulder.

"What?"

"Could it be okay that we don't talk about that stuff now? It's gross."

Bobby was out late on Friday night, taking care of business. His calling was complicated. Some tasks had to be tended to during daylight hours, helping people shape their lives. Other jobs required the cover of darkness. You didn't change the world while you slept.

Tonight he had something pressing on his mind.

"Wake up, baby, we need to talk." Fully clothed, Bobby sat on the side of his bed, shaking Amanda gently. "Come on, it's important."

"Bobby?" Her voice cracked with sleep and he started to get hard, but it wasn't time yet. "What's wrong?"

"Nothing's wrong. Just important."

Rolling over, Amanda rubbed her eyes, squinted at him, and ran her fingers lightly along his lower lip.

His penis grew a little more.

"It's not time for loving, Amanda," he said, pulling her hand down. He was God's chosen. He could do this. "It's time for baby-making."

The speed with which she was wide awake didn't surprise him. Amanda believed fully in the cause. Gave her life to it. Other than that brief lapse when she'd wanted to marry him, of course. But she was human.

She knew he'd never be able to take the risks he had to take for the cause if she was tied to him—if his actions could come down directly on her or his children. She knew he belonged to the nation, not to her. But still, for a moment, she'd yearned.

They were all human.

Including him. He had to get this over with, before the weak, sinful parts of him got in the way. "Come on."

"No, Bobby."

"He's here now, Amanda. You had a period two weeks ago, so you should be ready."

"Who?"

"It doesn't matter who. I determine that he's pure and that's all that matters. You know that. You would never have known about Jacob, if the blindfold hadn't slipped."

He pulled the black scarf out of his pocket.

"No!" She scurried across the bed. Bobby was so shocked that she almost got away.

"What's the matter, babe?" he asked, frowning.

"I hate it, Bobby. It makes me feel like a whore. I love you. I only want you...there."

His penis swelled again. "Ah, Mandy, I know that. We'll do it just like we did before. You'll be blind-folded, so you don't even have to look at him. And I'll be right here, just like I was the last time."

He dropped the bra and long winter dress he'd brought in with him on the bed. "Put these on, and I'll make sure he doesn't see anything and that he doesn't touch you with his hands or lips at all. I promise."

"Bobby."

"God wants this, babe. I've been up on the mountain tonight, waiting for him to come to me. He sent Gabriel this time. He told me who to choose. He told me you'll be greatly blessed for doing his work. And I'll be blessed as well, for allowing you to do this. He needs us."

Everything was in service to God. If Bobby didn't believe that, he couldn't do half of what he'd done. His strength came from God. He'd had that truth beat into him over and over while he'd been growing up.

Literally.

The fear in Amanda's eyes turned to a different kind of light. She reached over and cupped his enlarged penis. "I want *you* tonight, Bobby. I'm feeling turned on and I don't want to feel that way when I...do...that."

God wouldn't ask him to stand by and watch while Amanda had sex with another man. There were some things Bobby knew with the certainty of his soul. Yet he'd been so sure earlier tonight…

"And I don't want to do it here, Bobby," she continued. "I don't want to remember what it felt like having someone else fuck me while I'm lying in our bed."

Respecting that God had chosen this woman for him, Bobby paid attention. She was as smart and gifted as he was. Her intelligence had been what had first drawn him to her.

She continued to rub him and Bobby was fully enlarged, ready to bury himself inside her sweet warmth, to feel her wanting him. Only him.

"Have him pick me up after work one night next week." She lowered her head and kissed him. "I'm off until Tuesday. I don't want to know which night. I don't want to think about it. And Bobby, I don't want you there."

"There's no way…"

"I mean it." She put her finger on his lips. And then licked them. "I don't want you to see another man inside me, because it means nothing. If you see, that makes it something."

She pulled off her gown, unzipped his pants enough to set his aching penis free and climbed on top of him.

"Okay? You promise no more bringing him here? You'll do it my way?"

She moved on him and Bobby felt the peace she always brought him. And he felt her fire.

"Okay?"

"Yes," he grunted, holding her waist as he pushed farther inside her.

"What?"

"Yes!"

Bobby gave himself up, his love and his soul, to the woman his savior had made for him.

And thanked God.

_18_

Johnny was in town on Saturday and came by to take Jan and Hailey to lunch. After that, the three of them went back to Jan's house so Johnny could hook his electronic game system to Jan's television and teach Hailey how to play a new game that was all the rage.

While Jan wasn't happy with the violence in "Conquer or Die"—and vowed they'd never have it in their home again—she was thrilled to see Johnny taking an active interest in her life and in Hailey's.

"Did you see that, Jan?" Hailey stood with the controls in her hand, moving back and forth in front of the television. "I wiped him right out of there!"

"I saw." Jan smiled. It was only a game. The guns weren't real. Kids played these things all the time. She couldn't let her fears spill over onto Hailey.

Hailey handed the controls to Johnny, who lay on the floor taking his turn. He got blown off the cliff the second he ran up to it and Hailey giggled and started swaying as she chanted, "I win, I win. Oh, yeah, I win."

Jan laughed too, then, watching the two of them.

She'd never seen Hailey act so much like a carefree child.

Her cell phone rang as they started a second round.

"McNeil," Jan said into the phone, watching Hailey go first.

"Danny Ruple here."

With a blink, Jan tuned out the television set, her brother trying to grab the control out of Hailey's hand to make her lose and Hailey squealing at him to stop.

"Sorry for bothering you at home, but we've had a development you'll want to know about."

She hadn't talked to Ruple since Tuesday night. She assumed that, other than showing up for the trial as her expert witness, he wasn't working on the case at all. She hadn't turned the rest of it over to the cops yet.

"What's up?" she asked, preparing to hear him with a jaundiced ear. The man had already lied to her.

"Had a call from my informant this morning. She's scared to death—certain she's being followed from where she works."

"She?" Hailey and Johnny both stopped what they were doing to look over at her. At Johnny's raised eyebrow, she shook her head, mouthed the words "just work" and motioned for them to continue their game. "You testified that the informant was male," she said more softly.

"Because I was afraid of something just like this." Ruple didn't sound the least bit apologetic. "She's probably just imagining it, but what if she's not? What if someone found her out? We're dealing with lowlife here, Jan. They're merciless with men who fink. Would you like to imagine what they'll do to a woman if they find out she's ratted on them? The Ivory Nation sees them as little more than machinery. Think of how hard Hall's friends would've looked if they'd known their traitor was a woman—and how much more easily they might've been able to figure out who it was."

"You've jeopardized my entire case." Jan couldn't think about the woman now. The danger. Couldn't think about what Hall and his associates would do to a woman they considered an enemy.

If they ever got hold of her.

"I need the information on Hall's computer to prove the first three counts of fraud, let alone all the aggravators I'm going to get on him. Your testimony was the only thing that kept that information in. If they find out you lied…"

"Only about the sex of the informant," Ruple said. "And it wasn't her sex that convinced the judge that she was valid. Everything else I told you was true. Everything."

She wished she could believe him.

And didn't see that she had any other choice. Her entire case rested on Ruple's integrity.

Simon was out of his mind. He knew that—and didn't worry much about it, considering that his own life was the only one that he touched in any way that mattered. He'd been up most of Friday night, determined to speak with Jan, to set things straight.

And equally determined to stay away. By the end of Saturday's lone, impromptu workout at the Snowbowl, he'd convinced himself that Shannon's visit had been a blessing in disguise. Jan hated him now. And that was as it should be.

If she hated him, he couldn't hurt her any more.

As content as he was with the rightness of this turn of events, his guilt for having hurt her in the first place remained. He hit the free weights the second he got home, lifting, grunting, punishing himself.

While his marriage to Shannon wasn't really an issue, he'd made love to Jan knowing full well that he'd never have anything to offer her—not even close friendship. Shannon's unexpected appearance, the memories that had returned full force, only strengthened his eight-year resolve to remain alone. Only then could he rest at night—only then could he find any peace at all. Only if he was alone could he guarantee that he wouldn't hurt anyone else.

With 230 pounds in the air above his head, Simon froze, elbows locked, when he heard the roar of Johnny's motorcycle next door. He assumed Hailey was still there, too.

None of your business, man.

He let out the air he'd been holding, lowering the bar at the same time, setting it down with careful deliberation on the poles that held it. He lay on the black padded leather bench, staring at the plain white ceiling.

What had ever happened to those broom swirls he used to stare at as a kid? Or the popcorn crap that Shannon had wanted for the home she and Sam were building? Ceilings were nothing to look at anymore. Just plain flat blankness.

He wasn't finished working out. Wasn't going to sit at the computer at all today. But Simon needed a fresh bottle of water from the refrigerator, and he had to drink it somewhere. His dining room was halfway between the kitchen and the spare bedroom. It seemed like a fair place.

And while he stood there, draining the bottle, the eye was naturally drawn to the window. It was bright, big, right in the center of things. That was the only reason he saw Jan's car leave her driveway with Johnny at the wheel, Jan in the front passenger seat and Hailey in the back.

Just like a real family.

He was glad she had that.

And he had an exercise bike to ride. Music to listen to, a shower to take. Wrinkled pants and flannel shirt to put on. A sandwich to make. A motorcycle to watch out the front window as he ate that sandwich.

He'd promised Jan that he'd protect her. She probably hadn't put much stock in his ability, considering that he wrote textbooks and spit in his living room, but he'd taken the vow seriously.

There was no reason to resent Jan's brother. No reason to suspect him of anything. The guy had a key to her house. He'd left a grief book. Jan loved him. He'd checked out on every search engine he'd used—including one that required special clearance. Johnny McNeil no longer had his job, was on unemployment while he presumably searched for another, and that was the worst he could come up with.

Simon had lost all perspective. He knew that. Just as he knew he probably didn't have much time if he was going to search Johnny's bike. It was wrong. Unnecessary.

It was there. And he had to do something.

Judge Warren had set the case on his calendar for 10:30 Monday morning, to begin the jury selection process. Fifty-two people, ranging in age from early twenties to late sixties, filed in. Different races were represented. And income brackets from all across the spectrum. Thirty-two men and twenty women. They all stood to be sworn in.

Though Jan had noted his suit and tie and noticed that his tattoo was no longer visible, she had never once looked at the defendant's face. She was going to get six strikes, and her job was to make sure that anyone who seemed obviously biased toward the defense did not sit on this jury. No matter how much work, time and effort she put into this case, in the final analysis the outcome would rest on the twelve people picked that day.

By 12:30, when they broke for lunch, Jan's body was stiff with tension. Hall was led out, still handcuffed, but other than a peripheral glance at the defendant, Jan paid no attention.

She couldn't.

This was showtime and she was only going to get one shot at the part. She had to play it to perfection.

"Warren's going to excuse numbers 12, 25, 28, 13, 39 and 16," Andrew said, as they made their way to one of their favorite eateries across the street. "It would clearly be a hardship for them to serve."

Dressed in her black-and-red power suit, Jan followed him to their table. "And number 21. He's nuts," she added.

"Defense is going to strike the woman who was raped."

"We want number 34, but I don't think Michaels will argue that one because she's obviously right-wing." Jan didn't need to look at the menu. She could only eat French fries on the days she was in court. "She stared straight at Hall and wasn't the least bit intimidated."

"And we want as many women as possible, considering the aggravators," Andrew added. "From what we've already heard today, we need to come up with questions that'll make some of the men look worse. Number 14 is one, he's as liberal as they come—so let's get him to expound on his views of racism. That way we can bargain with Michaels. Hothead goes, female number three stays."

For the first time that morning, Jan relaxed. Andrew was in top form. She wasn't doing this alone.

* * *

Davenport's number showed up on Simon's cell phone Monday afternoon.

"I have a job for you, starting tomorrow night."

Dropping his glasses, he squeezed the bridge of his nose. "Starting?"

"It could be one night, might be four."

More than an hour or two. Did that mean he'd been promoted?

"What time?"

"Eleven." Not your safe little afternoon stroll.

He should care more than he did.

"Where?"

"The Museum Club. A waitress there, Amanda Blake, is the girlfriend of our client. He believes she'll be leaving with another man one night this week and he wants to know which night or nights and who the man is."

Simon grabbed a pen, doodled on the pad beside his computer, not surprised to hear that Amanda was in trouble. Sorry, but not surprised.

She was a sweet girl. Pretty. Smart. Had a lot going for her. He hated to see the waste.

And knew that this was the job he'd been waiting for.

"I'll be there."

Due to the sensitivity and the high-profile nature of the case, Jan had expected jury selection to last all day. Instead, by three o'clock Monday afternoon she found herself delivering her opening argument to a jury that pleased her, with a defendant who scared her to death boring a hole in her back. As always, she was quick, to the point, preferring to impress the jury with facts rather than emotional rhetoric.

Michaels expostulated, paced, paused, made eye contact and pointed to his client at least fifteen times in the half hour he took trying to hook the jury. He wanted them to believe that the money Jacob Hall had moved into his bank account had been donated funds he'd received for a mission he was leaving on for his church, and that the cash had moved out just as quickly, since he'd given it to the church for his arrangements. Judging by their faces, he hadn't convinced most of them.

Jan didn't put it past the defense team to have a church pastor somewhere who'd provide corroboration if called upon. She didn't intend to ask for it.

By 3:45 she had the floor again. With a queasy stomach, she called her first witness, Detective Danny Ruple, to the stand. Listened while he was sworn in.

And prayed that she wouldn't go to hell for putting on the stand a man she knew had lied to her.

"Detective, tell us the events that led you to arrest Mr. Jacob Hall."

"I was following up on a crime report. I was able to trace money that had been charged to the victim's credit card using an IP address that was registered to my informant. Upon questioning this person, I was told that Jacob Hall was responsible for the missing money. Hall asked if he could use this guy's computer one night when he was over and the guy let him, but at the time he had no idea what Hall was doing. At another point, he'd heard that Hall had written a virus that allowed him to hack onto infected computers and get any personal information logged there."

"Objection!" Michaels jumped up and in that split second Hall caught Jan's eye. And ran his tongue slowly along his lips. "That's hearsay, Your Honor," Michaels cried as if personally affronted.

"Objection sustained."

Jan rubbed her thumb across her palm, took a deep breath and forced a smile for the detective. "Please continue."

Ruple's face looked more grim than normal. He didn't like being told what to do.

"I was advised that if I looked on the computer in his apartment, I'd find all the information I needed to prove that he'd not only used the credit card, but that he'd also taken money from the victim's bank account, transferring it into his own account and then into another unnamed account. And I was also told that I'd find a list of roughly thirty other accounts that had been fraudulently accessed."

"And did you?"

"I did find the account numbers."

"Did you find any evidence that Hall had either written a virus or accessed information by the use of one?" Michaels would ask if she didn't.

"There was nothing on Hall's computer, or in his apartment, at the time of our search that could prove that. But when our specialist examined his hard drive, we found enough evidence to convince us that he could have done it."

She'd be calling a computer expert as a witness the next day.

"Did you ever find anything to prove that Hall had used the virus to access accounts other than those belonging to the victim?"

Jan brought the weakest part of her case into the open, taking the offensive. If she didn't, the defense would ram her omission into the jurors' brains so hard they'd be aware of nothing else.

"No, we did not."

"Do you have a theory about that?"

"We believe that Mr. Hall has that evidence on another computer that we were unable to locate."

"Objection!" Michaels jumped up again.

"Sustained. The last statement will be struck from the record, and the jury is not to consider it during deliberations."

Jan walked to the witness stand, stopping just in front of Ruple. Her heart was beating hard. She had to wipe the others in the room from her mind—making it just her and the detective—if she was going to be able to do this. "Are you familiar with the Ivory Nation?"

"Objection, Your Honor!" Michaels's voice boomed. "There's no relevance to this question."

"The state intends to prove Mr. Hall's membership in the white supremacist organization, Your Honor, and to establish that the Ivory Nation's beliefs and teachings were the motive for those crimes."

"Overruled."

"I'm part of a team that's been investigating possible ties between the Ivory Nation and several unsolved crimes in our city," Ruple said.

Jan asked several more questions to give the jury a general idea of the attitudes and belief systems of groups such as the Ivory Nation.

She didn't turn around. Didn't acknowledge anyone but Danny Ruple. To his credit, his gaze was forthright, respectful, as he responded, almost as if he was pulling her through the questioning rather than being led by her.

"Is there anything in particular about the way they dress?"

Ruple nodded. "They wear thick-soled hiking boots." He named a well-known brand.

"Do they alter them in any way?"

"Just the shoelaces," Ruple said. "When they're first indoctrinated, the laces are black. When they prove their loyalty to the cause, they advance to white. And when they've shed another's blood for the cause, they are awarded red shoelaces."

"Was Jacob Hall wearing these boots when you arrested him?"

"Yes."

"And what color were his shoelaces?"

"Red."

"Thank you, Detective."

Judge Warren dismissed them at five o'clock. Andrew offered to stay, but she sent him home to his wife and baby. Most of the staff was gone, as well. Jan didn't mind the quiet as she settled behind her desk, going over the notes she'd taken that day—and the ones she'd already composed for tomorrow's questioning. In addition to her computer witness, and a credit card fraud specialist, she planned to put the defendant on the stand. Her hardest work was going to come after the defense called his witnesses and it came time for her to cross. That was where her best tool would be quick thinking.

Grabbing the pile of mail Nancy had put in her box, she leafed through it—an invitation to a judge's swearing in, a retirement party, a brochure about a closing-argument competition being held at the law school in Phoenix. And, in the middle of the stack, a blank envelope with nothing but her address sticker on it.

With shaking hands, Jan dialed her secretary's cell phone.

"Did you sort through my mail this morning?" she asked, probably too harshly, as soon as the woman answered.

"Ms. McNeil?"

"Yes, Nancy. I'm sorry, it's been a long day and I hate to bother you on your way home, but I'm in court again first thing in the morning and I probably won't see you…"

"It's no problem," Nancy said, as supportive as always. "Yes, I went through your mail before I put it in your box. I always do."

Just as Jan had asked her to do years ago—she hated junk mail and Nancy disposed of it.

"Did you notice anything unusual?"

"Unusual how?"

Pushing her hair back from her shoulders, Jan stared out the window at the setting sun. "A plain envelope with no return address."

"No, ma'am. Everything was on court stationery, or it came through the postal service."

Everything but one envelope.

"Thanks, Nancy."

"Is there a problem?"

"Nope." As tired as she was, as lost, Jan didn't trust anyone at that moment. "Just got an invitation to one of those home jewelry shows and I'm supposed to know who's giving it, but I forgot."

"Not surprising with everything you have to keep track of. I wish I'd seen who left it for you."

"You were probably down the hall."

"I guess. I'm really sorry."

"Don't worry about it, Nancy." Jan would do enough of that for both of them. "I'm sure I'll remember."

More like, she was never going to forget.

Grabbing her purse and satchel, with flash drive inside, Jan locked the Hall files in her bottom drawer and headed down to the parking lot. She wanted to get out while there were still people milling around.

And home before it began to get dark. Especially now that Simon wouldn't be there to escort her inside.

She planned to ignore the fact that she'd neither seen nor heard from the man since his wife had hit town on Friday. What did it matter to her?

19

Simon stood in his dining room and ate a doughnut. And then he put some coffee in the grinder and went in to the dining room while it brewed. With a full cup in hand, he stood there and slowly drank the hot coffee he hadn't wanted in the first place.

And finally he just stood. Waiting. He'd given his word that until she was out of danger, he'd escort her into her house whenever she was alone.

Her car turned onto the street half an hour earlier than usual. He'd been watching her house most of the afternoon. Hall's trial had started that day—which could easily up the ante in terms of anyone trying to do her harm.

By the time Jan was out of her car, Simon was in her garage.

"Ah!" It was more a squeal than a scream.

"Sorry, I didn't mean to scare you." She looked tired. And far too beautiful for his peace of mind.

"What..." She glanced at him and then looked down. Grabbed her satchel out of her car. "I didn't expect you."

Her tone couldn't have been colder. For her sake, he had to keep it that way. But God, he'd missed her.

"Trial started today. And I gave my word."

"I'm not holding you to it."

"I am."

He expected her to argue further. And worried when she didn't.

Figuring he'd better not press his luck, Simon took the keys she held out to him, entered the house, turned off the alarm and checked every room. It shouldn't have made a difference that he'd slept with her since he'd last done this, but somehow it did. He noticed everything that had been moved since he was there—the jacket on her desk chair, the bedding in the room she'd designated as Hailey's. Her life had gone on as usual without him.

Which was as it should be.

"Looks fine," he said tersely.

Jan was waiting by the front door. "Thank you."

He almost walked through it without another word. "Jan…"

The hand she held up wasn't quite steady. "I don't want to hear it, Simon, okay? We both knew that night…was just that. One night. We made no promises and we owe each other nothing."

He wasn't sure if the speech was rehearsed. But he guessed not.

"I was going to ask you if anything specific had happened today that brought that pinched look to the side of your mouth. You seem to get it when you're scared."

She'd been standing straight, her hand on the door handle, and she seemed to shrink an inch as she dropped her shoulders.

"I got another letter."

"At the office?"

She hadn't checked her mail at home yet.

"What did it say?"

"Nothing. Just an envelope with my return address label."

"No stamp?" His adrenaline was pumping at top speed. Not healthy.

"Nope."

"Which means someone hand-delivered it."

She didn't say anything.

"I'm guessing no one saw anyone who didn't belong?"

"My secretary sits outside my door and delivers my mail. She didn't notice anything suspicious."

"Did you show it to her?"

"No, I said I'd gotten an invitation that someone forgot to sign."

His thoughts flew in circles, but they were beginning to form a pattern.

"You called Ruple?"

"No." She glanced outside, down at the floor.

"Why not?"

And then she looked straight at him. "Same reason I won't call you." Her voice was cold. Distant. "I have reason to believe I can't trust him."

The blow was low. And fair.

"I should never have touched you," he said, although he could have said so much more. "And you shouldn't trust me with your heart," he added, trying not to notice the way her chin rose—and trembled—as he said the words. "But you can trust me completely with your physical safety."

He considered the exchange a victory when she didn't argue.

"So tell me about Ruple."

She did. And Simon had to agree that the situation didn't look good regarding the missing files. He'd never met Andrew, but Jan spoke so highly of her assistant—and while Andrew had made mistakes, there was no evidence they were deliberate. Ruple had admitted to lying about his informant.

"I really wish you'd consider staying someplace else for a while. At least until the trial's over."

He thought she paled, but she didn't back down. "I will not be controlled by fear," she said. "I have an alarm system. I'm not going out alone after dark. I won't answer my door to another stranger as long as I live...."

He felt the dig.

"But I won't run and hide. It wouldn't do any good, anyway," she finished, her eyes looking tired as she peered up at him. "If this is coming from the Ivory Nation, they're professionals. They'll find me. And if it's not, an amateur isn't going to have the courage to do much more than scare me from afar."

Judging by the choice of scare tactics, Simon didn't think she was dealing with an amateur.

"Let's go check your mail."

Silently Jan walked down to the street with him, glancing both ways before she approached the road. She pulled out her mail, handed it to him without a word and took it back the same way.

"I'm right next door," he said as he left her at her porch.

She nodded. Stepped inside.

"Jan?"

She turned back. "Yeah?"

"If you have any reason to believe you're in danger, call me."

He didn't leave until he had her agreement.

Dressed in her gray suit, red silk blouse and gray suede pumps, Jan stood tall and straight, satchel on her shoulder, when she greeted Andrew outside the courtroom the next morning, treating him the way she always had—as a respected colleague. She hadn't slept well—another nightmare—and took comfort in her assistant's familiar smile.

Judge Warren had cleared his calendar so that their trial was the only case in his court this morning. Jan went over her notes, discussed a couple of points with Andrew and reminded her expert witnesses what to expect when she called them to the stand. She was prepared and ready to win.

"Your Honor, may counsel approach the bench?" Michaels stood and addressed the judge the second they were in session and on the record.

Exchanging a puzzled glance with Andrew, Jan approached. Jacob Hall, in another suit and tie, sniffed as she passed between the defense and prosecution tables. Jan didn't watch the jury, but she wondered if they'd noticed.

"Your Honor," Michaels lowered his voice. "The defense urges you to reconsider the earlier motion to suppress all evidence seized on the basis of the search warrant obtained by Detective Ruple. I have new evidence we believe will make a difference."

New evidence? What the hell was this?

Jan's stomach turned as Judge Warren nodded, and she went back to her table, shaking her head as Andrew's eyebrows rose in question.

Judge Warren called a recess, dismissing the jury to the jury room, and left the bench while they were escorted out. He returned five minutes later.

Andrew was fidgeting in his seat beside her.

Still on the record, but without the presence of the jury, the judge agreed to hear Michaels's issues.

"Your Honor, the defense has been informed that the testimony given to this court by Detective Ruple at the evidentiary hearing held earlier this month, regarding his confidential source, was false. Detective Ruple specifically testified in this court that his informant was male, when, in fact, his informant was female."

Ruple didn't move. If Hall hadn't known the sex of the informant before, he was about to. And the informant's fear might not just be due to an overactive imagination any longer—if it ever had been.

Jan didn't move, either. Only she and Ruple knew about this. And he would never have been responsible for this leak.

"Ms. McNeil?"

Andrew looked up at her as she stood. Waited for her to deny the allegations.

Johnny and Hailey had been in the room when Ruple had phoned her on Saturday. She couldn't remember exactly what she'd said on her side of the conversation.

But she knew she'd said enough that someone could have gleaned the fact that the detective's informant was a woman. And she knew that she could have just blown her entire case.

Jan shivered. Her face felt like ice. The room became indistinct and hazy.

Johnny?

"Your Honor, the state was recently made aware of this information, as well." She was an attorney. A prosecutor the state paid to serve the public. "The sex of the informant did not seem pertinent, as it was not used to sway the court, one way or the other. I have verified with Detective Ruple that every bit of pertinent information he provided under oath was valid and true. He apologizes to the court for any confusion, and asks the court's understanding in this matter, as he felt honor bound to protect the woman who had risked her life to assist the state with this case. Detective Ruple concealed her identity in the only way he felt he could while still serving the court and the state."

Michaels argued again. Jan responded. And the judge took a five-minute recess to look at case law before ruling on the issue.

Jan spent the five minutes locked in a stall in the ladies' room, afraid she was going to be sick.

Why would Johnny have done this to her? He'd been so concerned about her safety, so attentive since their mother's death. He seemed to genuinely love her. Had it all been an act?

Did he hate her that much?

What had she ever done to him?

Or was he just so desperate to have her off this particular case that he'd done what he thought was necessary to make that happen?

Judge Warren ruled that the evidence was in. At that time Michaels made an oral motion for a mistrial, claiming that the jury had been tainted by the morning's events. Judge Warren denied that as well.

He'd removed the jury immediately. They had no idea what had taken place. The trial would continue.

Simon didn't have enough to do. The energy coursing through his veins pushed him to action. His life choices limited his activities. Something big was coming down in Olsen's case, and right next door. And here he sat waiting to babysit. Jan between eight and nine. Amanda at eleven.

He was an investigator, for God's sake.

Pushed beyond endurance, he got into his car, went

to a local bookstore—one of only two or so in the city—and asked to speak to the manager.

He was obsessing. He knew that. Over a burger, he took stock of his actions, decided they were harmless, and drove on to the second store.

And when he'd gathered some information, he called the New York publisher for whom Johnny had worked as a sales rep. They weren't going to tell him why they'd fired one of their key nonfiction salespeople. They couldn't.

But Simon, in his old life, had been gifted with the ability to make people give up information without saying much at all.

By three o'clock that afternoon he knew why Johnny McNeil was no longer peddling books.

If she'd had any way out of it, Jan would never have attended the battered women's fund-raiser that evening. She knew she wasn't coping, couldn't trust herself to make small talk with any credibility, but had never learned how to say no when it came to donating her time, energy and talents. She'd been giving free legal advice to abused women since she'd graduated from law school.

But Tuesday night's dinner wasn't about free advice. It was about paying top dollar for rich food served in an elegantly appointed room on the Northern Arizona University campus. It was about the networking, fake laughter and keeping up with the Joneses.

Tonight, she couldn't keep up.

When a defense attorney she couldn't stand asked her out, she'd finally had enough. She'd paid for her ticket; money was really all the organizers needed from her. And she felt too sick to her stomach to eat.

All she could think about was getting to her computer and doing a search on her brother—discreetly, without anyone knowing.

Driving home just after dusk, she remembered her keeper next door. She wasn't alone for the evening yet. She'd told Simon she'd be home around nine.

Should she call him?

Ask him to meet her at the door?

At least she didn't have to worry about another impromptu visit from Johnny. He knew she was at the dinner tonight—and he was out of town on business anyway.

Johnny. How could he? Jan nearly melted against the steering wheel as waves of despair overwhelmed her. All that talk about the two of them being each other's only family... There had to be another explanation.

With only vague feelings of guilt Jan shut off her headlights as she turned onto her street, coasting the last two driveways, and let her garage swallow her up. She couldn't see anyone else tonight.

Particularly her married next-door neighbor.

Half an hour later, lying back in a mass of bubbles in the soft glow of lily-scented candlelight, Jan closed her eyes, listening to the piano music playing in the background. She was exhausted to the core. Emotionally. Physically. Mentally. Too tired to be scared.

Her security alarm was on, everything was just as she'd left it that morning, and she needed a night off from hell.

She needed to sleep.

The bubbles became soft cotton balls that made up a bed, and she was in the middle of it, surrounded by a cool breeze, fresh flowers and a gauzy white curtain to keep out the bugs. Birds sang in the distance. And the s'mores smelled great.

Opening her eyes, Jan chuckled, and sipped the wine she'd brought up with her. Where on earth had s'mores come from? She hadn't had them in years. Not since Girl Scout camp.

She took a deep breath. And stopped. What was that smell clashing with the scent of her favorite lily-of-the-valley candle? She recognized it. But couldn't place it. It reminded her of Girl Scouts. A campfire. Not the match she'd used to light her candle. Not melted wax or wick. But burning, for sure.

When a second sniff brought a stronger dose of the same scent, Jan grabbed her towel.

Her house was on fire! *Oh, my God.* Standing in her bathroom, wearing nothing but pajama bottoms and a sweatshirt, Jan saw the smoke coming under the door. If she opened it, would flames engulf her?

She'd called the fire department. Thank God she'd

been nervous enough to bring her cell phone into the bathroom with her. She'd been sleeping with it, too.

Trying to lighten up, to think, Jan hated the fear she heard in the involuntary sound she made. Was this it, then? Was this how her life was going to end?

The dispatcher had told her not to open the door.

Jan glanced at the small, narrow window up near the ceiling. She could get her head through there. At least then she could breathe.

Oh, God. She was going to die.

They'd warned her.

She hadn't let fear kill her.

Fire was going to do that.

"Help!" she screamed as loudly as she could. Mostly because she had to do something. "Help!"

She could call Simon. But he wasn't a fireman. And she couldn't take a chance that he'd come barging into God knew what, to save her.

She thought about calling Hailey. And started to cry as visions of the butterflies burning up in the next room floated through her mind.

Then she went completely quiet, listening for sirens. The closest fire station was only a couple of miles away. But the guys had to get their gear on and...

She glanced at the window again. Hauled a hardsided makeup case out of the cupboard beneath the sink, balancing it on the top of the toilet seat. Climbing up, she rocked back and forth a couple of times, almost fell, caught herself against the wall and finally threw a large, solid bar of soap through the window.

She dragged a towel from the bar beneath her, wrapped her hand in it and pushed out the rest of the glass, then hung her head out to breathe in the cold night air.

Simon was waiting for Jan to return from her charity, just about to win a game of four-suit spider solitaire, when he heard the glass shatter. He was outside, gun in hand, hugging the side of his house, before he took another breath. Sliding his bare feet silently along the grass, he listened with all his senses.

The sound had come from the master bedroom side of Jan's house. She wasn't home, but someone was. Someone was knocking out the glass in her bathroom window.

Which made no sense to him. The space was too small for entry or exit. Before he could round the corner, the smell reached him.

Jan's house was on fire.

Simon didn't think. He didn't reason. He ran— straight to her front door. It was cool to the touch, but it wouldn't have mattered to him if it'd been in flames. He jumped from the stoop to the window, broke the glass with his gun and cleared enough space to climb through. Barely registering the sharp sting he felt in his foot as he landed, he tore toward the bedrooms. Sirens sounded in the distance.

They'd better hurry.

Her bedroom door was open. Gun held at chest level, Simon rounded the corner of the room. One edge of the carpet beneath the window was burning, but the flames had only spread to the area in front of the attached bathroom door.

A closed door.

He heard the piano music. And what sounded like a woman's muffled voice.

And he saw the satchel Jan carried to work on the end of her bed.

She was in there.

Ripping her comforter from her bed, Simon flung it over the fire, then threw himself at the door and crashed into the bathroom just as two fully suited firemen appeared at the bedroom window with a hose.

Jan was standing on the toilet, face against the broken window, with tears dripping down her face.

The cause of the fire could have been a spark from a short in the electrical outlet beneath Jan's bedroom window. The window had been closed when the firemen broke the glass. The frame wasn't locked. Investigation would be ongoing, and would take a day or two.

Standing next to Simon in her living room, Jan nodded as the fire chief gave her a rundown.

One minute she'd thought she was burning to death. And now she was freezing. Had been ever since Simon had let her go.

"Your closet was open, but a good cleaning might save the clothes."

A picture of herself walking around with smoky-smelling pumps flashed before her.

"You won't be able to sleep in here tonight," the fireman said. "The smoke's pretty bad. Lucky you were home and called as soon as it started. Lucky, too, that the spark flew out and the fire didn't travel through the wall. It could've been a lot worse."

If she'd stayed at the dinner as planned, she would have lost her home.

"Air the place out, and you should be able to get back in by tomorrow."

It would be a while before she could use her bedroom. Though the fire hadn't traveled far, between the water and the smoke she was going to have to gut the whole room. Her satchel—and everything inside— had been ruined.

Jan felt the pressure of tears again and looked down at the floor, fighting for control. She was strong. The fire had been small—an inconvenience, really, not an insurmountable problem. She'd lost very little. She had insurance.

There was blood on the carpet by Simon's foot.

"You're barefoot!"

Simon stepped from one foot to the other, leaving another smear of blood on her beige rug.

"Simon, you cut yourself!"

He glanced down. "Well, shit, I'm staining your carpet. I'm sorry."

"I don't care about the carpet. Let's see your foot!"

It didn't need stitches, and by the time the paramedic on the scene had cleaned and bandaged Simon's two-inch wound, the fire department was done. They sealed off her master bedroom, told her there would an investigator coming by sometime in the morning, and then it was just her and Simon.

And the curious neighbors who'd gathered outside. In a community their size, news traveled, and this was the second time in almost as many weeks that Jan's house had been vandalized. They all knew what she did for a living. And undoubtedly they'd seen information about the trial in the papers or on local TV.

The Thorntons had been outside earlier, when Jan had stepped out. As soon as they'd seen her, they'd shaken their heads, hugged their baby close and walked away.

She didn't blame them. She'd brought the threat of danger into the quiet neighborhood where they were raising their baby.

"I guess I need to pack some stuff and get a hotel room."

Her toiletries weren't damaged. They'd been locked in with her.

"What'll you wear to work tomorrow?"

"My spring and summer suits are in the closet in the spare bedroom. I'll find something that's warm enough."

Simon's arms were at his sides, hands in his pockets. She remembered them around her, pulling her down from the toilet. Carrying her out of the room. Holding her until she was steady enough to stand.

"We need to talk."

His words weren't ominous, necessarily, but definitely serious.

"I don't have the energy for a lecture."

"I'm morally opposed to delivering them, so that lets us both off the hook."

Jan couldn't imagine feeling much worse than she did at that moment, barefoot, in a pair of baggy light-blue pajama bottoms and an NAU sweatshirt, her hair hanging damp and frizzy around her face, smelling like smoke. With a life that had almost literally gone up in flames. But the determined expression in Simon's eyes stopped the objection she was about to make.

"The smell's a little pungent in here."

"We can walk next door."

Alarm signals sounded at the thought of being inside his home. She'd never been there, so she couldn't picture him there—and it should probably stay that way.

"I have to find a hotel room."

"It can wait an hour."

Considering all the moderately priced chain motels on the main route past NAU, the train station and up to the Grand Canyon, she knew he was right.

"Let me get some things together…."

20

"I swore I was never going to speak about my past, but it's become obvious to me that it's necessary."

Jan shook her head. "It's okay, Simon. Your life is your own. You don't owe me anything." She needn't have worried about picturing him in his house. She'd gotten no further than the living room to the left of his front door. It obviously wasn't used much. There was a couch, on which she sat, a chair, on which he sat, and a coffee table. No stereo, no television, no books or knickknacks, not even a coaster to set down a drink—if you had one. No one lived there.

"I want you to consider a theory I have, and in order for you to be able to do that, you need to know the validity of the source. Namely, me."

Jan leaned forward, her elbows on her knees, clasping her hands together. "I'm honestly not sure I'm up for theories tonight."

His stare was unrelenting. "It's important."

She nodded.

"I lied to you."

Her head hurt. "You're trying to build credibility here?"

Simon didn't grin. The Simon she knew didn't seem to be in there at all. In his place was a somewhat imposing man she'd never met before.

"About being married, you mean?" She wanted this over with.

"About everything."

Jan was beyond the point of being surprised about that. Ruple, Johnny, Simon. Possibly Andrew. No one could be trusted. She was starting to get that message loud and clear.

She just wasn't sure what to do with it. How to live with it.

"Eight years ago, I was an undercover FBI agent working in Philadelphia."

Jan swallowed. Shivered. That would explain the gun. The questions.

"You don't write textbooks."

"Yeah, now I do, but I hate it."

He wasn't a writer. Nothing was as it seemed.

Jan didn't ask what had happened. She didn't care. She wanted to find a bed, lie down in it and sleep.

"I had a degree in law enforcement when I was twenty-three. By the time I was twenty-six, I'd been directly responsible for several arrests that made the news—though I was never in the news. I worked undercover. And I thought I was pretty hot stuff."

So he was here to hide out? "You in some kind of witness-protection program?" It would justify the lies.

"No." Simon sighed and the reserve on his face slipped, showing her a glimpse of the kind man she'd known all these years—but not the fun side she'd seen recently. This man was anguished.

At least, she thought that was what she'd seen.

"I'd been after a top hit man for a mob family. I'd been told that my cover was blown, but because the source was a man in the agency who was twenty years older than me and I was his boss and he had a problem with that, I ignored the warning. I'd been told there was going to be a hit. I stayed on the inside, anyway, positive I'd know if anything was amiss."

He dropped his chin to his chest. His hands remained still on the arms of the chair.

And when Simon looked at her again, his eyes were completely empty.

"What no one in the mob knew was that there were two of me. As far as they were concerned, the bullet hit its mark. And they left my identical twin brother dead in the living room of my home, thinking the agency would find me there and consider my death a warning to leave them alone."

Oh, my God. Jan's throat closed for the second time that night.

"You found him."

Simon's head fell slowly forward in acknowledgment of her last words and the tears Jan had been holding at bay during the past hour started to fall.

Compelled beyond reason, Jan went to him, sank

to her knees at his feet, laid both hands on his knees and gazed up at him—an identical twin.

"I'm so sorry."

He didn't seem to notice her.

"I don't remember a lot about the following months." He sounded almost as if he was reading to her. "I spent a lot of time with Shannon."

His wife. She had a hard time remaining where she was, but she wasn't sure how to pull away when he was reliving such hell.

"Of the two of us, Sam was the scholar. He was quieter, less aggressive, although athletic enough when he remembered to go outside. He had his Ph.D. and had taken a leave from teaching at a small Philadelphia university to write a textbook on economics."

A doctorate by, what, twenty-six? These were two talented men.

"*You* write economics textbooks," she said, puzzled.

"I finished Sam's. The first draft was done, as were revision notes on a hard copy. It just needed to be compiled. His editor agreed to let me take a stab at it."

He still hadn't made any acknowledgment of her nearness. Feeling awkward, Jan slowly backed up, sitting on the floor in front of him with her knees pulled up to her chest.

"Shannon was Sam's fiancée."

Jan felt sick, getting the picture now. He'd finished Sam's book, married his wife. The man was so consumed with guilt, there was no room for anything—or anyone—else.

"They met in junior high. Neither of them ever dated anyone else. Sam wanted his wife to be a stay-at-home mom, and that's what Shannon wanted, too. At the time of the… They were living together, planning the big wedding her parents insisted on."

"So you married her, instead."

Simon pushed his glasses up his nose, then dropped his hand back to the chair.

"That relationship didn't even last through the honeymoon. I might've looked like Sam, but according to Shannon I smelled different." He shook his head. "Everything about me was different."

He tried to grin, but the resulting smirk held far too much bitterness to be mistaken for humor.

"She wasn't attracted to me. And hard as I tried, I wasn't attracted to her, either. About a month after the wedding, I moved here."

"But you're still married."

"There was a lot of money because of Sam's death—from the government and from a life insurance policy our parents, who were both gone by then, had taken out on us when we were born."

Jan watched the faraway expression come over his face—and saw the moisture at the corners of his eyes.

"Shannon got half the money…."

Simon had probably given it to her. She and Sam hadn't been married yet.

"Before I left, we agreed that we'd stay married—unless she fell in love again—so that if anything happened to me, she'd get my half, too, without any hassle or questions. I couldn't bring Sam back. I couldn't *be* Sam. But I could provide for her financially, so she'd never have to work if she didn't want to. Never have to worry about material security."

Jan scooted back onto the edge of the couch, hands between her knees, watching a man who'd touched every inch of her body but was otherwise a complete stranger.

"So what do you do here all day, if you don't write?"

What did it matter?

"I do write. Sam's editor liked my style and he asked me to submit something of my own. I've been writing law-enforcement manuals ever since."

"Guess I wasn't that far off with the suspense idea, huh?" She needed to be alone. To cry until her heart quit hurting.

And, *when I feel like it, I do privately contracted undercover work for the FBI.* Simon thought the words he couldn't say. Very few people knew he was Olsen's source. His life, and the lives of those with whom he worked, depended on no one knowing he was anything but a bored textbook writer.

Bringing Jan to his home had been a bad idea.

"I told you all of this for only one reason—so you'd understand why what I'm about to say is something you should seriously consider."

Jan mattered.

After tonight he couldn't deny that.

But having her matter and playing an active role

in her personal life were two different things. It was up to him to keep that straight.

"Just one more question." Her expression was closed to him.

"What?"

"Why was Shannon here?"

"Because she's fallen in love and wants to get married."

He was relieved to see that his answer didn't seem to hold any significance for her.

"I'm sure there's a better way to do this," Simon said, remaining in his seat by sheer force of will. He needed to pace. To put distance between them.

He needed a sock and shoe on his throbbing foot.

"But I don't know what it is."

She waited.

And Simon had an inkling of how it must feel to be a doctor who had to tell a patient he was seriously ill.

"I suspect your brother was responsible for tonight's fire."

"Johnny?" She didn't jump up or scream obscenities. She didn't tell him to go to hell, as he'd half suspected she'd do.

"Hear me out, and if you think I'm wrong, then so be it. I've spent a lot of time these past eight years playing solitaire, not honing my detective's skills."

The fact that she just nodded convinced Simon that he was more right than he'd initially thought.

"Let's start with the envelope in your mailbox. Your brother was the only person, other than you, who'd been in your home shortly before that happened. All it would've taken was for you to make one trip to the bathroom to give him time to get some of your personalized address labels."

She still didn't argue. Didn't say anything at all. Didn't give him any hint of what she was thinking. And he understood why she was such a tough opponent in court.

"I have no idea how he got into your office, but since he's your brother, someone might've let him through."

Or maybe there'd been another person. An associate. Simon figured he'd better stick to the topic before he lost her.

"The day he dropped off that book on grief, he was in your house for about six minutes longer than it would've taken him to leave the book, write the note and go."

"Maybe he used the bathroom."

Simon shrugged. "Or maybe he tampered with the outlet in your bedroom. This might seem far-fetched, but I've seen remote-controlled igniters that are about as small as a flea. All he'd have had to do was scrape the plastic coating off one of the wires in that outlet, clip the bug on, and set it off whenever he chose."

He waited for further comment, and when there was none, he continued. He could be completely off the mark. Fine with him. He hoped he was.

But he'd lost a brother because he'd ignored warnings. He wasn't ignoring them again.

"He lost his job."

Her eyes opened wide at that.

"I'm guessing he didn't tell you," he said.

She shook her head. And gave him nothing more.

"The interesting thing there is, he lost it because he wasn't selling certain books on his company's lists. *The Black Road to Glory. The Power of Women. From Here to Jerusalem.* A store manager rattled off several titles for me, not knowing, of course, that Johnny was fired for not giving her the choice to carry them. They're very fond of him and they think he was telling them what he'd been told. Apparently the owner of the store had had several requests for one of the titles and when Johnny insisted they were back ordered, she called the publisher. They didn't challenge Johnny's story—just agreed to put a rush on the titles."

With clasped hands at her lips, Jan bowed her head.

"When I visited the second store, I found those same titles suspiciously missing from the racks. That, in itself, might not mean anything, but when you consider the fact that you're planning to expose a white supremacist group, it starts to concern me a bit."

"Today, in court, the defense brought a motion that could've lost me the case. It was based on information only Johnny could have given them. He'd overheard me on the phone over the weekend."

She didn't sound devastated. Or angry. Or sad. She sounded dead.

Simon wanted her out of the neighborhood, under twenty-four-hour guard.

"I have a list," she said, staring at her hands. "It contains names of businesses and their owners—all dead and defrauded—that was found on the defendant's computer." She glanced up at him then, and he knew they were working. Period. "There was an unusual number of independent bookstores on the list."

"Do you mind if I take a look at it? See what else turns up?"

Jan stood, moving toward the door. "It's at my office."

"I'll drive." He just had to get his shoes. And keys.

She didn't even look back. "You can follow me. I'll go on to a hotel from there."

Jan knew the second she unlocked her desk that something was wrong. She'd left the Hall file with some pages sticking up. Not on purpose, but because she'd been too tired to straighten them. They'd caught in the drawer when she closed it and she'd almost cried, forcing it shut with her knee.

The drawer slid open easily, the file neatly in its slot.

Simon was looking around her office, not with a curious eye but a suspicious one. "How often are you here alone?"

"Fairly often."

"You're a sitting target."

"No one can get in without a key card."

The answer didn't seem to satisfy him, but Jan had other worries at the moment.

At first glance, everything seemed to be in order. She was almost ready to convince herself that her hard slam of the drawer had settled the pages into place.

But after a more focused inspection, she frowned.

"What's wrong?"

Now that she knew why Simon was so damned observant, she didn't find it so endearing. She'd liked it a lot better when she believed it was because he was a writer.

"The names on this list have been changed." The third one down had been Darling. It had grabbed her attention from the very beginning. Ironic that someone whose name was the same as an endearment would come to such a tragic end, just for being a woman.

And the eighth had been King—as in Martin Luther. Neither name was there now.

Someone had gone to a lot of work, as the lists still basically looked the same, check boxes all lined up and checks changed to fit the revised information.

And the only someone who had a key to her desk besides her was Andrew.

God, will it never end? She'd known the Ivory Nation had a reputation for being everywhere—and nowhere. Had they gotten to Andrew, too?

Was no one immune?

Even as she asked the silent question, Jan was aware of the answer. She didn't know of a single human being on earth who was immune to fear.

And manipulating individual and societal fears was the Ivory Nation's greatest talent. Fear of physical harm. Fear of scarcity. Fear of those stronger, harder, more capable of violence. Fear of death and of the unknown. The unspeakable.

It didn't matter. Once fear took hold, the Ivory Nation was in control.

"Do you have another list?"

On a ruined flash drive. "I can re-create it," Jan said, taxing her overwrought brain. "I think. I deleted the files off my laptop at home, but I didn't clear my history. Last week, I did searches for every single business on this list."

She hadn't been sure Andrew would do his part.

And now she knew why. The missing file on that NAU student, Lorna Zeidel, hadn't been an accident. The forgotten grand-jury schedule. And the file Ruple had sworn he dropped off. Andrew wasn't merely preoccupied. He was sabotaging her. Now she knew it with absolute certainty.

But Nancy had confirmed Andrew hadn't received that file from Ruple.

So they had her, too?

"It'll take me a couple of hours, but I can probably pull them together for you."

Simon checked his watch. "I have an appointment to keep, but it shouldn't take long."

It was after ten. Jan didn't want to know what the appointment was for. She didn't have the emotional wherewithal to care.

At least not now.

Simon walked out of the building with her, holding all the doors. She wondered if he'd always done that, or if Sam had and that was why he'd become a gentleman.

"I'll follow you to your hotel."

She hadn't expected that. "I'd rather—"

"I need to know where to pick up the file."

Because that made sense, Jan nodded and unlocked her car.

"Come on. Come on," Simon muttered. "Let's get this show on the road."

The client, presumably Amanda's boyfriend, just wanted to know who she was with and when. Was he planning on ditching her once he could prove infidelity? Might be the best thing that ever happened to the girl.

Dressed in snug black, minimally aware of the throbbing of his left foot, Simon leaned against a wall across from the Museum Club, which gave him a view of both exits. Looking at his watch for the third time in as many minutes, he did his best to rein in his frustration. Eleven-fifteen. He could be there for another half hour. Or longer.

An eternity.

In his day, he'd been able to sit for twenty-four hours straight, ready and alert, without feeling a moment's stress.

Back then, he'd entertained himself with scenarios of bringing the bad guys down. He'd done it in every way imaginable, sometimes fighting weapons that had yet to be invented.

And he'd mentally bedded a few women, sometimes also in ways that had yet to be invented.

Tonight, all he could think about was Jan.

Until a familiar roar sounded down the street and Johnny McNeil's motorcycle stopped in the parking lot across the street. Attaching his helmet to his handlebars, the younger man adjusted his jeans, hooked his thumbs in his pockets and leaned back against the bike.

Simon's blood chilled. Johnny and Amanda were connected.

His mind raced. If, as he suspected, Johnny had Ivory Nation connections and was hurting Jan, and Amanda was Olsen's source on Diamond, did that mean that Amanda's boyfriend, the one she'd said had terrorist connections, was also connected to the white supremacist organization?

But even so, what business did Johnny McNeil have at the Museum Club that night?

Was he on stakeout, too? Someone from the inside their leader trusted? Someone to check up on Simon's loyalties? Had his cover been blown?

He didn't like what he was seeing at all.

Eleven-thirty, and she still hadn't come out of the bar. Simon considered going back inside to make sure she hadn't skipped on him, but he knew she couldn't have. And then he thought of the bullet that hit Sam. He'd been certain that wouldn't happen, either.

Edging along the wall, so as not to draw attention to himself, he was just about ready to push off when the back door opened. He heard voices, but only one person emerged.

Amanda Blake.

Staying back, Simon cleared all other thoughts from his mind as he went to work. The only other person he'd seen in the area was Johnny McNeil. So perhaps her man hadn't shown.

Or he was waiting in a car in the full parking lot.

Or around the corner.

Or Johnny McNeil was dumb enough to be stealing a "brother's" girlfriend.

Keeping an equal distance between himself and Amanda, and himself and his car, Simon followed her as she moved toward the employees' parking lot.

Johnny was moving, too. Straight for Amanda.

"Hey, babe," he heard the man say.

Amanda jumped but didn't turn around. "Don't call me that." She knew him.

"Why not? It's what your man calls you, isn't it? I've heard him."

"I said don't call me that."

"Whatever you say. 'Cause that's how we're going to do this, isn't it? However you say? You didn't want it the other night. Didn't want it in bed. So what do you say we take my motorcycle outside the city and see how much noise we can make?"

What in the hell was going on here?

Simon moved in closer. He hadn't taken Jan's brother for a rapist. Neither did this sound like an entirely unexpected visit.

Had Amanda told her boyfriend that Johnny was bothering her? And Simon was there to protect her, instead of catch her in an act of infidelity, as he'd assumed?

As far as Simon could tell, Amanda didn't reply to the other man. But she didn't try to move away when McNeil fell into step beside her.

"He wants to know which night or nights," Davenport had said. "And who the man is."

Simon piled up the facts, but nothing was making sense. Had he been set up? Was this some form of test? Or was it really a lovers' tryst and the interplay between Johnny and Amanda what they both wanted? What turned them on?

"We have no choice about doing this," Johnny was saying, his voice a drawl. "But we sure can choose to have fun while we're at it."

No choice about doing this? What was this? Having sex? Leading him on? And who was forcing them?

"No."

"You don't want to have fun?"

"I'm not doing it."

Johnny stopped dead, and then hurried to catch her. "You can't mean that," he said, his voice completely different now. Filled with unmistakable fear.

Bravado to fear in the space of seconds. Simon's mind started to click.

"Bobby will kill us both."

Bobby? Was Amanda's boyfriend Bobby Donahue, leader of the Ivory Nation?

"I don't care." Amanda accelerated her pace.

"Well, I do, bitch!" Johnny grabbed Amanda's shoulder, pulling her into the bushes. Holding her with one arm beneath her neck, he reached for the button on his pants. "We'll do it right here if we have to, but I'm not going back till you take my seed…"

Now it *was* rape. Simon's head didn't have time to spin. Nor to consider his assignment.

McNeil was so busy pulling at his clothes and Amanda's that he didn't even hear Simon run up.

"Get off her, you bastard," he said, yanking the man up so hard Johnny's head snapped back.

Amanda's shirt tore.

"Hold it!" Simon froze, recognizing the tone from behind him even before the man identified himself as Flagstaff Police. He pushed Johnny away, glad to turn him over, and then instinctively jumped after him as the younger man fled.

"Don't move!" A second officer stood to the right of him, a gun pointed at his head.

Hands on his head, Simon stopped.

And looked straight into the eyes of Detective Danny Ruple.

"This the man that ripped your shirt?" he asked Amanda. If the detective remembered him, he didn't acknowledge that fact.

Amanda stood up, straightening her clothes as best she could. Simon waited impatiently for her to admit that he'd been saving her from a vicious rape so they could all get some answers. "Yeah, that's him."

Hell's bells.

She'd turned on him. To protect Johnny McNeil. He'd read the signals between them right the first time.

Feeling the clap of iron at his wrists, Simon knew one thing.

He'd been away from the job too long.

21

It took another hour for Olsen to be tracked down and to get his ass over to the station where Simon was being held. By that time, Johnny McNeil was long gone.

And Simon, through Olsen via Ruple—who now knew, in strictest confidence, who Simon was—had heard far more about Amanda Blake than he'd wanted to know.

The young woman, consumed with fear, had spilled her guts.

Believing in Bobby's cause, loving Bobby, she'd been blind to his brainwashing in the beginning—and still was to some extent. But unlike most of the other extremists, she had enough of a conscience to be bothered when crimes were committed under her nose.

And she was so afraid of Bobby's tentacles that she'd trusted no one. She'd been working with Ruple, to begin with, at Bobby's request. Her earlier information had been fed to the cop to lead them away from big-time activity with tidbits concerning other smaller jobs. And then, when Ruple had discovered her connection to Jacob Hall, she'd worked with Ruple at her own behest. Without Bobby's knowledge.

She had a son to protect, and she wasn't going to be implicated for the sake of the cause.

But when she'd heard talk of a terrorist trainer working with some of Bobby's buddies, she'd been afraid to go to Ruple, afraid Bobby would figure out what she'd done.

That was when she'd called the FBI—and connected with Olsen.

Simon had apparently been called in that night just to certify that Amanda had sex with Johnny, as Bobby had ordered.

Simon figured he should've stayed at his computer playing solitaire.

Listening to the ring of Jan's cell phone, at close to one o'clock that morning, Simon figured she'd turned it off so she could sleep.

He was heading to her hotel, anyway. He'd sleep in the car outside her room, if that was what it took, but he wasn't going to leave her.

And he had to speak with her before she went to court in the morning.

"Hello?"

"Am I too late?"

"No, I'm still up."

"I'll be at your door in ten seconds."

"I'm sorry," Simon said, as soon as she opened the door.

"I don't want to hear it," Jan said, taking in the tight black clothes that she'd never seen before.

She'd explored that gorgeous body, but she'd never seen it fully clothed in anything that showed it off.

Not that she gave a damn.

He should've taken off the clothes before embarking on wild adventures with whatever woman had entertained him. He was a mess.

And that wasn't any of her business, either. "I don't want to hear it," she repeated.

"Yes, you do," he said, throwing his leather jacket on one of the two chairs in front of her window. He followed it.

"Or at least, you *need* to hear this."

Jan didn't have the energy to argue. Taking the other seat, she tossed a CD case at him. "The list is in there."

Simon left it on the table. "Do you mind if I wash my face and hands?"

They were filthy. "Of course not." She thought about grabbing a bottle—too small a bottle for too large a price—from the minifridge across the room. And then she did.

By the time Simon returned, she'd opened two of them. One vodka. One scotch.

"Take your pick. It's either that or whiskey."

He chose the scotch, sipped it warm and straight from the little bottle.

Jan twisted the top off the bottle of orange juice she'd also brought over, sipped enough of it to make room and then poured in the vodka.

"You been playing in the dirt?" she asked, when he said nothing. She didn't want to know. Didn't want to care. Didn't like the fact that she was too weak to stop herself from asking.

"I was arrested."

Jan's drink splashed as she set it down. *"What?"*

Her head swam as she listened to Simon recount the events of the past couple of hours.

"I don't get why you were there in the first place."

"Amanda is a girl I met a few months ago."

A "lady friend?" Which still didn't explain why he'd been waiting outside the bar for her.

"I'd heard she was having problems with the guy and wanted to make sure she got to her car safely."

Okay. Maybe.

She'd showered and changed into a pair of jeans and a fleece-lined long-sleeved shirt as soon as she'd arrived at the hotel. Her feet were still bare. She wished she'd at least put on some socks. The bareness was too intimate.

"So this guy starts to attack her, you go to save her, Ruple shows up and she names you as the bad guy."

It was almost inconceivable, on top of the night she'd already had. And yet it all seemed about to make horrifying sense.

Simon watched her, his lids lowered, probably as much from fatigue as anything else. "Too much to take in, huh?"

She wanted to say yes. To suggest they lie down and rest and face the world in the morning.

But she was afraid to go to sleep. And after two hours alone in the hotel room fighting her fears, she wasn't too eager to be alone, either.

"There's more."

"I figured." And she knew she wasn't going to like it.

Or maybe she would. At this point anything that made sense might be more welcome than this disorientation.

"Amanda Blake is Ruple's informant."

A huge piece slid into place—as another huge hole opened up.

Jan's skin chilled. Hot and then cold. She couldn't find equilibrium. "She'd called Ruple to tell him she was being followed," she said.

"And because he felt responsible, he'd been pulling off-duty night watches."

That she could believe. Which was saying a lot these days. She gulped her vodka and juice.

"She was right. Somebody came after her, but when it came down to fingering him in front of the cops she chickened out," she surmised.

"Correct."

"And it's just a coincidence that you also happened to know her."

"She works at the Museum Club. I go there for burgers. This town isn't all that large."

And in her job, she'd learned that coincidences were red flags.

"How'd you get out of jail so quickly?"

He'd emptied his bottle. Tapped it against the table.

"Ruple wouldn't leave Amanda there in the dark, in case there was more than one of me waiting in the bushes."

"What about the other guy?"

"She'd said he was trying to save her. They chased him, finding it odd that he'd run off, probably wanting his testimony, but they'd lost time and he was gone."

She sipped. Tried to think over the roaring in her head.

"Still doesn't explain why you aren't in jail."

"Ruple interrogated Amanda, and either he scared her into talking or being at the station made her feel safer—I don't know." He glanced over. "She had a lot to say. To Ruple and some other officers."

Jan knew he was giving her a chance to go to bed. To hide—at least for the night.

To shore up some energy.

"Tell me."

"Amanda's boyfriend is Bobby Donahue."

Damn Danny Ruple for not saying so.

"Ruple was as shocked as I was to make that connection," Simon said, as though reading her mind. "He'd arrested her for picketing unlawfully once, but the other couple of times had been for possession of drugs and drug paraphernalia. She'd told him her time in prison had straightened her out. She was clean. She'd fallen in love. Had a baby. Was getting her master's degree. And she thought she owed Ruple for saving her life."

"But that wasn't true?"

Simon sighed, peeled at the paper on his bottle. "Not in the beginning. She really believes the crap this Donahue spouts about God giving him revelations to save the world. When Ruple was getting close to exposing the Ivory Nation, Donahue convinced Amanda that she had to go to the cop, tell him her story and offer to give him some information. The stuff she passed along was true, just not all that significant. It was supposed to distract Ruple. And it did.

"Then the whole thing with Hall broke, and she wasn't going down with them. She has a baby to care for."

"And she's probably scared to death of Donahue," Jan guessed.

"I'm sure she is. They offered her protection tonight, but she refused, saying she'd never get her baby back if Bobby knew she'd talked to the cops.

"It seems every decision she makes is based on fear. She told Ruple about the fraud—after she'd found out that Jacob Hall had used her computer—but she doesn't trust anyone enough to put all her eggs in one basket. She'd heard of some other activity that alarmed her, apparently a whole separate part of the operation, and she tipped off someone else to that."

Pulse speeding up, Jan sat forward. "Do we have enough to bring them in?"

Holding up his hand, as though telling her to slow down, Simon continued. "That's not all. Bobby, who was hell-bent on populating the world with pure—

324 Tara Taylor Quinn

read white—blood, turns out to be sterile and so he chooses loyal men of the cause to impregnate Amanda for him and plans to raise the kids as his own."

She should have been shocked. Maybe she would've been if she'd been more rested. And if she hadn't read about such atrocities in her years of researching white supremacist movements. There was nothing that would shock her now.

"Her son isn't Donahue's?"

Simon shook his head.

"Whose is he?"

"Jacob Hall's."

"Shit."

"That's not all."

Jan's head weighed a ton.

"The guy who was there with her tonight…"

"The one you tackled?"

"Yeah. He'd been chosen as the next surrogate."

A foggy brain didn't quite spare her. "Do I know him, too?"

Simon nodded, his eyes grave.

And she didn't have to be told.

Simon was just a man. He could make decisions. He could give his word. He could stand by it. But he had a breaking point.

He kept himself in his seat for the first couple of minutes, while tears rolled down Jan's cheeks. She didn't sob. Didn't even sniffle. Just sat there letting emotion pour out of her.

And it wasn't over yet.

"Come here," he said, leading her to the bed. He meant to lie with her, hold her, give her a respite before she had to face another day. She lay down, but instead of moving to give him room, instead of responding to the pressure of his hand trying to slide under her, she turned her back, curled into a fetal position, and cried herself to sleep.

Simon considered the other bed in the room, then went back to his chair.

It was going to be a long rest of the night, any way he looked at it.

The pool of blood was there again. She recognized it. And feared it at the same time. She tried to run away, but every time she looked back it had followed her. Into the grocery store. At a playground. Sitting in class.

It had never followed her before.

She tried to tell someone—kept looking at everyone around her, but no one was familiar.

Finally she recognized someone. Simon. No, it only looked like Simon. He'd let someone else use his body. She called out to him, saw him turn. He was holding a gun. She tried to scream, but no sound came.

Simon turned into Johnny, smiling at her—with a gun in his hand. And behind him, Andrew came. He held a gun, too. His hand was shaking as he looked at the trigger.

Jan tried to scream again. She lifted a hand to her mouth, and that was when she saw the gun in her own hand.

* * *

"Hey, Jan… Wake up. It's okay. Wake up."

She was conscious for a full minute before she opened her eyes. Lying still on the bed, Jan tried to place where she was, how Simon came to be speaking to her. Tried to figure out what to do now.

She'd never had to explain a nightmare before. Johnny and her mother had always known about them.

"Jan…"

She moaned and turned onto her stomach, burying her face in the pillow. Maybe he'd assume she was still asleep and go away.

She wasn't a coward.

Scooting to the opposite side of the bed, Jan sat up, her back to him.

"Sorry if I bothered you," she mumbled, needing the bathroom and not wanting to pass him. "I didn't realize you were still here."

"I didn't feel safe leaving you here alone."

As she recalled, she hadn't felt safe either.

The room was dark except for the dim light coming from a lamp on the table.

"What time is it?"

"Five."

Late enough to get up. So she did. And locked herself in the bathroom. With her things still there from the night before, Jan opted to shower and dress, hoping Simon would be gone by the time she came out.

He'd found coffee instead. "No one was serving breakfast yet," he said, pouring a cup for her from his seat at the table.

"I'm not hungry."

"You're going to work?"

She'd only brought the one suit—a light cranberry-colored one—to the hotel.

"Trial starts at ten."

Jan appreciated that he didn't argue or suggest that she wasn't in any shape to go to work. Work was going to save her.

It was all she knew.

"I can't bring Hailey into this." She sat down, considering the coffee. Thought about its warmth sliding down her throat. Wondering if she'd be able to feel it. "Not with the trial going on. Not with Johnny loose."

"I took the liberty of using your laptop during the night."

He'd found something.

"And?"

"Every one of the businesses that wasn't a bookstore was in a strip mall that had a bookstore."

Johnny would've seen them, even frequented them, on his route. They weren't random women-owned businesses. They'd been handpicked.

"And when I ran a search on the name Jacob Hall, I found an article about an independent Phoenix bookstore—not on your list—that hired him to write a computer program to help him track sales of both new and used books using ISBN numbers."

Whatever he had to tell her, she could take it. It couldn't be as bad as them all pointing guns at her. At least this way there was no blood.

"You think Johnny met him there."

"Just a guess."

Probably a good one.

Jan didn't touch the coffee. She was afraid to move. Simon was watching her, and she looked back at him for as long as she could.

"Can I trust you to keep this to yourself until I can figure out how I want to handle it?"

He was a private citizen who had information, not a cop with a duty. She wasn't asking him to break the law.

"You have to ask if you can trust me?"

The question sounded rhetorical. Jan might have laughed, if she had had the ability.

"You've been investigating me, my life, my brother, without my permission or knowledge. Until recently, you were a textbook writer I had sex with. Now you're a married ex-cop. At the moment, I feel like I can't trust anyone."

Simon stood. "I won't say a word until I hear from you."

She rose as well, putting her face within inches of his, their eyes locking for several tense seconds until she moved away.

"Thank you."

He left without looking back.

She waited for Andrew in his office.

"What's going on?" he asked, stopping in the doorway when he saw her sitting behind his desk.

He gripped the briefcase in his hand, the sides of his twill coat open to reveal the shirt and tie underneath.

"I need to talk to you."

"Sure." He seemed concerned but not guilty, as far as Jan could tell.

Although no one else was on the floor yet, Andrew closed the door and sat down in the lone chair opposite his desk. Andrew's furniture was similar to Jan's, but his windowless office was not. It was half the size and twice as clean as the space she normally occupied.

"You took the Zeidel file."

His face visibly paled. And another dark seed of disillusionment dropped from Jan's throat to her stomach. She stared him down.

"You purposely neglected to get me on the grand jury calendar the week my mother died."

He didn't speak.

"You tried to lead me up the wrong path on opening arguments."

He held his briefcase in his lap, denying nothing.

"You left the blank envelope with my return address label on my desk, after I told you about the one that had been left at my home."

He swallowed. She'd just been guessing on that one—but it wasn't hard to see how he could have done it. He had access to her desk. And she kept a few personal labels there.

Jan tossed a file on his desk. "And you tampered with the list of dead women, so that I'd be discredited when I produced false evidence in court."

Andrew's chin dropped to his chest. He still said nothing, either to disavow the horrible accusations or to excuse himself.

"What I don't understand is why. If I fail, you do, too."

His eyes narrowed as he raised his head. "I had phone calls on my unlisted home number. They were watching Jenny and the baby, and they knew when they'd been out of the house. If I didn't do as I was told, they were going to do more than watch."

She'd figured as much. Could almost even understand. But nothing could make it okay.

"Did you call the police? Have a trace put on the line?"

"They told me not to. I know just how elusive these guys have been—eluding the law for years—and I wasn't willing to risk my family on the chance that this time we were going to nail them."

"And after all our years together, you didn't know me well enough to trust me? To realize you could come to me?"

Andrew lifted his hands from his briefcase and let them fall. "The threats against you didn't faze you. Didn't stop you. And I was supposed to think the threats against me would?"

They wouldn't have stopped *her.* "I would've moved you off the case."

"They didn't care. They, whoever *they* are, knew that you trusted me. I was their man."

Because anyone could be bought—if the price was right.

Anyone could turn traitor—if the motive was great enough.

* * *

Holding the magazine open in his palm, Detective Grady Soine stared at the pictures of naked women, turned the page and spit an orange seed into the trash can at his feet.

Sitting at his computer Wednesday morning, Simon typed nonsense. The manual was close to being done. He had no desire to write another.

No desire to do much of anything. Like this sorry-assed fictional detective who'd appeared on his monitor that morning, he had nothing left to lose.

The phone rang and he ignored it. The second time, he took out the battery.

What if Jan called? She might be through with him, but her problems weren't over—not by a long shot.

And neither was the danger.

He'd barely clipped the battery back in when the damn thing rang again.

Olsen was nothing if not persistent. "What?"

"Amanda Blake's car was found about five this morning, rammed into a tree just off Route 66. There's no sign of a body."

Simon didn't spare the agent a string of expletives. "Did someone call the boyfriend?"

"He's devastated, naturally." Olsen's voice was drier than the desert after a 100 day drought. "And has an airtight alibi."

He would. His kind always did.

"What about the kid?"

"Legally his. He's listed as the father on the birth certificate."

"You got guys helping the local cops look for her?"

"Yep. And I don't give 'em a snowball's chance in hell of finding her."

Simon stared at his blinking cursor. Soine could've found her. "Davenport called, after my session with Diamond this morning. Apologized for last night's mix-up. My cover's still good."

"Or if it isn't, they're letting you believe it is. I'm pulling you out."

"Diamond is at least associated with Bobby Donahue, training part of his force. He's also got other clients— probably terrorists in training. We can't just walk away."

Well, he could but...

"We don't intend to. But we're going to come up with another plan. One that doesn't involve you."

And that's how it worked.

"We'll be watching Diamond and every single one of his clients. If they train with Diamond—they're on our radar."

"He's an independent," Simon guessed. "No loyalty to Donahue or anyone except himself."

"Now that we're sure Amanda Blake was telling the truth," Olsen said, "we're going to put men on every one of Diamond's clients—track 'em to their source. We'll get these guys." He paused. "Diamond will probably go free. He's just a trainer, selling his services to anyone who offers enough cash."

"He'll lose his business."

"I'll shed a tear for him. In my next life."

"Is Ruple bringing Donahue in?"

"For what? Having a girlfriend who got in a car wreck?"

For hiring Davenport to have a private investigator follow his girlfriend to see if she's with another man? If that was a crime, a fair percentage of the country's wealthy citizens would be in jail.

"People like Bobby Donahue always cover their tracks," he said derisively, thinking of the men who'd killed his brother and had never been charged. "They can't pin anything directly on him—and now that Amanda's out of the picture they have no testimony."

Simon knew full well how the game was played.

But if Jan was strong enough to play until the end, Ruple would soon have another thirty murders to investigate—another thirty chances to implicate Bobby Donahue.

Simon didn't think it would happen. Hall would go down. Johnny McNeil would go down. Amanda's body would never be found.

And Bobby Donahue would continue to serve his God.

"Chief of police asked me if you'd be interested in joining the Flagstaff team. Head of criminal investigations."

Soine didn't give a damn about the pictures, didn't taste the orange. Hadn't smelled flowers in almost a decade, either. The once-great detective was all washed up....

"I'll think about it," Simon said. Maybe. Someday.

22

At eight-thirty, the time Judge Warren's staff was due to report to work, Jan rang the judge's office.

"Christopher, I had a personal emergency last night," she said to his judicial assistant. "I need a continuance for one day…"

As soon as she had confirmation that the judge had been notified and his judicial assistant was calling the jury to let them know they wouldn't be needed that day, Jan left the office and headed home.

Dizzy, sick to her stomach, she was tempted to crawl into Hailey's bed, pull the covers over her head and sleep. Maybe she would have, if sleep had been in any way a friend to her.

She should have called her insurance company—started making arrangements to have her bedroom repaired.

Instead, she spent the day holed up on the floor of her spare bedroom, going through the years of photos she'd brought from her mother's home. So many memories. So much love and support. So much pain and confusion.

So much anger.

And guilt.

If she hadn't loved Johnny so much, she would've seen the signs sooner. The Ivory Nation preyed on young men in their mid to late teens—often connecting with them over the Internet. Boys who had self-esteem problems. Young men who didn't have solid families or father figures. The group—and others like them—supplied a strong sense of purpose and belonging, all in the name of righteousness. They taught these kids that women were inferior.

And they filled them with enough anger to last ten lifetimes. Or took advantage of the anger they already had built up inside.

At five o'clock, when she heard a key in her front door, Jan didn't jump. Didn't pick up her phone.

She wasn't really surprised he'd come.

Surrounded by photographs of the little brother she'd adored, she sat on the edge of the bed and waited.

Five minutes after Johnny entered her home, she heard his footsteps in the hall. And was held captive, frozen, by a fear worse than any she'd known before—the terror of being hunted down by her own sibling, a man she'd trusted with her life. She could hardly breathe, couldn't move, couldn't help herself. She loved him.

He rounded the doorway, stopped when he saw her and just stood, watching her, his right hand in the pocket of his black leather jacket.

"You didn't ride your bike." There'd been no roar out front. And he wasn't wearing the cowboy boots he'd had on every other time she'd seen him recently.

He wore hiking boots. With red laces.

"I traded it for a friend's car," he said, walking those laces farther into the room—closer to her. "I had some things to move."

That was his version. It didn't really matter.

"I saw the news this morning, Jan," he said, the bed sinking with his weight. The laces were right beside her. "They said you named the Ivory Nation during trial yesterday. Everyone's talking about it, wondering if they have any neighbors involved, if their kids are safe. Fear's spreading across the city."

He was exaggerating. "The danger's been there all along," she said quietly. "Now is when they're finally going to be safer."

"But you aren't!" Jan jerked as Johnny leaped up. "You've got to drop this thing, Jan. Your house was on fire last night. What more do you need to make you see sense?"

The house fire was known in the neighborhood. It had been kept out of the news on purpose.

She didn't ask him how he knew. What was the point?

"I can't."

"By God, woman, yes, you can!" He spun around.

"No, I can't. Not if I want to live with myself."

"Yes, you can." His voice lowered. "And you will." The words were even, cold. And that's when she saw the gun in his right hand. Their father's gun. Pointing at her.

Staring at that gun, Jan couldn't get words past her dry throat. Her heart was beating so hard she thought it would explode in her chest. She was in her nightmare, living the hell, only this time there would be no waking up.

"Now, Jan, you make the call." He motioned to the phone. And Jan had a memory of their mother's face as she told Jan there was nothing wrong with her.

And another, of her mother holding Johnny as a newborn. She could remember, even now, how that look of love and joy and happiness on her mother's face had made Jan feel happy and safe inside.

"You set the fire, didn't you?"

"With a remote igniter." He seemed almost proud of what he'd done.

"And left the envelope in my mailbox?"

"All you had to do was listen. Just once. But you couldn't let it go, could you, Jan? Couldn't stop being the crusader long enough to save your own life."

"Why does it mean so much to you, Johnny?" She knew the love she felt for him had to be shining from her eyes. She did nothing to disguise it.

He faltered. Only for a second. His eyes dropped, the gun tilted slightly downward. But it was enough to break Jan completely. The little boy she loved was still in there.

"Make the call. Now!" The anger in his voice, when he hollered the last word, coursed through her heart.

She didn't move. Wasn't sure she could have. "Why do you hate me so much?"

His scrutiny was prolonged, the expressions that crossed his face ranging from frustration and anger to disgust. There was no softness there. No acknowledgment that he'd ever loved her.

"You really don't remember, do you?"

Remember? She was supposed to know what she'd done to deserve something this horrible? It didn't seem like something one would forget. "No."

He laughed then. A sick, cruel sound. The gun never wavered from its position, pointing at her forehead.

"I hate you because you deprived me of my father and got away with it," he said, almost conversationally—if she could discount the remorseless pleasure he seemed to be taking in the words. "Mom always protected you, treated you like you were something special, some fragile thing, while I grew up without a father. Or much of a mother… What you did, what she did, made her go crazy." He scowled. "Because of you, I didn't have an old man to teach me sports or how to drive…." The self-pity in his voice was palpable.

He wasn't making any sense. "Because of me? I deprived you?"

Their father had been drunk. Planning to go hunting. She'd been four years old. And she was somehow supposed to have prevented him from cleaning his gun?

Johnny took a step closer, and the room started to spin.

"How does it feel, big sister, to be looking down the barrel of this pistol? To have someone you love holding it to your head?"

"Johnny…" Her voice broke as she started to cry. "Put it down, please. You need help. I love you. I'll do anything I can, and I'll stand beside you the whole time. The murders, the fraud—we can probably win with an insanity defense. We'll get through this."

"Insanity! You and Mom are the crazies and you want to pin that on *me*?" He raised the gun. "Look at it!" His spit splattered on her cheek as he drew closer. "Look right here." He pointed to the tip of the barrel. "This is where the bullet's going to come out and then you won't be able to look any more." He heaved a deep breath and shook his head. His voice dropped to almost a whisper. "They took me in, Jan. Gave me something to live for, something that mattered. And you don't even care. Bobby Donahue's the brother I never had. I needed him—and he needed me. And now you're trying to take that away. Just like you took away my father…"

Grabbing her stomach, Jan moaned.

"I hoped I was wrong about you." Johnny's voice changed, lightened. He stepped back, glaring at her. "I hoped that this time you'd listen to me. That you'd do what I asked—drop the damn case. But you just couldn't do it, could you? You couldn't sacrifice yourself for me like I had to do for you all those years. You had to destroy my new family, too. You don't care about me. I never came first with you—or Mom."

"Johnny! I *do* care. I always have! I'll do anything…."

"Fitting, though, that you should die by the same gun you used to kill our father."

He'd lost his mind. She was staring at a madman.

"I wasn't even in the room," she told him. "I'd been taking a nap and—"

"Shut up!" He took a step closer, the gun held steady. "You women are all alike. Bitches every one of you. Dumb bitches."

She felt so sorry for him. And terrified. Tears streamed down Jan's face as she sat there, afraid she was going to die by her brother's hand.

"You were there, all right." His words were deliberately spoken. "I came home drunk one night during my senior year and Mom flipped out. You were away and she was screaming and crying and rolling around like some lunatic. I called Clara and she came running over. She expected me to just go to bed and sleep off my good time, when my mother had just lost her mind. I heard them talking, heard Mom telling Clara that she couldn't get that day out of her mind. At first I didn't know what she meant, but Mom just kept talking until I could see it all so clearly it could have been an instant replay. According to her, Dad was abusive and alcoholic—but I figured she just said that to protect you. He'd hit Mom, I don't know what she did to make him mad, and you picked up the gun he'd had out to go hunting, this gun…" He shoved it closer to her face, filling her nostrils with the scent of gunpowder and old metal.

"And you shot him, point-blank. He didn't even know what'd hit him."

"No!" Jan flew off the bed, bruising her nose in the

process. "You're ill, Johnny. Sick!" She was screaming. And she didn't know how to stop.

"Sit down!" With careful aim, he caught her in his sight again, held her there.

"No, Johnny. Please, give me the gun." She took a step closer. "Please don't do this. Let me help you."

"You and Mom are just the same," he sneered, not seeming to care that his prey was getting closer. When she knew he was going to shoot her before he'd turn over the gun, she stopped moving. "You can't just leave well enough alone. And then, when you get what you deserve, you say you're going to help me. *Me!*" His expression, the tone of his voice, was vile.

"Mom caught me in her closet, trying to get the gun, that day before she died. She said she'd help me, too. Stand by me while I went for counseling. Well, the time for helping is past. You both had your chance. I took care of her that day, and I'll take care of you now."

Jan was shaking so hard her teeth were chattering. "Johnny, Mom committed suicide. The autopsy confirmed it."

"And why did she do that, sis?" he sneered. "You're the smart one. You tell me."

Chills spread through her. "I don't know why."

"Because I told her I was going to tell you the truth. You're a murderer, Jan. You think you're better than the rest of us, when really you're nothing but one of the lowlife criminals you take such pride in pinning to the wall."

Jan slid to the floor, her knees hitting first, and

then she fell back against the wall where her head came to rest. The air in the room was cold against her tear-stained face. She couldn't focus.

"That's it, sis. Sit there and take it like a good girl."

The click of metal against metal as he pulled back on the hammer sounded loudly in her ears.

"Put the gun down or I'll blow your fucking brains out."

Jan knew that voice. Or a voice like it. She was dreaming again. Only the dream was backward. It started with the gun this time. Johnny had it. And then Simon, right behind him. She didn't have a gun. And she didn't wake up. Men in uniform were there, coming through the door of the bedroom, one right after another, taking the gun away from Johnny.

Simon disappeared someplace.

And then he was in front of her. Pulling her away from the wall, lifting her. Her legs flopped over his arm, her neck fell back against his other arm. Her head just hung there.

And in this dream, Simon had tears in his eyes.

Tony Littleton was a good kid.

"Thanks for meeting me on such short notice," Bobby told the boy as they sat down at one of Bobby's favorite family restaurants. Tony reached over and helped strap Luke into his high chair.

"Hi there, big guy," he said, amusing Luke while Bobby clipped the seat belt across his son's waist and adjusted the tension.

"I heard about Amanda on the news," Tony said, his mouth pinched. "I couldn't believe it, man. I'm sorry."

Bobby ran a finger lightly down his son's cheek, checking his tears. He nodded.

"I only met her that once, but…God…she was so perfect. Beautiful, smart. Understanding."

"They'll find her." Bobby wiped his eye. Knowing the lie would be forgiven. It was only him and Luke now, until God sent him another woman to help him raise loyal followers of the cause.

Tony surveyed him silently for a second. Bobby waited him out.

"Right," Tony said eventually. "And get the bastards who did this to her."

Bobby opened the plastic container of dry cereal, spread some on Luke's tray. "No one knows if anyone did anything," he said. "She crashed, probably hit her head." He had a little trouble with that one, but kept talking. "She might be concussed, wandering around lost in the woods."

And if the police ever caught the two men who'd lain in wait for his lovely traitor, his own Judas, they'd never be able to track them to Bobby.

"Oh." Tony turned his head slightly, regarding him with serious eyes. "You really think so?"

"How could I be sitting here eating anything at all if I believed differently?" Being human allowed for errors in judgment. And sometimes the lure of free will.

Hall had fallen. Johnny McNeil was done, too.

They'd have to be replaced. It happened that way sometimes. He'd lost men before. But God's war continued.

And Bobby was far enough removed to avoid implication at this time.

Tony sighed. "I can't tell you how relieved I am, man. That's great. I was sure—"

Bobby motioned for the waitress before Tony could complete a sentence that was better left unsaid.

He ordered for himself and Luke. Made sure his son's grilled cheese would be made with American cheese, that he had a lid on his milk, and that he had applesauce instead of French fries. And spent the rest of the meal talking to Tony about his future.

The kid was looking at colleges, getting scholarship offers. He'd been planning a career in English—until Bobby convinced him to major in political science.

Life came. Life passed. And life went on.

Jan slept for more than twelve hours. Simon spent most of that time watching her. He'd taken her to the hospital, but other than providing the names of some therapists—and a supply of sleeping pills—they'd been little help.

He hadn't known who else to call.

"Where am I?" He'd been staring out the window, but now he turned to see that she was wide awake watching him.

"My bed."

"I don't remember getting here."

"They gave you a shot to calm you down at the hospital. It made you pretty groggy."

"I don't remember much about being there, either."

They were going to have to talk about it. He had no idea how to begin.

Jan sat up, glanced down at the wrinkled extra-large T-shirt she was wearing with a pair of his workout shorts.

"You weren't going to be comfortable in that suit all night." He nodded toward the other chair in the room.

Her gaze followed his movement to the dirty and wrinkled suit, which had been pristine the morning before. So long ago.

"Where'd you sleep?"

On the bed for a few hours. "Mostly here."

She nodded again, got up and grabbed her suit.

"Where are you going?"

"To shower." She said the words over her shoulder as she headed for the door.

Simon jumped up. She couldn't simply walk out like this.

He caught up with her in his dining room. "Jan, wait. We need to talk."

She wouldn't look at him now. "I remember a lot of uniforms," she said, glancing out at the street. It would be another hour before the kids assembled for the first bus. "I'm assuming Johnny's in custody."

"Yes." He wasn't sure how much to tell her. Or what she remembered. It'd been a long time since he'd been responsible for another person's life or well-being—even temporarily.

She moved to the door, turned back.

"Thanks."

"Jan…"

Unlocking the door, she pulled it open.

"I'd like to take you out to breakfast, after you've showered."

"I can't." She was halfway through the door. "I have to get to work."

She was a grown woman. He couldn't stop her. Had no right to interfere.

He stood, watching after her, feeling utterly useless.

And worried sick.

By the time Nancy arrived that morning, Jan had her personal things packed and loaded in her car. She also had three copies of the resignation letter, effective immediately, that she was going to be turning in that afternoon.

With her door shut, her sweaty palms the only indication that she wasn't as composed as she appeared, she picked up the phone.

"Gordon?" Michaels had answered on the first ring. "Jan McNeil here."

The black cloud around her was closing in. She just had to hold on a little longer—had to get through this last piece.

"I have a plea offer."

"I'm listening." He was going to take his flesh, too. She'd expected that.

"I've got new evidence. At least thirty murders to

charge. Your client will be implicated." She gave him some of the details, and then added, "Hall testifies against the murderer, giving me dates, times, everything he has, and I drop the charges to a class-three attempt, with lifetime probation and mandatory relocation to another state."

"Send it over."

Jan faxed it herself.

And twenty minutes later had the call back. Hall had accepted the offer.

His testimony might help send Jan's little brother to death row.

Soine turned another page, exposing the next set of firm and tanned female breasts, nipples erect, the belly button ring, and shaved skin where a woman should never be shaved. And again. And again. Every page looked the same. Cold and distant. Unreal. A man who went for the real thing, which included a little imperfection, he'd never understood the appeal of these rags, but now that he was barely more than a rag himself, he'd figured he'd give it a try.

One more page, and Soine stopped. Stared. Turned the magazine, getting a better look at the ear on one side of that provocatively tilted head. The tiny scar was there.

It was her.

Dropping the X-rated periodical, he grabbed his coat, checked purely out of habit for the gun in the hidden holster at his waist, and headed out the door....

Simon, who'd spent the morning alternating between pacing, staring out the dining room window and trying to get this aggravating Soine character out of his head, stared at the blinking cursor.

What was Soine doing? His life was over. So where the hell was he going?

And who *was* this woman? Why did she matter? How could she matter to a man who'd used up all his chances?

Because he didn't have anything better to do, Simon continued to type.

Clara Williams was at home Thursday afternoon. She had a smile on her face when she opened her door and gave Jan a bright hello and a long hug. But her smile quickly faded.

"What's wrong? What's happened?" She stood back, eyeing Jan up and down—something her mother would've done, too.

Jan couldn't think about that now. "I need to know the truth."

Clara's expression suddenly deadpan, she studied Jan. "Come in."

And in that instant Jan didn't need to. She'd just had all the confirmation she needed. She'd murdered her own father. She turned to go.

"Jan?" Clara took her hand, pulled her gently inside to a seat on her light blue couch. The same color her mother's had been when Jan was little. "I promised your mother that if you ever came asking, I'd tell you the whole story. She and I are the only ones who knew. I was hoping the knowledge was going to go to my grave with me."

Jan sat, folded her hands in her lap. Shook her head when Clara offered her something to drink.

Her stomach wasn't in good shape.

"Your father was a good man," Clara started, taking a seat beside Jan on the couch and holding her hand. Clara's grasp was the only warmth Jan felt. The rest of her might have been frozen. "A hard worker and good provider. And then, just after you were born, his company downsized and he lost his job. The economy wasn't so good and he couldn't find another position, so he took odd jobs. And he started drinking. And the more he drank, the meaner he got."

Jan stared at their clasped hands. And saw her father's big hand holding her tiny one. Felt the warmth. The security. And saw it raise...

"He beat her," Jan said, with no emotion whatsoever. "He used to hit her with the back of his hand, over and over. He'd start with her face, and when she'd turn away he'd hit her back."

"You remember."

23

Jan hardly saw the kind, watery eyes of the older woman. "Only just now. Only that."

"Well, you're right. He used to hit her so hard that sometimes she couldn't sit or lean back for weeks. I used to beg her to get help, but he was always so contrite afterward, begging her to forgive him." Clara shrugged, staring into space as if answers that had always eluded her might suddenly appear.

"She loved him. And she was afraid to leave him, too. She kept remembering the man he'd been. And hoping he'd find himself again."

Jan's arms felt weak and she could barely lift them. She wanted to get up and leave, to run until she collapsed and someone else could take over.

"Then Johnny came along, and with another mouth to feed, more doctors' bills and diapers, things got worse.

"One Sunday, he went out drinking while your mom took you and the baby to church. By the time you got home, he was drunker than a skunk and ready for battle. He had his pistol out, said he was going hunting. Your mother begged him not to, afraid that he'd hurt himself or someone else. He swung at her with the gun still in his hand, hit her across the chest and broke a couple of her ribs. You were right there— and Johnny, too. Your mom screamed and Johnny started to cry. That's when your dad really went crazy. He dropped the gun to grab the baby, and said if he didn't shut up, he'd shut him up."

Jan's head spun, caught in another living nightmare. She was awake, and dreaming at the same time.

"I was afraid he was going to kill my baby," she said, recognizing that her voice sounded almost childlike. "I screamed and kicked him and he dropped the gun. I picked it up. It was too heavy and I had to hold it in two hands. I had my fingers by the trigger, like I'd seen him do, pointing it at him like he'd done with Mommy. It always made her stop whatever she'd been doing, and then he'd put the gun down."

"He pointed that thing at her?" Clara's voice was real. Loud. Too loud.

Jan nodded. "But he didn't stop like Mommy did. He came after me. Told me to give him the goddamned gun. I shook my head and held on tighter."

She could hear the bang again. And then her mind went blank.

"The explosion knocked you back into a wall and you hit your head." Clara's hushed words penetrated the shadows.

Jan was only now aware of the cushiony warmth

against her cheek—Clara's chest. The older woman was holding her, stroking her head.

And Jan remembered that, too. When she'd regained consciousness all those years ago, Clara had been holding her just the same way. And the first thing Jan had seen was the pool of blood on the floor where her father had lain.

Her mother had told her—and the police—that Jan had been taking a nap when the accident happened, when, in truth, the "accident" had caused her unconsciousness.

A not-so-minor point that changed everything.

Shaking, she got up. Thanked her mother's friend, assured her she was fine, although she didn't even know what that meant anymore. And left. She saw no point in telling Clara that Johnny also knew about that tragic day so long ago. Saw no point in telling her about the overheard conversation, or explaining the real reason her mother died. Clara had suffered enough anguish.

She drove straight to the county attorneys' office, left an envelope for her superiors. It contained her resignation and Hall's executed plea agreement; all the documentation they'd need to charge and convict her brother, including her own written statement; and the new, expanded Zeidel file, with a recommendation to charge the case. It also contained legal documentation, with a request for Nancy to disperse it for her, backing out of the adoption, urging CPS to find another home for Hailey as soon as possible, and requesting the delivery of an enclosed letter to Mrs. Lincoln.

The little girl needed someone far more balanced than she was.

And she turned in a statement documenting every wrong step Andrew had taken. He'd be disbarred, without doubt. Maybe do some prison time for obstruction of justice. She couldn't think about that now.

Without speaking to anyone but a receptionist on the first floor, she left the office and drove home, took off her clothes and curled up on the couch with a blanket. She couldn't go into her room. Couldn't face the butterflies in Hailey's. Would never open the door to the spare bedroom again.

She couldn't ask for help. Didn't know who to ask.

All those years, the nightmares—she'd known all along. Her mother had lied to her. Worse yet, she'd lied to herself.

How could she trust anyone else to show her the way, when she couldn't even trust herself to see it?

All these years, her own mind had been a traitor.

Jan went to sleep.

Simon had seen her come home Thursday afternoon. She'd gone straight into the garage, closing the door behind her. She hadn't checked her mail. He knocked on the front door. And then again an hour later. He called.

And when she didn't answer, he accepted that she had no obligation to see him. She was entitled to be alone if she chose to be.

Entitled to grieve alone.

But the thought was killing him.

* * *

By Friday afternoon, his patience had run out. He'd written fifteen pages. He'd paced and drunk far more coffee than he needed. He'd been at her house at least four times. She could be dead in there, for all anyone knew.

Another life lost while he blithely ignored the signs.

By the time the second school bus had come and gone and all the kids had disappeared into their homes, he'd made up his mind. Pulling on his jacket in case he was out there for a long time, he marched over to Jan's front door and knocked. He continued to knock for half an hour.

He'd give her another five minutes and then he was going in, if he had to break the law to do it.

Technically, he didn't have to break the law. When he finally tried it, her front door was unlocked.

Jan heard him come in. She'd heard him outside her front door, too, calling to her. His voice growing louder and more frustrated as time passed. She'd forgotten that the front door wasn't locked. She'd gone for a walk sometime around three in the morning. She'd been unable to sleep, and unable to work up any fear for her safety, either.

With a peanut butter sandwich in hand, she'd walked the neighborhood.

And wondered how many of the homes were really happy ones. How many had moms and dads who made the right choices and were dedicated to their children. Two-stories, one-stories, rundown, expensively appointed, all of the homes told the same story. Everyone could be bought.

On her way back, she'd passed the Thorntons, thought of baby Mark and the couple's joy at having a son. She thought of their zealous beliefs in raising the boy right and of their cold shoulder the night of her fire. And she hoped they'd be a happy, normal family.

"Jan?" Simon's voice was getting closer.

Tightening the blanket around her, she burrowed deeper into the back of the couch and closed her eyes.

"Jan!"

He came around the sofa, feeling for her pulse.

"Go away."

"Thank God!" He sank down on the edge of the sofa. "Why didn't you come to the door?"

She thought the answer was obvious.

"Have you eaten anything?"

Turning over, Jan looked pointedly at the napkin and paper plate on the table. Breakfast dishes.

Simon's eyes darkened, and she remembered she hadn't showered or put on makeup since the day before. Her eyes were undoubtedly swollen, too. She didn't care.

Jan didn't like the funny look that came to his eyes as he stood. He didn't understand.

"Time to get up," he said, pulling her blanket until it caught on the tennis shoes she still had on from her walk during the night.

She wore her sweatpants and jacket, too. She couldn't seem to get warm. But she lay there trying, anyway.

"Come on, Jan. Sit up."

"Go away."

"Nope. Either you sit up or I'm going to sit you up."

The strange voice was back. The one that had told Johnny he'd blow his brains out.

Jan sat. Sighed. "It's not as bad as it looks," she said. "I'm not taking anything. I'm eating. And I'm catching up on my rest."

"It's best, when you're resting, to get up and do something now and then."

"I made breakfast." She'd peeled an orange a couple of hours ago.

"Tomorrow's Saturday—your day with Hailey. You'll probably want to get this place spruced up."

"She's not coming."

"Why not?"

"I'm not adopting her."

He stood over her, and even though she wasn't watching him she could feel his frown. "You're going to prove to her that she was right all along? That she's not good enough for you?"

If she'd been able to feel, that might have hurt.

"How much did you hear the other day?" She wasn't even sure which day it was.

"I've put the bits and pieces together. Enough to know that your brother thinks you're responsible for your father's death."

It sounded so…human…when he said it. Nothing like the terrifying black chasm that loomed before her every time she woke up.

"I killed him." Jan sat still as the horror engulfed her again. She was getting used to the sense of suffocation.

"Accidentally."

She contemplated that. "I didn't know the damage would be so…permanent," she said eventually. "But I meant to stop him in his tracks. I wanted him gone. He'd beat up my mother and he was hurting Johnny."

Had she realized the consequences of her actions, she might still have pulled the trigger.

"You were four years old. Your mother and baby brother were being attacked and you were the only one who could save them. If you hadn't done what you did, he might have killed all three of you."

That had come to her, too, sometime during the hazy hours since she'd left Clara's home. Her father had hit her, too.

"I know that even if my mother hadn't lied about what happened, I still would not, at the age of four, have been prosecuted. That doesn't change the fact that I did something most four-year-olds wouldn't have done—*couldn't* have done. Something in my makeup allowed me to cross that invisible line that separates the species into those who can take lives and those who can't.

"I've worked in the justice system a long time, Simon," she said wearily. "I know the laws, and I wouldn't give Hailey to me. She needs stability, emotional security. Those aren't things I can give her. I don't trust myself."

He was listening, really listening.

"I understand it's not going to help her to have the adoption fall through. But I believe there'll be another chance for that soon, and in the larger scheme of things her disappointment will be momentary. If I take her, the damage could be much more permanent."

Jan pulled her feet up quickly before Simon sat on them. He perused her for several long seconds.

"Have you considered counseling?"

She nodded. "I called yesterday morning. I have an appointment on Monday."

The day she was supposed to be bringing her daughter home.

"So where does this leave you?" He spread his hands. "Just prosecuting and living alone?" He made it sound so bad, when in fact, working and living alone was just the life he'd carved out for himself.

"I quit my job."

His silence was unnerving. But then her head was still pretty foggy.

"I'd feel like a fraud, standing up in front of a judge, asking him to take thirty years of a man's life for doing something I've done myself."

"Give yourself some time," Simon said. "Once the shock wears off, you'll have a different perspective."

"But the facts will be the same." Jan couldn't budge on this. "Felons are not allowed to practice law in this state," she told him, holding up her hand to forestall his objection. "I know, I wasn't prosecuted, but the spirit of the law still applies here. I can't prosecute others for a crime I've committed myself."

She believed in the law. Had dedicated her life to it. Even if upholding that belief meant losing the life she loved.

"But…"

"Please don't," she said, her gaze as implacable as her heart. "I've just betrayed my own brother, given them the evidence to put him to death, because I believe in our justice system." Her voice broke and tears sprang to Jan's eyes, even though she'd been so sure she was cried out.

She had to believe in the system because there was absolutely nothing else she could trust.

Two weeks and two days after Jan gave her brother's life to the authorities and quit her job, she went to see him.

"What are you doing here?" he practically spat at her, hands cuffed behind his back. Since he was at the county jail until he went to trial and was sentenced, they could sit together at a small table during visiting hours.

She'd cried all the way over.

"You've been indicted," she said, as if he didn't already know that. He'd confessed to all thirty murders. "And there's no bail." She was listing the facts, as any good lawyer would have done.

"Get out of here." Johnny's voice, though quiet, had lost none of its intensity.

"I've hired the best defense attorney in the state…" Not caring that it was going to cost her dearly. "There's a chance he'll be able to get you down to life in prison. And if you cooperate, we might be able to sell an insanity defense."

Johnny didn't even seem to hear her.

"I love you, Johnny." Her voice broke again as her arms ached to hold him. "I've always loved you so much."

Johnny looked straight at her, taking her breath away with the anger apparent in his eyes. He stood, called for the guard. And glanced back.

Jan stood, too, hopeful that, in their last second together, he'd soften. That they'd share the unconditional love they'd had growing up.

Johnny spat on her and walked away.

Simon heard a bit about the incident when he saw her at the mailbox that night, though he suspected he was missing much of it. As she was collecting her envelopes from the box, Jan merely mentioned having seen her brother to tell him about the attorney she'd hired.

"So, have you officially decided to be a lady of leisure?" he asked her in an attempt to keep her with him, however briefly. He anticipated these moments with her from the time he rose in the morning. As far as he could tell, they were all she gave anyone. "Because if so…" He moved slightly in front of her when it appeared that she might walk away. "There's an official welcoming initiation that we stay-at-home bums must bestow on you…"

Jan grinned at him, as she usually did, but the expression carried no spark. No life. Those empty eyes were haunting his nights. "Sorry to disappoint you and the other…bums," she said. "But I'm making plans to open a small private practice, handling battered women's cases only. My counselor suggested it."

It was more real conversation than she'd had with him in weeks.

"Well, it's going to tax me and the other bums, but we'll have to find a way to throw a grand opening party, instead."

"No parties, Simon," she said, waving as she walked toward the house.

He went home and threw a party for Soine, instead. The man had seen the first sign that the woman for whom he searched was still alive.

Saturday morning, while Jan was going over her budget, working out exactly how much rent she could handle for an office, the phone rang.

"Mrs. Lincoln?" She stood up from the new desk in her dining room as the woman identified herself. "Is something wrong with Hailey?"

"She's run away, Ms. McNeil. She hasn't been out of her room except to do chores and go to school since… Well, anyway, it's Saturday morning and I thought I'd let her sleep in, but when she didn't come down I got worried and went up to wake her. Her window was open and she wasn't there."

"Have you asked Derek about it?"

"He's as upset as I am. He's been trying to get her to play his video games every night, but she won't even talk to him."

The rush of emotion hit Jan so hard she had to sit back down. She'd been doing so well, maintaining an even keel, feeling no joy, but no great despair, either.

"Have you called the police?"

"She hasn't been gone long enough for them to do anything."

Jan reached for her purse. "I'm on my way."

She didn't get any farther than her driveway before she saw a familiar little figure traipsing tiredly up the road. Her jacket was unzipped, revealing nothing but jeans and a T-shirt beneath. She was wearing the clogs Jan had bought her, and limping as if she'd developed some blisters.

Backing down the street, Jan pulled up even with the child, pushing the button to roll down her passenger window. "Get in."

Hailey immediately complied.

"You're on probation, young lady," Jan said the second the girl was in the car. "Do you remember what happens when you break the rules?"

Hailey nodded, her eyes wide but unblinking.

"You don't care?" Jan shot her a glance as she stopped in the garage, so tempted to haul the precious child into her arms and keep her there.

She'd missed her so much.

Hailey shook her head. And Jan decided she'd better wait until they were inside to finish this conversation.

Hailey seemed to have another idea. She got out

of the car but refused to even stay in the garage. Out on the driveway she folded her arms across her chest and glared at Jan.

"I'm not goin' in there. I just had to ask a question, that's all."

Shivering in only her black turtleneck and jeans, Jan faced her. "Then ask."

Simon, seeing Jan's car backing down the street, slipped on a pair of thongs, grabbed his jacket off the door handle and went outside to see if she needed help. He paused when he saw Hailey get in the car, figuring out pretty quickly that the child must have come of her own accord.

He waited for Jan to turn around and take the child back, and then, when she returned to her house, he waited for the garage door to close behind them. It didn't and he decided to join them, slowing just short of the front porch when he heard the little girl's voice.

"I just...just want to know," Hailey said, sounding angry, but as she continued, Simon could hear that she'd been crying. "Is it true what Derek told me, that he heard his mom and dad say you can't take me because you shot your own dad? Did you tell Mrs. Lincoln that?"

Simon sucked in a breath, forcing himself to stay where he was when what he needed to do was interrupt the two of them and find a way to make them laugh.

"Yes."

He could see Hailey's back from his perch on Jan's front porch. He couldn't see Jan at all.

"Well..." The little girl paused, hunched her shoulders, but then lifted her head toward where he assumed Jan was standing. "Then I have one more question."

Simon admired the child's grit. If he'd ever had a kid...

"What?" Jan didn't sound nearly as bland as she had since Johnny's arrest.

"If you're such a bad person now that you can't even take me, 'cause you did something when you was a girl even littler than me, and you done it for a better reason, then how can I be a good person when I even got caught and persecuted?"

"You were prosecuted, not persecuted." Jan's voice was soft. Simon would have given anything to see her expression.

"And it's very, very different."

"Hailey!" Simon blurted out. "What a surprise! The only person I ever see around here anymore is Jan and she's pretty boring. Can you stay a while?"

Not his best effort, but Simon had been spending too much time with Soine these days. The detective didn't have an idiot bone in his body. Or humor in his soul, either.

Hailey wiped her eyes and nodded, but she didn't seem at all sure of herself.

"Good, because I could use your help," he said, ushering them both into Jan's house. "See, I've been trying to talk to Jan for days and she just doesn't listen to me as well as she does to you."

Jan hadn't said a word and Simon avoided looking

at her, avoided giving her a chance for any silent communication that might kick him out.

"Because I overheard what you were saying just then, about Jan not being bad, and I agree, but I haven't been able to convince her of that."

He hadn't actually tried, not to her face. She hadn't let him get that close.

They were standing in the kitchen and Hailey was staring at him. "So why do you think, considering what she did, that she's not gross or something?" he continued, hoping his babbling wasn't coming across as idiotic as it sounded to him.

"Because of why she did it," Hailey said, completely serious as she explained things to him. "It's *why* someone did it, not what they did, that makes you a kind of person."

Simon chanced a peek at Jan, saw the beginnings of tears, and turned back to the child.

"Where'd you hear that?" he asked.

Hailey pointed, stating the obvious. "From her."

Taking Hailey's hand, he stepped up to Jan. "Any questions?"

The child was tucked beneath her butterfly quilt, sound asleep. Simon waited in the hall while Jan took a last peek and then followed her back to the living room where they'd all had pizza and watched Hailey's favorite movie, *Annie*. The little orphan girl who found a home.

It had been a couple of weeks since Hailey had

shown up at Jan's house and proved to her that she still had a heart. She'd seen the child every day since then. That day, CPS, who'd agreed to reopen Jan's file, had petitioned for an adoption court date.

Jan straightened the room, threw pillows back on the couch, and then stood, facing him, as though she expected him to leave.

He had every other time he'd been over in the past weeks.

"I'm not good at speeches," he said, not sure what to do with the sudden fear he felt. Courage had never been a problem for him—or rather, not one he'd been aware of.

"As a matter of fact, I'm not all that good at speaking, period. I do better with words on paper."

"I thought that was Sam's area."

He shrugged. "I guess we shared more than just good looks."

She didn't smile. He didn't either.

"I've been writing a novel." He spit it right out there, before she could decide he was hiding something from her.

Which, of course, he was.

Jan looked impressed. "Good for you." She also looked like it had nothing to do with her.

Her hair was down and he loved her jeans and sweater and...

"I didn't mean to, didn't set out to."

"So? Mark Twain started out writing for a newspaper."

"Soine's really irritating, more than anything."

"Soine?"

"The star of the show—I think. I'm not that far yet. He's a detective."

Jan did smile then, crossing her arms over her beautiful breasts. "I can't wait to read it."

Simon swore. "What I'm trying to say, and not doing very well at it, is that as galling as this guy is, he's taught me some things."

Her eyes darkened. "What things?" Her voice had changed ever so slightly, as well. Or he was dreaming it had.

"I promised myself after Sam died that I'd continue to live, but only by assuring that I never, ever hurt another human being."

Jan didn't move.

"I thought I could do that by making certain no one ever got close to me again." He wondered if his words sounded as asinine to Jan as they now did to him.

"How'd it work?" Her eyes were glistening.

Simon shoved his hands in his pockets. "Not too well. And I gotta tell you, that really kind of pissed me off."

She grinned. And Simon could breathe again for another moment. "I'm getting ahead of myself, here. Can we sit down?"

"I guess."

She chose the chair.

He settled for the couch by himself. "I have something else to tell you."

"You don't owe me anything, Simon. You've been

the best friend I've ever had, and I'll be grateful for the rest of my life."

He didn't want her gratitude.

"I wasn't just looking out for Amanda that night because I knew her. I was working undercover for the FBI."

She paled. Nodded. Didn't show an ounce of surprise.

"An agent I knew in Philadelphia transferred here several years ago. He's tried repeatedly to get me back to the agency and while I know for certain that I will never, ever live that life again, I have, from time to time, gone undercover for him—as an outside contractor, not an agent."

"You were investigating the Ivory Nation?"

He wondered if he'd ever again see the vitality and passion that had driven Jan in the early days.

"I was looking for suspected terrorist activity." He explained his early role with Amanda and Diamond—the eventual connection to Johnny and Bobby Donahue.

"If you're about to tell me that Bobby Donahue isn't being charged, that there's not a trace of evidence leading to Amanda Blake's body, that the Ivory Nation's implication is only reaching as far as Jacob Hall and Johnny, I already know that."

He wasn't surprised she'd kept herself informed.

"I was dismissed from the case the night that Johnny was arrested. Olsen was afraid my cover had been blown. It's pretty obvious with Amanda's disappearance—without her baby—that they knew she'd gone to the police and they silenced her before she could testify. But who knows what she told her captors before they did whatever they did to keep her quiet?"

"So why are you telling me this now?"

"Two reasons." He was tempted to pace, to stare out the front window. To make a sandwich he had no appetite for. "First, because I don't ever again want to give you reason to doubt me. No more secrets…"

Jan started to interrupt and he talked over her. "And second, because after that last night, Ruple offered me a job with the Flagstaff police department."

"You're going to be a cop? Here?"

He shook his head. "I turned them down this afternoon. I talked to a publisher who's interested in seeing Soine, and thinking about a possible series. I want to give it a try."

He'd also agreed to testify against Davenport. So far, they hadn't been able to pin anything on him regarding the Ivory Nation, but they brought him in on an unrelated charge—conspiracy to commit murder. Had Simon continued to work for Davenport, he would've eventually been given the job of hitman.

"Good for you!" Jan's smile was sincere. And so impersonal it made him mad. *Patience, man,* he reminded himself for the hundredth time in that many hours. He moved to the end of the couch. Their knees were almost touching.

"That night with Johnny, when I saw him pointing that gun at you, and afterward, when I was scared to death that I'd lost you to some private hell of your own, it was all I could do to stay in my skin with the regret eating away at me. It was the same after Sam died. Because I'd refused to take action, to deal with the threats, I lost the person I loved most in the world—and I inadvertently caused the great love between him and Shannon to be cut short."

Her lower lip was trembling.

"And here I was again. Having failed to act, I might be losing the second person I loved most in the world."

There. He'd said it. No matter what happened, that was done. Simon had hoped he'd be able to breathe a little easier at that point.

It didn't work that way.

He held his breath, waiting for someone else to show him whether his future held possibility or despair.

"I…" The trembling in her lip spread to her chin and Simon dared hope that life was soon going to right itself after a very long, painful battle. "I just can't do this, Simon. I'm sorry."

Johnny McNeil was found dead in his Flagstaff cell the third day in December.

Home from her new office only for a moment, Jan closed her cell phone and hung on to it, holding it tight, as tears poured down her face. And when she could, she opened the phone again and called Simon. He was due to pick her up in an hour.

"Can you come over?"

"Now?"

"Yeah."

"I'm on my way."

The crack in her heart was growing ever wider, and beginning to fill as well.

He showed up in wrinkled pants, a sweatshirt and tennis shoes. He obviously hadn't yet dressed for the 10:00 a.m. court date he'd been invited to attend with her and Hailey.

"What happened?" he asked, his face creasing with concern as soon as he saw her.

"Johnny's dead." She still couldn't believe it. She was thirty-four years old and she had outlived all her blood relatives. Was alone in the world.

Her baby brother was gone.

"Someone got to him?"

"No." She was going to face this head-on—had to face it head-on. She had life left to live. "He committed suicide, apparently with a dagger made from a spoon. He left a message out of his own blood on the wall—*loyal to the cause*."

Simon wrapped his arms around her and Jan sank willingly against him, unaware until that moment how badly she'd needed him to do just that.

"He chose to die rather than allow his trial to expose the Ivory Nation."

"No defendant, nothing to prove," Jan agreed—and knew in her heart that he was right. And that, for now, Bobby Donahue and his cause would continue to move across the state of Arizona.

"You want me to call someone? Postpone today's hearing?"

Jan didn't even think about it. "No." She straightened, gripped Simon's hands before she stepped away. "I have a little girl across town who's trusting me to show up today, to stand in court and tell the world that I'll be her mother." She could feel the tears coming again, but continued on. "What kind of a mother would I be if I wasn't there for her? If I put my own troubles before her own?"

Simon leaned over, kissing her gently before he said, "I'll go get ready."

Jan licked her lips, and then touched them. She hadn't been kissed in a while—since the night with Simon she'd tried so hard to forget.

She'd missed it.

And him.

"The court finds that it has jurisdiction and that all requirements of state law have been met. The court further finds the adoptive parent is a fit and proper person to adopt. The court finds it is in the best interest of the minor child to allow the adoption. It is ordered changing the name of the minor child to Hailey Ann McNeil. It is ordered granting the petition for adoption.

"From this date forward the petitioner and child shall and do bear toward each other the relationship of parent and child."

Jan was a mom.

Someone in the small courtroom let out a whoop. Jan lost track of everyone there as the little girl who'd been so solemn and mature all morning turned, threw herself against Jan and started to sob.

"I love you, Hailey," she said, hugging the child.

Hailey's eyes were blurred, her words coming in spurts as she asked, "Is it real, Jan? It happened and you're my mom, now? Forever and ever?"

"It really happened."

"You told me to believe, and it was really hard, but finally I did and you were right…"

The judge, a man who'd taught one of her law school classes in Phoenix, congratulated them. Simon congratulated them. Pictures were taken. And then Hailey and Jan and Simon went home—to Jan's house—where they spent the afternoon eating popcorn and playing Monopoly, a game Hailey had seen in the closet and wanted to play.

Simon offered to take them out to dinner, but Hailey wanted to stay in, not ready to leave her new home yet—not until she had to the next day to go to her new school. She wanted hamburgers.

And Simon ended up out in the cold, grilling them, though Jan told him several times she could do them perfectly well on the broiler.

What kind of game you playing? He asked, cursing the cold. And himself as he flipped burgers and tried to find warmth in the gas heat.

She'd told him weeks ago that she wasn't interested in him. And still he hung around like some besotted puppy dog.

She was starting a new life—it had been solidified today.

Tomorrow he'd start his.

Just as soon as he figured out how to do it without her.

"Don't go."

Jan waited, chewing her lip while Simon studied her later that evening. Hailey was in bed. There was no reason for him to stay.

Except that she wanted him to. She wanted to live. If she could find the courage.

"You need something?" he asked, and she didn't blame him for his hesitancy. Simon had saved her life, been her constant friend, there whenever she needed him—and she'd shunned him.

She took a deep breath and faced the toughest jury of her life. "At first, I needed time to absorb it all, to heal enough to be able to feel anything at all. And then I needed to be sure that what I was feeling for you—or you for me—wasn't somehow messed up with sympathy and gratitude."

"And now?" He hadn't moved from the door, his winter jacket unzipped.

"Now I..." She stopped when her throat was too dry to speak. Swallowed. And thought about saying good-night. Until she saw all of the other good-nights that would manifest in her future.

"I love you." She was scared to death. And alive.

She could see his frown even in the dim lighting of her foyer. "I hear a 'but' there."

"I just don't know if I can do it, Simon. You, Hailey... I want to so badly. I want it all. But I'm scared to death of what I don't see. What I might miss. What I might tell myself just so I don't have to deal with reality."

"We're quite a pair, aren't we?" His voice, a half whisper, was deep and gravelly. He took a step closer. "Both of us conquering the world on the outside and scared to death where no one can see."

She raised a brow. "You, too?"

"We've both seen too much of the dark side to pretend it's not there."

"So how will we ever be happy?"

"Well, there's something Soine told me recently," he said, and Jan knew she had to meet this detective. "We all do the best we can to cope, but the truth is, we're all going to fail somewhere along the way. We're human. We're fallible. And nothing we ever do— hide away in a life with computer games and grass, or prosecute within one inch of our lives—is ever going to be able to change that."

"You aren't convincing me about the happy part."

"It's the love," Simon said, sliding his hands along either side of her, nudging her closer. "Love doesn't take earning or doing or creating. It's just there. It's stronger than evil, lasts longer than life, is infallible. And we all have the capacity for it."

Jan's body weakened, and then filled with such strength she couldn't understand the sensation as he kissed her.

"Love is what saves us, Jan," he whispered against

her lips. "It allows those who feel it for us to support us. To understand us, even when we goof. Don't you see? Love makes up for the mistakes."

It had taken her a lifelong journey through darkness to get here, but Jan was finally beginning to see— people were going to let her down. She was going to let herself down.

But she loved and was loved.

And that made her happy.

REQUEST YOUR FREE BOOKS!

2 FREE NOVELS FROM THE ROMANCE/SUSPENSE COLLECTION PLUS 2 FREE GIFTS!

TARA TAYLOR QUINN

32194 HIDDEN   ___$6.99 U.S.   ___$8.50 CAN.

(limited quantities available)

TOTAL AMOUNT	$ _____
POSTAGE & HANDLING	$ _____
($1.00 FOR 1 BOOK, 50¢ for each additional)	
APPLICABLE TAXES*	$ _____
TOTAL PAYABLE	$ _____

(check or money order—please do not send cash)

To order, complete this form and send it, along with a check or money order for the total above, payable to MIRA Books, to: **In the U.S.:** 3010 Walden Avenue, P.O. Box 9077, Buffalo, NY 14269-9077; **In Canada:** P.O. Box 636, Fort Erie, Ontario, L2A 5X3.

Name: _____

Address: _____ City: _____

State/Prov.: _____ Zip/Postal Code: _____

Account Number (if applicable): _____

075 CSAS

*New York residents remit applicable sales taxes.
*Canadian residents remit applicable GST and provincial taxes.

MIRA®

www.MIRABooks.com   MTTQ1006BL